ARKANA

The Child and the Serpent

Jyoti Sahi was born and brought up in India, and after studying and teaching art in London returned to India to join Dom Bede Griffith's experimental Christian Ashram in Kerala. He spent three years there studying Indian philosophy, and later began work as a freelance artist, moving to Bangalore after his marriage in 1969. His previous publications include *Meditations on St John's Gospel* (1978).

THE CHILD AND THE SERPENT

Reflections on popular Indian symbols

JYOTI SAHI

ARKANA

ARKANA

Published by the Penguin Group
27 Wrights Lane, London W8 5TZ, England
Viking Penguin Inc., 40 West 23rd Street, New York, New York 10010, USA
Penguin Books Australia Ltd, Ringwood, Victoria, Australia
Penguin Books Canada Ltd, 2801 John Street, Markham, Ontario, Canada L3R 1B4
Penguin Books (NZ) Ltd, 182–190 Wairau Road, Auckland 10, New Zealand

Penguin Books Ltd, Registered Offices: Harmondsworth, Middlesex, England

First published by Routledge & Kegan Paul Ltd 1980
Published by ARKANA 1990
10 9 8 7 6 5 4 3 2 1

Filmset in 11/12 IBM Journal by
Hope Services, Abingdon, Oxon
and printed in Great Britain by
Unwin Brothers, The Gresham Press,
Old Woking, Surrey

Made and printed in Great Britain by
Richard Clay Ltd, Bungay, Suffolk

FOR MY PARENTS

CONTENTS

< vii >

ILLUSTRATIONS

FOREWORD
by Father Bede Griffiths

From a snake stone in Srirangapatnam

Most people find Hindu mythology utterly bewildering. It is like a forest in which one soon finds oneself lost. It is infinitely fascinating and obviously full of meaning, but it is so vast and apparently chaotic that one despairs of finding one's way. It is one of the great merits of this book that it provides a clue to this mystery; it opens up a path through the forest. Jyoti Sahi, who is an Indian artist engaged in exploring this symbolism in his art, takes as his starting point the

< x >

symbol of the child, known under so many names in Hindu mythology, as Balakrsna, Skanda, Murugan, Ayyappan and Ganesa, and
seeks from this point to unravel the threads which make up the
intricate pattern of Hindu mythology. But his search takes him
beyond what is specifically Hindu to the basis of all symbolism,
which he finds present in the religion of the Indian village. He has
been living for some years in a village outside Bangalore, and it is the
study of the religion of these villagers which has led him to discover
the basic pattern of symbolism underlying not only Hindu mythology, but the ancient primeval religion on which Hinduism itself
rests. Hinduism is a cosmic religion and its mythology rests on the
cosmic symbolism which underlies all ancient religion.

The basis of this symbolism is found first of all in the five elements,
earth, air, fire and water, and the akasa, or space, and their manifestation in sun and moon and stars, earth and sky and sea, rock and
tree and animal, and then in the cycle of human birth, marriage and
death. Now the characteristic of this symbolism is that it always
involves opposition. Nature is composed. of light and darkness, life
and death, creation and destruction, and the same symbol will signify
both these aspects. Water brings life to the earth, but it also brings
destruction by flood or by drought when it is withheld. Fire is the
element which cooks the food and gives heat to the body so that it
can bring forth life, but it also burns and destroys. In Hindu mythology Siva is the God of destruction, but he is also the renewer of
life, who by his grace recreates what he has destroyed. It is this ambivalence of the symbol which makes it so bewildering, yet once the
basic pattern has been discerned it is seen to have its own logic.
Nature is a conflict of opposites which is always seeking an equili-
brium, always seeking to harmonize the conflicting forces within her
and to restore the primal unity from which everything originally
came.

This leads to the discussion of the nature of symbolism itself and
perhaps the greatest value of this book will be found in the profound
understanding of what a symbol is and how it underlies all human
experience. The word symbol comes from the Greek word *symballein*
meaning to 'throw together'. The idea behind it is that the world has
been broken into pieces and the function of the symbol is to put
these pieces together. Behind this again lies the idea that nature
springs from a primordial unity — the 'mulaprakrti' of Hindu tradition — which is the darkness of the womb and the tomb, the darkness from which life comes and to which it returns. Consciousness is
the light which breaks into this darkness, dividing the light from the
darkness. Consciousness is thus essentially a force of division. It is

< xi >

the mind which distinguishes, separates, analyses and synthesizes. This is a necessary process in the growth of nature, but the harmony of nature depends on the balance between these opposing forces of unity and division, life and death, darkness and light. The symbol is the power which unites these opposites. The symbol is not something static; it belongs not to the world of 'fact' — of what has been done, which is finished and completed, which is also the world of death — but to the world of 'actuality'. A symbol is an 'event'. It is something which grows out of a situation, out of life itself. It has a life of its own, as every poet or artist knows. The rational, analytic mind separates the light from the darkness, the meaning from the event, and expresses itself in abstract concepts, which have a fixed meaning but no life. The symbol reunites meaning and event, understanding and life.

The study of the symbol thus leads to an understanding of the very process of life and thought. All life proceeds from the darkness of the unconscious, in which all meaning is hidden, enclosed as it were in the womb. The meaning of life is lived before it is understood. Nature herself is one vast symbol, in which the forms of life emerge from the unconscious and manifest themselves in the forms of the elements, in sun and moon and stars, earth and plant and animal and man. Man himself is at first enclosed in the womb of the unconscious. But as consciousness emerges it begins to divide the light from the darkness. The forms of life come up into the consciousness and it is the symbol which expresses this consciousness of life. The meaning of nature begins to be expressed in gesture and dance, speech and song, ritual and myth. The symbol is the bridge between body and soul, mind and matter, feeling and intellect, knowledge and life. It is this symbolic language which lies behind all the great religious traditions of the world from the most primitive tribal religion to the advanced religions like Hinduism and Christianity. It is for this reason that the study of Hindu mythology can be of such fundamental importance in the understanding of the meaning of religion itself. We cannot understand a religion until we enter into its symbolism, and such 'entering' is not merely an abstract understanding, which would eventually dispense with the symbol altogether. On the contrary it is a participation in the creative process of religion, by which the ultimate meaning of life is discovered.

The study of the symbol thus leads the author to the fundamental problem of the modern world. In the last few hundred years the human mind has developed the powers of the abstract reason further than ever before, but it has largely lost the capacity for symbolic thought. Most people today regard mythology as 'superstition' and

< xii >

imagine that they have got beyond it. But without symbolism (which puts things together) the mind loses its contact with life. The terrible destructive forces released by modern science and the imbalance of western civilization are evidence of this triumph of the dividing consciousness over the powers of life. It is only by a rediscovery of the symbol that we can recover the health of the mind. Many Hindus today, under the influence of western rationalism, reject the mythology on which Hinduism is based, and many Christians leave the Church because the ancient symbolism which enters into both its doctrine and its ritual has ceased to mean anything to them. The recovery of the meaning of symbolism, not merely as an abstract theory but as an experience of life, is therefore one of the greatest needs of the modern world.

Jyoti Sahi has answered this need in this book, which is not merely a description of Hindu mythology or a theory of art, but a creative work, in which the ancient symbols are made to live again. He writes as an artist, who is engaged in discovering the meaning of this symbolism for his own art, and as one who, living in an Indian village, has been able to discern the working of this symbolism in the lived experience of the villager. All of us, both Hindu and Christian, need to make this discovery for ourselves, and we could find no better guide than this, which unfolds the mysterious process of the symbolism of Hindu mythology in such a way that we are able to share in the process ourselves and discover its meaning hidden in the depths of our own unconscious life. He has brought together in his work the child and the serpent, for, as he says, without the serpent (who represents the life of the unconscious), how could there be vitality in creation, and without the child (who represents birth into consciousness) how could the world-process ever be transformed?

Bede Griffiths

< xiii >

AUTHOR'S NOTE

As a matter of general convenience, diacritical marks have not been used in the main body of the text, but have been included in the index. C and s are generally pronounced soft, as ch and sh; exceptions may be found in the Index (e.g. soma).

< xiv >

INTRODUCTION

Another version of the child Krsna dancing, inspired by a small bronze figure seen by the author in Tanjore museum

TENSION BETWEEN SCIENTIFIC AND MYTHOLOGICAL
INTERPRETATIONS OF REALITY

As an Indian artist I have over the last few years been trying to find the roots of my culture. I have felt that it was not sufficient merely

<1>

to go back to the past and try to revive an antiquated culture, how-ever great that culture might have been. And yet India at the present time is passing through a great cultural crisis which is part of the process which is called 'modernization'. Foreign influences in the form of advanced technology and an empirical approach to life and its problems have created a cultural élite which no longer feels in sympathy with the ancient Indian world-view. And yet this very élite feels alienated from the vast majority of Indians, and deeply longs to find its own roots amid its own people. In a search to find a relevant culture in modern India, the traditional viewpoints of the people have somehow to be integrated. The present is very much the child of the past, and its own future, the child of its dreams, will only truly fulfil the present when the past has been rediscovered and integrated.

It is from this standpoint that I want to begin in my study — as a modern Indian in search of himself. In the intuitive language of dreams this search has been portrayed as the child within — for the child is all that the heart 'hopes' for, symbol of the future. He is in some way a fulfilment of the past, for he is 'father of the man' in the same way that seed goes before the full-grown tree. He has a whole-ness. In the very innocence and newness of the child we feel the presence of a tremendous wisdom and mysterious 'age' that carries the bloom of eternity. As cur search is going to be a journey through symbols, it seemed to me that the best way to give unity to my theme is to take the child as a central motif in all the various figures that I hope to explore.

I have wanted to find the main spirit of Indian folk art, because I felt that such an art is by definition unaffected, arising spontaneously out of the life of the people. I hope therefore to find in this art a spirit which is both old and new, and capable of ever new interpreta-tions. I have therefore tried to concentrate on the favourite symbol of what one might call a popular Indian religion. Here also I found the centrality of the child motif, for the child or youthful deity seems to be deeply appealing to a popular religious culture. As in the West, where the theme of the nativity and the childhood of Christ has offered a perennial source of popular inspiration, Indian folklore has also elaborated on many charming myths concerning a youthful god who is close to the heart of every one. This god has been given in India many names, because in a culture which has deeply rejoiced in children it has seemed that the mystery of childhood has many faces. The various names of the deities who charm the heart of the people are numerous. We might name a few popular ones — Sanat Kumara, Skanda, Balasubrahmanya, Venkatesvara, Kartikeya,

< 2 >

Balakrsna, Murugan, Ayyappan, Ganesa and so on. There is a tendency in India to say that all these are in fact the names of one child god, though certain different myths apply to the different aspects of this deity. I myself will assume that, although the origins of these different gods may go back to different ethnic groups and cultures (some Aryan, some Dravidian), in the context of the present pan-Indian culture we can say that all these different sources have integrated to provide for the richness of the popular Hindu idea of a child god. Individual Indians might take this or that deity as their 'ista devata' or deity of preference, but all concepts of this child god flow in and out of each other.

THE ROLE OF THE SON IN RELATION TO ANCESTOR WORSHIP

Hindu culture has stressed the importance of having a son (putra) because without a son the soul of the ancestor cannot be assisted in the after-life.[1] The word 'putra' means 'he who protects from going to hell'. It is the son who is essential in carrying out the funerary rites which will assist his parents into after-life. It is essential to understand this connection of the child with death if we are to interpret the various symbols and world-view which are embroidered round the central figure of the child god.

The tendency among many is to think of the child in the womb as something passive. In the act of giving birth we think that it is the parent who is doing all the work. But in many ancient mythologies it is the child who is thought to be the active agent. It is he who like a young hero struggles out of the womb and takes hold of the destiny of his own life. In many myths concerning the hero this basic pattern of thought is found to underline the significance of his symbolic journey. The hero overcomes the enclosing, imprisoning womb and breaks out into the world of life and light. There is a constant relationship between womb and tomb, and the child hero has to encounter the forces of death in the very act of coming to birth.

Perhaps one of the most deeply meaningful hero figures of Indian thought was the boy Naciketas. On one occasion when his Brahmin father performed a great ritualistic offering, this youth was led to question the meaning of such actions. He thought to himself, 'What is the use of offering these old toothless cattle and these cows past bearing? If my father wishes to offer something dear to him, surely he should offer me?' So he said to his father, 'To whom will you offer me?' His father ignored his question, so he asked again, and then a third time, and finally his father, angered, said, 'I offer you to

< 3 >

Death.' So Naciketas went down to Death, to the god Yama. Yama kept him waiting for three days, but then, to make up for this sin of having so disregarded a Brahmin child, he offered to grant him three boons. The first boon Naciketas asked was that when he returned to earth the anger of his father should be appeased. This was granted. Then he asked to know the secret of the sacrificial fire which leads to heaven. This also Yama granted, and further granted that the sacrificial fire should be called by the name of Naciketas. The third boon Naciketas asked was that he should be initiated into the mystery of life beyond death. This at first Yama was not willing to grant. He offered the boy all possible earthly joys, but Naciketas refused them, and was steadfast in his request. Pleased with the child's firmness, Yama then revealed to him the mystery of the Atman, and that path of wisdom which leads beyond the cycle of birth and death.

The apparent curse of the father which led to the boy Naciketas descending to the house of Death, was in fact the moment of his initiation, and hence spiritual birth. Elsewhere in Hindu mythology we find this theme repeated, as in the curse of Siva resulting in the beheading of his son Ganesa and impaling of his son Andhaka, or, again, the curse of the goddess Parvati against Viraka. There is a tension between birth and death, what is new and what is old, the present and the past, and yet the one is deeply dependent upon the other.

> Look forward, how (fared) the former ones
> Look backward, so (will) the after ones
> Like grain a mortal ripens!
> Like grain he is born hither again.
>   [Katha Upanisad]

The basic significance of the Katha Upanisad is that it reveals the way in which the cycle of birth and death is overcome by the young hero and in this way, as in other ways also, it is closely linked to the Bhagavad Gita, which is also the story of a hero and his conquest of the meaning of existence.

Note that the second boon granted to Naciketas was the knowledge of the sacrificial fire. We shall see later how important the idea of fire has been in the cycles of myth which revolve around the symbol of the child divinity. The third boon, knowledge concerning the result of dying, leads the child hero beyond the cycle of birth and death. Through his own experience of the process of coming to birth, the child has a secret access to an understanding of the process of life itself, which it is thought enables him to escape from the natural generations of life-cycle, which is encompassed by death.

< 4 >

THE CHILD AS A SYMBOL OF INTEGRATION

People in a highly rationalistic and scientific society are feeling a deep need to rediscover their mythic experience, because whereas history or science can try to discover what is factual, they cannot convey that living experience which we call actual. What is actual contains within itself both the subjective and objective, the experience and that which is experienced.

For this reason I have in various places drawn on the insights now available to us through psychoanalysis. I do not expect that these are anything more than insights and interpretations which always have to be qualified. Still, in so far as modern psychology is scientific discipline and yet hopes to throw some light on the workings of the subjective mind, it can perhaps help us bridge the gap between the objective and subjective, or history and myth, not that these are in any way equivalent, but they both represent 'opposites' in our human consciousness of reality which we now feel have to be integrated.

'For Jung the child is an archetypal figure of the self. Certainly all over the world we could find myths concerning a child hero who reveals the way to a higher life. The popularity of this figure indicates a deeply felt need. It is obviously dangerous to generalize or universalize this figure as we find it described in myth or art. Though there are certain common features, there are also differences.

In the following pages I wish to study the various symbols as described by mythic incidents which seem to group themselves around the figures of the divine child. By studying these symbols I hope also to delineate certain common features of popular Hindu iconography. I also hope to outline a symbolic vocabulary which could show to us the patterns of Indian folk experience.

We might ask, then, what is the event which the image of the child celebrates? Surely it is the act of coming to birth. At this point myth and history meet, because birth is the stuff of history. The images of the child, even where it is described purely in mythical terms, represents the intersection of history and eternity.[2] Though it lies outside the purview of historical verification, it is nevertheless historical in its intention, because it gives meaning and purpose to the world-process. Above all it is unitive, revealing samsara as non-distinguishable (and by that we do not mean identical) from moksa. The child event in Indian imagery is not unique but it is crucial.

< 5 >

THE PROBLEM OF WORLD-VIEW AND A METHODOLOGY
FOR INTERPRETING SYMBOLS

The study of iconography generally tends to be descriptive, that is, it concerns itself with the objects of art, the particular images which are to be found. This approach leaves out the problem of symbolic language as such, and the relation of what has been described to what has not. That is to say every person who is trying to express himself through the medium of images, manages to express partly what for him is an experience, but also finds himself unable to express a great deal. The image is itself only a 'pointer', for it is something dynamic, on the move. There is a Zen Buddhist saying: 'It is with a finger that one points to the moon, but how absurd were one to take the finger for the moon!' The iconographer often falls into the folly of simply describing the finger. 'What is the intention of the image?' is certainly an important question when dealing with images. There are many conditions which make the image more or less inadequate. For example, a child when painting a picture uses certain symbols which attempt to put down on paper what he wants to say. But everyone knows how often what he wants to say, and what he manages to convey intelligibly to others, are in fact different. And this problem is not only with the child — the fully adult and even professional image-maker has the same problem, though perhaps at a different level.

Here as in every other discipline concerning communication, we have the problem also of conscious and unconscious motivations. Is even the image-maker very clear about what he wants to say, let alone what he is saying? As an artist I know that in the process of making an image, the very effort to create is part of my discovery of what I want to express. It has been suggested, for example, that word (and this applies to image also) is coextensive with thinking. When we look at the efforts of someone trying to express himself, we are in fact looking at his effort to think. For the purpose of distinguishing coefficients in this process we say there is a thought (idea, pattern, intention or whatever) and then there is an image. But it is dangerous to proceed from this and speculate which comes first and which comes afterwards. We must realize that these coefficients function together.

I wish in these reflections to view iconography dynamically as a process of growth, not statically as the fixed objective end. When we see a god represented in this or that form, we are not merely dealing with a god, but with a conception in symbolic language. And this conception, like everything born into the world, is mutated by circumstances. At this point arises the problem as to how far the intelligibility

< 6 >

of the image, the experience it evokes in the viewer, lies within the bounds of the artist's technique, his skill in descriptive portrayal.

AN ESSENTIAL ICONOGRAPHY

The problem of skill will always remain at the descriptive level. But ultimately we might ask whether however perfected the means of expression might become, they could ever ultimately contain an experience. The experience remains somehow elusive.. The film producer Eisenstein, whose theoretical works have deeply influenced the art of film-making, points out that the image in its descriptive detail is ultimately only a configuration which gives rise to an experience, but is never the experience itself. In other words, all imagery is only evocative. An atmosphere, a sort of preparedness, is built up which can situate an experience but cannot define it.

This really raises the issue of control.[3] Skill is, of course, control over the means of expression. It includes a capacity to predict processes and situations, and to have some command over an end in view, but not total command of the ultimate experience.

Let us take a concrete example. The artist wants to make an image out of a lump of stone. Looked at from one angle, the artist is working on the stone, using every technique he knows of to control the material beneath his chisel. But looked at another way, the image is coming out of the stone; what was latent in the stone is being revealed and that revelation 'points' to an experience in the artist which he communicates to others. No matter what skill the artist might have, if the image was not already in some way latent in the material, he could not bring it into being. The artist cannot make something out of nothing. Every artist knows that his skill is to a large extent a knowledge of the nature of his material. That is, he is able to recognize what are the latent images within matter: he sees in a particular way. No one would suggest that because a man can 'see' a phenomenon, he has created that phenomenon out of his own head. The image is part of the matter, only most people cannot see it there. The artist points out the image in such a way that it becomes intelligible to others. In other words he communicates his experience, his way of seeing, to others, so that they also begin to see reality as he does.

This idea is the basis of what we are now proposing as a method of understanding images. We suggest that, below the image, something is being born out of nature itself. Perhaps in this particular image it is only partly seen; in another image it is more clearly manifested.

< 7 >

But leaving aside the problem of unveiling the image, the image is already present in the primordial structure of things.

Let us take another example. I give a child a lump of clay. What does the child do? He plays with the clay, feels it, discovers intuitively what clay can do. He then finds to his surprise that he can roll the clay out into a long sausage. The fact that the clay can naturally be worked in this way has something to do with the nature of clay, with its molecular structure. You cannot roll a ball of sand out into a long sausage. The child is delighted with his discovery. At this point you ask the child what he has made — and he answers immediately 'a snake'. Here we see symbolic thinking working spontaneously. Of course we see his point — but what gave him the idea? What primordial structure of his mind responded to the structure he had created out of clay, to make of it this metaphor, this symbol? Let us watch the child go further. He finds that by twisting his long snaky line of clay round and round in a spiralling form he can make at first a plane. This plane is even structurally much stronger, and much less likely to crack than if he had flattened his ball of clay out into a flat pancake. But he can do more. He can spiral his long sausage upwards, making a vessel. This is an invention of great importance — one of the turning points in the history of human civilization. It was as important, probably, as the discovery of electricity; it enabled neolithic man to make his first vessel in which he could store things.

We might go on like this showing how the image and matter, and ideas, all work together. In the artist a threefold process is going on. First of all the artist experiences matter. Then in and through his play with matter he begins to know the primordial images hidden in matter. At this stage his capacity to develop skills also enables him to know more precisely, more effectively. He begins to distinguish and differentiate images from what in matter seemed to be all flux, confusion, chaos. And then the artist himself stands back and looks at what he has done — he 'sees' what has been revealed to him. He sees the image, but he is not the image. But the image becomes now part of him. That is, it becomes his experience of matter.

EXPERIENCE AND THE DEVELOPMENT OF A CULTURE

What is here referred to as 'experience' is not something which can be defined in terms of dogma, or fixed religious institutions. And yet the experience of an individual always has its context, its social determinants. These comprise a 'world-view' or 'culture' which give meaning to life. Man wants to give meaning to the world in

< 8 >

which he lives. What is meaningful to the villager, for example, arises out of his own deep-rooted understanding of the structure of the world in which he lives, a structure which has been built out of a cultural heritage, a tradition. There are many things which go to make up this heritage — already existing images which are used by the community, stories, games and rituals. A culture expresses a man's corporate identity with a society in which he can communicate. Right from childhood a man's mind is formed by environment, by the myths he is told, by the poems and dreams he enjoys. In order to understand him we must penetrate to the conditions in which his mind has been formed, and try in the light of his youthful fantasies and games to imagine what it is that he finds meaningful in the world around him.

A culture therefore becomes a religious language and, like any other language, it has its own vocabulary and syntax. Culture is not peripheral to man's experience of reality — in fact he experiences the world around him through his culture, and so to a certain extent what he experiences is determined by his culture. More and more we are becoming aware of the fact that a world-view is not only determined by the experience of a people, but it also determines what experiences they have. Their world-view becomes a medium through which their own experiences are interpreted to them. This world-view could be empirical and historical, or it could also be mythic.

On several occasions when I have talked to groups of people about folk symbols I have got the response, 'Do they really still believe in things like that? How can we liberate them from such superstitions?' I find it difficult to tackle such an attitude. I myself do not believe that the villagers have 'superstitions' in that sense. As Coomaraswamy points out,[4] superstition comes from the Latin word meaning 'to place above'. In that sense it is we who are superstitious, not the villager. The villager is closer to what the Taoists call 'the original mind' than we are. He is often simpler and more direct, and so his beliefs are really often what we believe deep inside ourselves, but have tried to ignore, or reject, because of our conscious rational superstition which does not allow us to accept a world-view which does not seem 'logical'. And so I stress that to understand the world-view of the villager we must not see him as somebody 'out there in the backward areas' — a man ignorant, lacking in true perception, who has to be educated by us. But rather we have to see him as a person having certain intuitions which are valid and which we can share. This also does not mean that everything the villager believes is an intuition, or that his intuition and understanding of life cannot be deepened. Our attitude should take into account that nothing

< 9 >

is static, and that we are all trying to grow in our understanding. We must view culture itself as a growing process, not as a mere deposit of tradition, but as a movement which is constantly trying to reach out to a fuller and deeper awareness.

THE COMMON CULTURE OF VILLAGE RELIGION

My family and I live in the countryside outside Bangalore city. Our home is situated between three villages. These villages are of different religions. There are Hindus, Christians and Muslims. The Christians are all in one village while another village near to us is nearly entirely Hindu, and a third village has a sizeable community of Muslims who live all together in a section of the village. Formerly my wife and I used to live in a similar mohalla of Muslims in another part of Mysore State. What I have been observing is that, whereas there are these religious differences, there is a common culture underlying credal distinctions. It is almost as though the held beliefs of the villagers are only a veneer, beneath which there is really only one religion, and that a very ancient one. Often, because credal differences have alienated cultural exchange between religious groups of villages, a particular group of villagers does not know that many aspects of its cultural and liturgical life have in fact their roots in a common archaic faith which underlies the religious practices of other groups as well. Thus, for example, in the Christian village at the time of Christmas and the New Year the villagers prepare pots containing a number of kinds of seeds which have sprouted and which they place near the crib. This ritual of preparing sprouted grain belongs to village cults, and in general is believed to indicate what should be planted in the fields in the coming year. Those seeds which are most successfully sprouted in these New Year rites are the ones which are thought to be most auspicious. The Christian villagers seem to have no idea that the rite is derived from local village culture and claim that they do it because when Joseph fled with Mary to Egypt he scattered seeds by the roadside and that they are commemorating his act. Thus they have made a myth of their own to explain a rite which goes deep into the village unconscious. The yearly practice of making a decorated cart in which the figure of Mary or some other saint is carried around the village and is left overnight in each house in turn as a blessing on the home is also obviously a Hindu idea which has been 'christianized' quite effortlessly by the people. Again the Christian festival of Epiphany falling close to the Hindu festival of Sankranti, or Pongal as it is called in the south, is celebrated in our

< 10 >

village with the decorating of all the cows and their blessing in front of the Church. Many other examples could also be given.

The Muslims in the village region are also very close to primitive religious attitudes. This manifests itself in the form of an interest in magical forces. For example, a Muslim villager whom I got to know believed in all kinds of spells and herbs which could cure or harm. He believed that the tulsi plant would repel snakes, and would die if the shadow of a woman who is passing through her menstrual cycle should fall on it. He had in his little hut a diagram for dispelling dark forces which resembled magical diagrams to be found elsewhere in folk culture. He had a whole stock of stories of Muslim holy men and their magical powers which obviously derived from a Muslim sub-culture whose roots were really in old village religion. In the same way the Hindus in the villages, though adopting various well-known gods and goddesses of the Aryan pantheon, have really their roots in a pre-Aryan religion. These and many other instances have led me to conjecture that when speaking of different religions we are in fact forgetting the cultural and existential unity between the village people to whom the theological and credal questions are of less importance, the most important thing being their common world-view.

Kolama patterns drawn by women in front of their houses, probably representing the interwoven pattern of the three strands of life symbolizing cosmic vitality

< 11 >

CHAPTER 1

The dynamism of
the symbolizing process

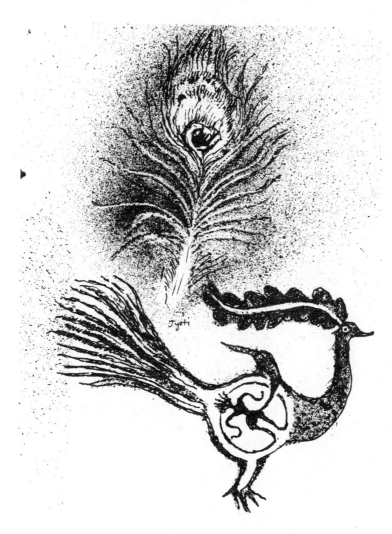

< 13 >

[OVERLEAF]

The peacock feather showing the 'eye' in the feather.
A motif derived from Harappan decoration' of pottery
showing the peacock with the soul of a human being in its
womb

< 14 >

The entity which I call a 'coin' lies between the two opposite faces which I might term the head and tail of the coin. Actually these two faces, though they seem obvious enough — so obvious that we are quite capable of only seeing the coin in terms of its faces — are in fact abstractions. The coin is a unity — its faces give it the impression of being a duality, of having an 'up' and a 'down', a manifest face and a hidden face.

I have been trying to describe the field of symbolism. There is no way in which I can describe this field except in terms of the oppositions that delimit it. But these oppositions are not static but constantly interacting. As when we toss a coin now heads come up, now tails, so also with the oppositions between which the field of symbolism operates. At one time this aspect is dominant, at another time its reverse. The dynamics of the symbolic field is characterized by a repeated process of inversion. And always in the effort to describe this process, we are in danger of speaking of the part as if it were the whole. We refer to the coin as if it were only heads, or only tails, because whichever side we see represents for us the whole coin.

But let us take our analogy further. What is the value of the coin? We might assume that this particular coin is the one and only coin — but the fact that it is a coin means also that it is part of a much much greater system of coins which are used, exchanged, amassed or spent. There is always a tension between symbolism (which is a system, having its own economy) and the individual symbol which is part of that system. We may be tempted to say 'this symbol means so and so', like saying 'this peacock' means regeneration.[1] Are we dealing with a language here? Is this a sort of intricate code? Take, for example, the process of sending a telegram. The words are written out on a form as a specific 'message'. This is handed over to the telegraph office. There it is converted into morse code. This is transmitted over great distances. It is received by another telegraph office where again it is changed from a code message back into a written message. When this message reaches its destination, the final receiver reads the message and, once he has read it and absorbed its meaning, he throws the telegram away. Here we have a concrete example of how meaning is transmitted through a code system. The code is in a one-to-one relation to its meaning. But when we say of a specific symbol that this peacock means regeneration, we find that having got the meaning 'regeneration' we are still not in a position to throw away the peacock, like the man who received a telegram was able to throw away the written message, once he had received the message. The peacock is something in itself which a language message can never be. Further, the peacock may mean something quite different on another

< 15 >

occasion. It may mean for example 'showing off'. I know somebody who has this meaning so fixed in his mind that wherever he sees a peacock symbol he understands 'showing off', so the idea of the peacock being a symbol of regeneration, or eternal life, or the rainy season, or Krsna, are all unacceptable to him.

A symbol is something very concrete. It is part of the world. As a result it has certain qualities, which are part of its nature. A peacock is a bird with blue feathers, and sheds its feathers in certain seasons. Further, it has a very beautiful tail which displays a certain pattern. It is known to dance in the rainy season which is the period when it mates. It is also known to attack serpents. All these 'facts' are part of what we might call the encyclopaedic knowledge which we have about peacocks. Note, however, the difference between encyclopaedic knowledge and semantic knowledge. The word 'peacock' means the bird which we find in nature. That is our semantic knowledge of the word. This bird, however, has a certain nature, certain facts about it (as listed above) – these constitute our encyclopaedic knowledge of this creature. The word 'peacock', while conveying the meaning 'a particular bird' tells us nothing about it – its colour, habits, shape, etc. Thus semantic knowledge and encyclopaedic knowledge complement each other. The symbol, for example 'peacock', is derived not from the semantic knowledge we have of a word (except in certain cases where etymology plays a significant role in the configuration of a symbol) but rather from encyclopaedic knowledge. Knowing the bird, its colour, shape, habits, etc., we take these into account when dealing with the symbol. Thus the peacock who is by no account 'musical' cannot be a symbol of the 'music of the spheres'. However, the peacock dances very beautifully and so it could be a symbol of the 'cosmic dance'.

From this we can see clearly that the symbol-maker whom Lévi-Strauss calls a 'bricoleur', meaning 'a handyman improvising out of random materials', does not make his symbols out of anything, any more than a handyman makes his artifact out of anything.[2] How does a handyman work? True, he looks at what might appear as a useless assortment of odds and ends, but he considers, like every good artist, the essential nature of these odds and ends, what I call their basic structure, what they can do. The reader will recall that when we considered a child at play with a lump of clay, we found that his 'play' consisted of finding what the clay could do, which was after all determined by the very molecular structure of that substance which we call clay. Every artist knows, as every handyman does also, that the materials he is working with are not indifferent – each material has its own use. I am convinced that no one will understand a symbol

< 16 >

who is ignorant of the technology of symbol construction. Every symbol-maker has to become familiar with the materials at hand from which he has to make his images.

My own approach to symbolism is the approach of an artist whose job it is to make symbols. I agree with the structuralists who see the symbol not as a thing, having a meaning, in the way a word has a meaning, but as part of a total structure of symbolism, in which every symbol relates to every other within a total overall economy.[3] I understand this because as an artist I am often asked, 'What does this symbolic picture of yours mean?' I myself don't know what it means! Having painted it, I sit down and look at it, and contemplate it, much as anybody else might contemplate it. I don't have a key to explain the picture. If I did, the picture would become useless — all I would need to do would be to keep the 'key' and throw the picture away, because after all what use would a picture be if it could be 'explained away'? The explanation would be all that we would need. Unfortunately this is exactly what often happens when I am asked to 'explain' my picture — interpret its meaning. What my interlocutor often really wants to do is to 'dispose' of the picture, by getting me (the artist) to dispose of it, verbally. With this explanation safely in his pocket, he can just walk off and forget about the picture. But symbols are more awkward than that: they just can't be explained; they can only be used, in the same way as a coin cannot be explained, but is used by people in the market every day.

Having shown how much I as an artist am in agreement with the structuralist I must also add that I would disagree with anybody who says a symbol doesn't mean anything. That would be saying that the symbol has no content at all; it is only form. I feel that too often the structuralist is just a critic — he is not an artist, not a symbol-maker himself. When I start to make my image, I am very aware of 'meanings' in symbols, as I am also aware of 'uses' in materials.

Let us return to the problem of explaining the picture which I have painted. Suppose I tell my interlocutor, 'The picture means nothing at all, it is just a structure of colours and lines'; he is naturally rather disappointed, because he doesn't know what to do with my picture. Either it is significant, or it isn't, either it is saying something, or it is a waste of paint and a crashing bore. So I don't myself so rudely dismiss the man who asks for a meaning. I know how important meaning is, how much a part of our life-movement it is, how meaning gives 'intention', 'direction', 'order', 'logos'. Meaning points to what lies beyond the manifest world in the dimension of pure signification. Without meaning we would be back to the static. The idolater is a man who gets stuck up in a thing without meaning.

< 17 >

So I try (it is an effort for me) to find the meaning. I look for meaning in the very colours, shapes, lines, the arrangement of the composition. But my explanation is an 'exposition', not a decoding of a very intricate and obscure 'message'. The exposition is an exploring of the symbol, an entering into it, a becoming part of it. Searching for the meaning, the image is no longer a 'thing out there', but rather a world opening up before me, into which I am being incarnated, and which is being born forth into me. When I interpret a symbol the interpretation is itself symbolic, and will very soon itself require further interpretation. 'Meaning' then reveals itself as nothing other than the symbolic field itself. Meaning here is not static, fixed, as in the semantic, but it is evolving, growing, expanding. In the process of discovering the meaning of the symbol, I find the meaning itself is being unveiled — the meaning of everything, the meaning of life. That ultimately is what the image is pointing to.

In my approach to symbol, as now becomes very clear, I am not a logician. I cannot even claim to have a theory concerning epistemology. I approach the symbol intuitively. And yet even in this intuitive approach lie the very seeds of a conscious order (logos) and a knowledge. It will be noted that I have tended to use the words 'symbol' and 'image' as though they were interchangeable. It is perhaps necessary now to distinguish between these two terms more precisely. Symbol comes from a Greek word meaning 'to throw together' (*sym* — together, *ballein* — to throw). So it carries precisely the meaning which Lévi-Strauss tries to convey by the term 'bricolage', something which a handyman 'puts together'. The symbol is thus the objective structure, the ensemble of odds and ends which confronts the mind with the problem — 'What does it mean?' 'Image', on the other hand, is more subjective, being the thing 'seen' and reflected upon. As I sit looking at the symbol, it appears to me as an image. This distinction at least helps us to understand an important aspect of the symbol or image, or whatever we call it — its power to be a 'focus' or a 'perspective' through which we see things.

Consciousness is a focusing on a set group of objects which are conceptualized. Even the handyman, however irrational his patched-up job might seem, does bring to consciousness what had presumably been discarded as 'bricolage' He goes to the rubbish bin of civilization, picks up something with apparently no use and finds a use for it within a structure. I am reminded of the play of an imaginative child who goes around collecting bits and pieces — string, nails, bits of wood, etc., and then with the tremendous effort of the handyman, brings them together, making something out of nothing. This is the symbol. To do this he 'focuses' his attention and draws from the

< 18 >

unconscious bric-à-brac meaningful configuration. Already in the 'image' meaning is latent. When we ask of the symbol, 'What is its meaning?', we have begun a process of extending the symbol beyond the mere physical existence of its collection of odds and ends, into meaning, which is (as we have noted) itself symbolic, because it has to be interpreted. Let us give an example. The peacock with the child god Kartikeya riding on its back, and holding a serpent in its beak, is a symbol. The question is asked, 'What does it mean?' And, by way of exposition, the answer is suggested — rebirth, regeneration, beauty, overcoming of the world cycle. There are a number of interesting oppositions. Child-snake. Bird-snake. Child-bird. At this point we begin to recall (and here perhaps the image is emerging) that when women want a child, they worship snakes. Further, snakes crawl on the ground, but birds fly about in the air. Further the bird is 'twice born' and children are sometimes thought to come 'from above' (the proverbial stork which brings the baby?). The child god is thus in a way both born of the earth (snake world) and the spirit world (the bird) — on certain ancient funerary urns the souls of the dead are represented in the womb of a peacock (see p. 38). Further, both the snake and the peacock renew themselves, one by shedding its skin, the other by shedding its feathers, and both are thus symbols of re-birth. However, the peacock kills the snake, perhaps also it even eats the snake, swallowing it as Siva swallowed poison.[4] The peacock, like Siva, has a blue throat ... and so on. The interpretation, which begins to give 'meaning' to the symbol, is only a way of 'focusing' and understanding the structure of the symbol with a view to making it more conscious. The explanation, however, explains nothing at all, because the interpretation is itself symbolic, and requires further interpretation. How, for example, do we explain that the shedding of its skin by the serpent, and the shedding of feathers by the bird are both symbolic of rebirth. What exactly is being said? Focusing itself also implies 'seeing out of the corner of one's eye'. Anyone who has tried to focus his attention, finds that he becomes more aware of all those things which he catches a glimpse of on the periphery of sight and which he tries to avoid as 'distractions'. Symbol is seeing out of the corner of one's eye, not quite distinctly. It is thus both focusing and being more sensitive to peripheral half-seen reality.

In conclusion here I would like to return to an idea which came up earlier concerning the symbol as something which is done, and which takes into account what materials can do. There is rather an endless and sterile controversy concerning the relation of myth to ritual. According to one school of anthropologists, myth is closely related to ritual. This has been discounted by those who have a very specialized

< 19 >

Kartikeya and peacock with serpent in its beak — drawn after a stone sculpture seen by the author in a small village temple south of Madurai. The child god represents beauty and energy

< 20 >

understanding of ritual, as something institutionalized, as in the case of rubric. I myself would like to understand ritual in a much wider sense as the type of consecrated action in which all drama originated. The myth is dramatic, as is every symbol in a subtle way. The symbol reveals in a way the mystery of a thing done, of an action. It has been pointed out that poetic expression concentrates more on the verb and adverb, that is on the process of transformation, rather than on the noun or thing acted upon. It is more poetic to describe movement and change than static things, whose description, like an inventory, is utterly prosaic. This introduces us to another central theme of symbolic thought, that of transformation. As symbol, however irrational it might seem, is the effort to give order and focus to all that reality which we 'discard' for one reason or the other as 'indigestible', so magical transformation is the primordial effort of man to transform matter, which is chaotic, into a higher mode of being. Thus alchemy laid the foundation for modern chemistry and physics. The symbol, as we have described, is a dramatic process whereby everything is thrown together into the witch's cauldron (a new aspect of 'bricolage') and cooked and stirred until something new — a new consciousness, new meaning — emerges. In this way what belongs to raw nature is transformed, through the magical power of energy-heat, into culture, higher consciousness. The culture of man has arisen out of the symbolizing process.

< 21 >

CHAPTER 2
Symbols of opposition

< 23 >

[OVERLEAF]

View of a typical village in Karnataka, showing village shrine which consists simply of a small cubical structure with only one door and no windows, often containing an old ant hill and some simple stone images. In front is a round pillar used on occasion for sacrificial purposes. A grove of sacred trees is present with here and there a constructed platform on which are erected snake stones

< 24 >

Tagore stressed the 'wholeness' of the child. He wrote in 'The Poet's Religion' (in his book *Creative Unity*):

> Growth is the movement of a whole towards a yet fuller wholeness. Living things start with this wholeness from the beginning of their career. A child has its own perfection as a child; it would be ugly if it appeared as an unfinished man. Life is a continual process of synthesis, and not of additions. [pp. 22-3]

This attitude towards childhood characterized his whole approach to children's education. In his set of poems entitled *The Crescent Moon,* he pictures the children playing on the sea-shore. 'On the sea shore of endless worlds children meet.' But this sea-shore is itself the meeting of what the poet describes as 'death-dealing waves' and 'the smile of the sea beach'. By this image the poet evokes the secret of childhood. It is the meeting of opposites. The child is itself the 'image' — 'pratima'. It is the symbol of integration.

When we ask villagers about the meaning of their symbols, they are often unable to explain these in rational terms. This is not because the symbols have no meaning for them: the very fact that they play such a role in their lives shows how important these symbols are for them. Rather, we must remember that the villager has not developed his thinking process along rational lines, and often does not have the vocabulary to express what he feels intuitively. There is also a certain fundamental difference between word and image. Word builds up a whole through what we might call a discursive method. The very nature of a descriptive process is to try to work outwards through analogies towards a definitive statement. But the image works in the opposite way. In the image we see everything that has to be said at once. Many layers of meaning are to be discovered in an image, and these layers of meaning can even be contradictory. An image begins with a wholeness which is its strength and appeal. It is for this reason that a diagram is much easier to assimilate than a long explanation, however subtle and comprehensive that description might be. A description in words is made up of parts which are interrelated and thus attempt at a whole. An image begins with a whole in which it is possible to differentiate certain parts.

The process of making an image is the process of division. Thus the etymology of the word 'maya' which is the substance of creation, shows an Indo-Aryan concept of 'measuring'. To say then that the world of facts and events is 'maya' is to say that facts and events are terms of measurement rather than realities of nature. W. D. O'Flaherty in her source-book of Hindu myths writes concerning the myth of the dwarf (Vamana) taking three strides:

< 25 >

By far the most important Vedic myth of Visnu is the story of his three steps, a creation myth based on the Vedic concept that to measure out, to spread, or to prop apart the elements of the universe is to create.

That is why iconometry is so important in Hindu thought, because the creation of the image is based on correct measurement or proportioning. We read in the canons of pramana, 'Gods and goddesses become fit to be worshipped only when they are set up with correct proportions' (Silpa Sastra, Ch. 40.13). In fact, the artist beginning to create the 'wholeness' of the image, starts by dividing the spaces, which is the primary act of composition. It is also, mythologically speaking, the act of creation — the dividing of the yarrow stalks in the practice of the *I Ching* (Book of Changes). Creation myths follow a general pattern of describing how the primary void (hiranya garbha, sunyata, bija) is divided. Even the creation myth which we find at the beginning of the book of Genesis follows this basic form. God is shown as dividing the night from the day, earth from water, woman from man, and so on.

The child is perhaps the most perfect symbol of this process of creation. The process of birth is itself parturition — and that process continues through life as self-discovery through differentiation. He is a unity, and yet he has within himself tremendous polarities. He has been compounded as it were out of the intermingling of all that is opposite. This symbol reveals with a clarity which no words could do, how a unity and duality can in fact be aspects of the same reality. The figure of the child, with supple rounded form, has constantly suggested the mystery of the void.

The child is thought of as being both creative and destructive, pure and dirty. The child in play mirrors the play of life itself, a humorous-serious drama in which the world-cycle (samsara) is itself understood as playful (Lila). The thought is close to that of Plato, who said, 'What I would say is this: serious things must be treated seriously, but not those that are not serious. In deed and in truth, however, it is God who is worthy of all our deepest and most blessed seriousness, man, on the other hand, is a plaything in the hand of God, and truly this is the best thing about him. Everyone, therefore, whether man or woman, must strive towards this end and must make of the noblest games the real content of their lives.' The child in his play both creates and destroys. He also gets very dirty. When Yasoda, the foster mother of Krsna, was told that the child Krsna had been eating mud, she scolded him and looked into his mouth. But when she looked in she saw,[1]

< 26 >

in his mouth the whole eternal universe and heaven and the regions of the sky, and the orb of the earth, with its mountains, islands and oceans; she saw the wind and lightning and the moon and stars and the Zodiac; and water and fire and air and space itself; she saw the vacilating senses, the mind, the elements and the strands of matter. She saw within the body of her son, in his gaping mouth, the whole universe in all its variety, with all the forms of life and time and nature and action and hopes, and her own village and herself. Then she became afraid and confused, thinking, 'Is this a dream or an illusion wrought by god? Or is it a delusion of my own perception? Or is it some portent of the natural powers of this little boy my son?

We see here the process by which the image opens itself up, and unfolds the whole universe which lies within it. In the same way the apparently insignificant games of the child are all full of meaning and reveal the universe as it really is. We find that what appears at first simple, is complex. What is small and insignificant, is huge. The macrocosm is the microcosm. The child playing by the sea-shore in Tagore's image, using for his imaginative games sand, water and shells, is in fact playing with the very stuff of the universe, and his game creates in microcosm all that is.

The child has come into being through the interplay of male and female, Purusa and Prakrti. He is thus mysteriously androgynous. He carries within himself the image both of his father and his mother. Hindu myth plays a great deal on this essential ambivalence in the child, asserting sometimes that the child has been created only out of the mind and seed of his father, or only out of the womb of his mother, who remains a virgin. This sort of subtle tendency towards one or the other parent makes for the essential tension between Kartikeya and Ganesa. Kartikeya is more of his father, whereas Ganesa is more of his mother. Here also there emerges the archaic anxiety concerning a deep jealousy between the parents centring on the son. The son on the one hand tries to usurp the position of the father by becoming his own mother's lover, and is consequently punished by his father (this happens both in the case of Ganesa and Andhaka): and on the other hand the mother gets her son to watch the father lest he should have adulterous relations with other women (as in the case of Viraka).

The child emerges as both wise and foolish, weak and vulnerable, yet also extremely strong. Like Vamana, he is at once a dwarf and also able in three strides to cover the whole universe. In this connection there is a popular myth concerning the youthful rivalry

< 27 >

between the brothers Ganesa (also called Ganapati) and Kartikeya. Their parents Siva and Parvati offered to give a prize of a fruit to whoever should go round the universe first. Kartikeya dashed off with all the energy and enthusiasm of the modern astronaut to go round the whole cosmos. Ganesa, on the other hand, being more clumsy and stupid, went round his parents. It was Ganesa who won the fruit as prize because he had demonstrated that his parents were in fact the universe, and related action should be intensive rather than extensive. It may be remarked that the fruit itself is a symbol of the round universe.

The folly of the child is repeatedly his supernatural wisdom. And because his world-view seems so upside down from the point of view of the worldly wise, he becomes the archetypal trickster. His 'maya' power seems to make him into a magician. Even here the ambivalence of destructive–creative aspects in the child comes into play, because part of the trickiness of the child is his capacity to put obstacles in the way of people, upset their plans, and destroy the things which they hold to be precious. He is the 'jinx' which seems to destroy every sensible adult enterprise. In this aspect he is Vinayaka, the obstacle. Because of his irrational magical capacity to destroy the cosmos unexpectedly, he must be propitiated before any enterprise is begun. This is certainly one of the most popular appeals of the trickish laughing god Ganapati.[2] He must be humoured, or else he might spoil the actions of a well-intentioned person. And so everywhere he is invoked at the beginning of every day, and the beginning of every enterprise.

The child deity is thus two-faced, and like the god Janus whom the Romans worshipped at the beginning of the year (January), his two faces look backwards and forwards. He is past and future, he is negative and positive, dead and living. He comes to us as the fulfilment of all that is over, and the dawn of all that is to begin.[3]

OPPOSITION OF THE ONE AND THE MANY

One of the most fundamental experiences of man who is close to nature is an awareness of the great multitude of forms. He feels the proliferation of entities which he concretizes in the form of a polytheism in which every potency of life is given a divine nature. He has a tendency to make everything which strikes him as uncanny — a stone, tree, ant hill, water tank, etc. into a manifestation of the sacred which has its own guarding deity. Not only that, but each family and many of the articles of the home, have their own peculiar deities. In

< 28 >

this almost endless assortment of deities it might seem impossible to find a unifying principle. And yet, though there is in all folk symbolism a stress on the manifold nature of the universe, there is also an almost contradictory assumption that the universal itself is one, not many. The one which we are speaking of here is not a part of the many, but rather the many find their fulfilment and ultimate completion in the one. The universe, in order to be fulfilled as above the particular and limited, must transcend the multitude of its forms and become the single or one. In nature itself, while confronted by the abundance of variety, there is to be discovered a certain unity of intent which is the cementing reality; the universal within the fragmented. The crowd aspires to a unity which is fundamentally and dialectically beyond its diversity. And this unity is mysteriously not in its collective unconscious force which tends to fragment, to create and destroy — but rather in a particular conscious authority to which it adheres.

The villager's view of the universe is essentially hierarchical, governed by a strongly centralized authority. The whole thrust of nature is understood as a movement inwards and upwards, whose centre as functionalized in society is a person, the hierarchical head of the community. At a more differentiated stage it becomes, in the process of individuation[4] in the psyche of the individual, the 'ista devata' or indwelling Lord, the archetype of the self. The force which draws the many together also pushes them up to a higher mode of being. And so the unification and universalization of unconscious forms is also their development into higher realms of consciousness.[5] This upward-pushing movement which is also inward-moving is characterized by the male principle, the secret pillar at the world centre, the lingam in the womb-house.

In Karnataka you will find the ant hills worshipped. There you see in a very clear symbol the effort of many (in this case the multitudes of ants) creating this upward-moving structure, so mysteriously characteristic of nature as a whole. Whereas the 'many' is characterized by movement, turning wheels, flowing waters; the single is conceived of as the still, fixed, immovable. The eternal is 'acala' (non-moving).

MYTH OF THE BATTLE OF DARK AND LIGHT

Everywhere in Indian art one finds an intuitive understanding of the interplay of opposites — movement and stillness, light and darkness. The figures seem to emerge from the deeply chiselled out stone with

< 29 >

Symbols of opposition — Buddha in meditation, the perfect yogi ascetic, is tempted by Mara. The figure of Mara in this sketch is derived from a carved, wooden village spirit god (Bhuta) from a temple on the Canara coast

< 30 >

their full forms, thrown into relief against the nascent darkness of the mother rock. This impression of form and colour emerging from the drama of light and darkness is particularly realized in the golden era of Indian culture, under the Gupta dynasty. The magnificent examples of this dialectic of light and darkness are to be found in the compositions of Ajanta, Ellora and Elephanta (see pp. 65-6, 143-4). The dark spaces of cave architecture are particularly appropriate for such treatment. Through the conscious use of the tension between light and darkness, a sense of aesthetic and spiritual wholeness is achieved. Also the epic themes so favoured by classical Hindu art are based on extremely ancient folk legends in which the battle of light against darkness, good against evil, forms the warp and woof of existence.

In mythology the battle takes the form of the battle between Asuras and Devas which, in its most primal form, seems to be the battle of light against darkness. Certainly in the archaic notion of the liturgy of the year, whereby the whole of nature is thought of as a constant interplay of light and darkness, days and nights, summer and winter, the war between the forces of light and darkness is ritualized. The ancient festival of Dusehra belongs to this category, though it is variously interpreted, either in the light of epics (Ram's battle at Lanka, or the Pandavas who after the battle of Kuruksetra give up their kingdom to live incognito) or in the light of the Puranas, where it is believed to commemorate the battle of the Mother, Durga, or more particularly Camundeswari against the buffalo demon Mahisasura.

The ten days of Dusehra are a yearly re-living of the battle between the goddess and the buffalo demon. During the nine days of Navratri various festivals take place. An important festival falling within these nine nights called Ayudha Puja is an old agricultural ritual in which agricultural implements are worshipped. In modern times this has developed as the festival of the implements, that is, the machine (yantra). It includes the worship of all vehicles — cars, motor-cycles, and any machine from pump sets to computers. In this tradition we also see the strong village feeling about the opposition between the cultivated area of the village, and the wilderness beyond the boundaries of the village which is supposed to be inhabited by bloodthirsty ghosts of the dead. It is important to understand the relationship in folk thought between apparently cruel and aggressive sport and fertility. Destruction is itself a part of the creation of a new order. Elements of this viewpoint are to be found in popular festivals such as, for example, in the festival of Holi in the north, when hierarchies are reversed and complete licence is given to return to the chaos of the release of ambivalent emotions. Again, in the rites

< 31 >

of Ayudha Puja pumpkins are broken open by dashing them against the ground, and their fleshy interior is painted red with powder colour, further accentuating the impression of violence and blood. In fact, the pumpkin is always a symbol of the womb with its many seeds. And so its ritualistic breaking open is a bringing to birth. The fearsome deity Siva, the destroyer, who dances upon the burning ground, destroys in order that he might liberate. Destruction here is not simply negative, but is preparatory to recreation.

Ganesa, the child of Siva, is thought to be an old agricultural god. He is known as Ekadanta or one tusk, which also indicates a connection with the plough. In fact the theme of his one tusk appears in another name which is given to this god — the southern name Pillaiyar, meaning noble child. This comes from the word pille meaning child, but curiously pallu, or pella, means tooth in the Dravidian languages, and pillaka was the old Pali name for a young elephant.[6] A verse attributed to an ancient source in the Laws of Manu says, 'Siva is the god of the Brahmans, while Ganesa is the god of the Sudras, that is, agriculturalists.'

An interesting myth explains why one of the tusks of the genial god Ganesa is broken. Once Ganesa fell off his rat mount and the moon laughed at him, the spectacle seemed so incongruous! Ganesa became so angry that he looked around for a weapon to attack the moon and, finding nothing to hand, broke off one of his own tusks and struck the moon with it. He revealed his 'fearful aspect' or 'Kirtimukha' which means 'face of Glory'.[7] This terrible face is often represented on the reverse side of the genial childish Ganesa showing that he too is ambivalent. This 'alter' side of Ganapati is sometimes known as Vanaspati, that is, the Lord of the Forests.[8] Another explanation of this broken tusk of Ganapati is that he, being an 'auspicious' sign, a sign of the good, averts the evil eye (in this case of the moon) by the imperfection of his own broken tusk.

The village god is invariably ambivalent, having a good, kind, peaceful, aspect together with a dark, terrible and fearful one. The mother is a good example of this. She is the curer of all infirmity but also the giver of sickness. Thus smallpox, a much feared sickness in rural India, is characterized as the 'Kiss of the Goddess', the pockmarks being called 'pearls given by the goddess', and in many primitive communities a person who has contracted the disease is thought to be in some way favoured by the goddess.

< 32 >

Kolama pattern with intersecting arcs, probably signifying the intersection of heavenly and earthly spheres as in the orphic mandorla

< 33 >

CHAPTER 3
Womb–tomb symbols

< 35 >

[OVERLEAF]

A representation of the maze which Abhimanyu entered but from which he could not emerge — from a village shrine abounding in fertility symbols at Bannergatta, south of Bangalore. Worshippers walk through the maze which is marked out with stones on the ground, as they feel that this will aid them face the trials of life

< 36 >

FOLK ORIGINS OF CONCEPTS OF BIRTH AND DEATH

As we have already noted, there is a relationship between the child
and death — the very contrast between the two seems to bring them
together as 'yin' and 'yang', light and darkness, creating a unity out
of their very opposition.[1] The child stands at the very navel of the
universe — he becomes a symbol of centrality, of the hub of the life
wheel, whose outer circumference is the enclosing and limiting container of death. The transcendental God appears either in the form of
the child or the old man — both are aspects of the same eternal wisdom. Zimmer retells a story from the Brahmavaiverta Purana, at the
beginning of his *Myths and Symbols in Indian Art and Civilization,*
which gives an idea of the Hindu concept of time. Here we hear how
Indra, after constructing the universe with the help of Visvakarma
(the Indian Pantocrator), was confronted by a pilgrim Brahmin child
who pointed out a procession of ants, and revealed that each of these
ants was in fact an Indra, who in turn had created a cosmos, though
each had passed away, and only he, the child, had remained to see
the one following upon the other. This child was followed by a very
old man, who appeared to be a hermit, and called himself 'hairy'
because he had a patch of hair on his chest. This wise old man also
revealed that with the coming and going of each Indra and cosmos,
one hair dropped out from the hairy patch on his chest.

The same two figures (the old sage and the child) meet in the
myth of Markandeya who found the eternal child playing peacefully
in the trackless ocean of the cosmic void. It is the child who through
his playful fantasies creates one universe after another. Often the
figure of the wise old man, or ancestor, and the child, or first mortal,
are confused, forming two aspects of one person.

It is thought that the myth concerning the churning of the cosmic
oceans belongs to one of the oldest strata of cosmology (see p. 49).
The story is very familiar, and upon it is based the very popular
Kumbha Mela. According to this myth the gods of light (Devas) and
titans of darkness (Asuras), representing the two cosmic opposites,
churned the waters in the hope that the life substance would rise
from it. This motif of churning can also be noted in connection with
the kindling of fire. The word 'kindle' means to 'bring forth' and
in German the root concept has developed into the word 'Kind',
meaning child, from which we also have many related words like kin
and kind. What the waters brought forth after being churned was
both poison and elixir of eternal life (amrt), in other words death
and life.

Here also we find the basic idea of food so connected with the life

< 37 >

within the womb. Much of the symbolism behind fire is also related
to this sacrament of life. Fire is the transformer of matter into food,
and food generates in the organism energy. One could identify two
cosmologies, one which bases itself on air (prana) and the other on
food. The very drive of samsara is hunger. The child is driven from
the womb by hunger, and its cry is a demand for the food of life. In
the myths of Krsna we find that the baby was at one time nurtured
by the demoness Putana who gave the babe her breast which was
filled with poison. The child drank the poison, even as Siva drank
the poison which came out of the cosmic ocean. He not only drank
the poison, but he drained all the life out of the demoness so that
she was destroyed. The festival of Holi is linked to this myth, as the
festival of Sivratri commemorates Siva's action of swallowing the
poison generated from the cosmic ocean. Both myths probably relate
to an ancient concept of recreation by swallowing, but here food is
given a negative value — as poison it cannot be absorbed, but has to
be transformed through a ritual death.

Krsna's childhood hunger for curds and sweets which motivated
him to many childish pranks has thus a cosmological significance.
We are told that the child Krsna (Balakrsna) was for ever stealing
curds out of earthen pots, and often breaking the pot in the process.
This pot containing sweet life substance is in fact the purna kumbham,
or overflowing vessel of life which is described as emerging out of the
cosmic ocean. The pot itself is at once a symbol of life and death.
Sita is discovered as a baby in a pot, but again pots figure in funerary
rites as the urns in which the remains of the dead are stored. Everything emerges from the pot, and then goes back into it again.

In pre-historic times the whole continent south of the Vindhyas,
and even somewhat north of them, was characterized by a culture of
cists (stone tombs) and megaliths. Even in Harappa we have an important graveyard whose funerary urns are painted with peacocks in
whose wombs we see depicted the souls of the departed. I would
conjecture that the peacock is always the vehicle of the dead; in
Christian bestiaries it is described as the bird of immortality. If I
were to describe most briefly that which is most characteristic of
what I have called folk religion, I would say it is this interest in the
dead.

We find in the stone cist tombs of southern India that the tomb is
constructed on womb symbolism. To begin with, it is round, dug
into mother earth. It is a room with a place for the dead person to
lie. Provision is made for his being fed with pots containing ceremonial food. The whole idea of giving 'drink' to the souls of the dead
in Hindu funerary rites links up with the feeding of a baby. Finally,

< 38 >

there is the exit, or porthole, cut into the stone and facing south from which presumably the soul of the dead person can be 'born again'.[2]

In Hindu thought Yama, god of the dead, rules over the south. To my mind the relationship of the dead to the south is most probably connected with solar symbolism. The sun has always been a sign of that which dies and is born again, entering the womb of Mother Earth at night, to rise again the next morning. The megaliths are often arranged with reference to the cardinal points of the compass. From the pre-historic megalithic culture of the south of India we have apparently the symbolism which inspired the form of the Buddhist stupa.[3] There too a circular funerary mound has gateways facing the main points of the compass. At Sanchi, whose complete structure is the earliest Buddhist stupa that we have, it appears that the gate to the south is the oldest and most important gate, for it is in front of this gate that the steps lead up to the harmika in which the funerary urns containing sacred relics are kept. The harmika of the stupa in Katmandu has eyes painted on it, connecting it even more intimately with sun symbolism, for the sun is the eye of the heavens.

Ancient rituals of the dead have been one of the most enduring features of the traditions of rural India. Burial is still common among the lower castes and outcastes, especially in south India. The earth is the Mother, and burial in her is a return to the womb.

The relation of womb symbolism to sacrifice is interesting because it relates to another aspect of village culture — that is the festivals when animals and birds are sacrificed, and their blood sprinkled on the fields, in order to make the fields more fertile. We find that these sacrifices bring about in the villager's mind the sense of a return to the first beginning of creation when all nature was in the womb of time. The stream of blood which is allowed to soak into the earth, and which is jealously guarded is itself a sign of the mother blood which feeds the womb. This blood is allowed to soak into mounds of cooked or sometimes raw grain, especially rice, which is then put into baskets and sprinkled over the village and its fields, with the cry 'food, food' in the belief that this will fertilize and bring abundance. Anyone who has seen this unpleasant mixture of rice and blood will understand its connection with the unformed substance of the womb, where the seed is fertilized, and the foetus is fed with the mother's blood. In fact the basket is itself a symbol of the womb, as is clearly seen from songs such as we read of in Verrier Elwin's account of the Gond tribes.[4]

Much of this symbolism lies behind the making of the Hindu

< 39. >

temple. We are told in the sastras that traditionally the temple was built in the image of a human body — the body of the primal man Purusa, who, it is thought, was sacrificed, his body cut into pieces which were then sprinkled over the earth in a fundamental act of creation. These pieces of the body of primal man are the squares of the Mahapurusa mandala on which every Hindu temple is based.[5] Also, the ritual for building a temple begins with ploughing up the earth and planting a pot of seed. The temple is said to rise from this planted seed. Again, the symbolism is connected with the same ideas which lie behind the legend of Sita (the name means 'furrow') who was found in a pot which was buried in the ground and which was turned up by the ploughman.

In the light of these ideas we can see why the central holy of holies of the temple is called the 'garbha grha' or womb house. I also feel that it is possible that the great interest shown in cave architecture also goes back to this primal concern for a return to the womb. Classical Indian art very largely owed its development to the carving in rock initiated in the great cave monasteries of Buddhism. Before these, apparently, stone was not used for temple art because it was thought to be a material proper to the dead. In Vedic times we presume that temples were made out of wood, and related a great deal to tree symbolism.

SYMBOLISM OF THE FOETUS IN THE WOMB, AND THE NAVEL

The centrality of the navel is of course a concept belonging to the whole birth-death syndrome of symbols. In folk religion we find frequent reference to navel stones planted at the centre of a village or sacred place, generally over a buried sacrificed animal (or, in more primitive societies, even a sacrificed human being, especially a baby). These navel stones are probably very much connected with the later development of the flagstaff in the Hindu temple. They represent the axis of the universe, and are ultimately connected with the womb of creation. The popular figure of Visnu as Padma-Nabha pictures the whole of creation as proceeding from the navel of the sleeping Lord.[6]

It is interesting here to note the very elemental significance in the villager's mind of the grinding stone or kitchen quern which is found in every household. Kosambi points out that this instrument belongs to as far back as the Stone Age, and has come down from that time to the modern village home, almost unaltered. Anyone who has lived in India is familiar enough with the Indian grinding stone. The typical

< 40 >

Womb-tomb symbols — a roundel from the Bharhut stupa railings, probably representing Brahma. The theme is closely related to the later Padma-Nabha, a creator figure from whose navel emerges a flowering lotus stem, symbol of the universe

< 41 >

grinding stone, as we find it for example in the south, is an oblong, smooth oval stone, like a grain of rice much enlarged, which stands very often in another stone in which a hollow has been chiselled out. It looks, therefore, rather like an egg in a cup. The villager uses it to grind together rice and pulse, or spices, rather as one might use a mortar and pestle. Whitehead, in his study of village gods of south India, notes that in certain village traditions, the earth is compared to the hollowed out, mortar-like stone, and the sky to the grain-smooth oval stone which is used for grinding. Kosambi describes a village ritual, which he claims is widespread but unknown generally to caste Hindus, in which on the 6th, 10th or 12th day after a baby is born, the smooth muller stone is passed around the baby's cot by village women, to ensure that the child will grow up as free from blemish and as enduring as the stone. This stone is even dressed to look like a baby, with a baby's cap on its top, and necklaces. The stone is also generally painted red. In Dravidian languages such as Tamil and Malayalam, the grinding stones, that is the muller and the quern, are called Kuzhavikal (baby stone) and Ammai or Ammikal (mother stone) respectively. During the marriage rituals the grinding stone is used as a symbol of stability, both husband and wife standing on the quern and looking towards the pole star.

One suspects often a relationship between those stone forms which seem to attract the villager so that he paints them red as a sign of worship, and an unconscious association with the form of the foetus. The red colour is itself the colour of life and blood. The ritual of anointing stones, or pouring different liquids over them, is also a sign of investing them with life. Ganesa is worshipped on occasion as the formless stone — svayambhu murti. There is a myth concerning Viraka, a son of Siva, who was cursed by his mountain mother to be born of stone.

Stones which are oval, egg-like in shape, or, as the traditional description goes, looking like a grain of rice, are often painted red, and worshipped as the emblem of god or goddess. There is a description of the 'hiranya garbha' or golden egg from which the whole creation came, even in the Upanisads. Whitehead describes a south Indian village myth about the goddess Ammavaru who is believed to have existed before any of the other gods came into being.[7]

Even before the existence of the four Yugas, before the birth of the nine Brahmans, three eggs were laid by Ammavaru in the sea of milk, one by one in three successive ages. The egg laid first got spoilt, the next filled with air, and only the third hatched. This egg had three compartments, from which came the Trimurti Brahma, Visnu and Siva.

< 42 >

In the Buddhist stupa the round dome is called the anda or egg. This egg is equated with sunya, India's great metaphysical concept of the void. Ultimately speaking this sunya is wholeness. It is the great egg which could be thought of in one way as empty, void, but in another sense in the fullness of the womb from which everything comes forth. In the symbol of the egg, both life and death, womb and tomb are signified.

SYMBOLS OF THE CYCLE OF LIFE AND DEATH

In the Mahabharata there is a story concerning Abhimanyu, the hero son of Arjuna. When he was in his mother's womb he heard the Lord Krsna describing to his mother (who was Krsna's sister) the secret concerning how to enter the maze, which the Kauravas had devised. But unfortunately Abhimanyu's mother fell asleep after hearing Krsna describe how to enter the maze, and so Krsna never finished telling about the maze — he never explained how to get out of it. Later, in the battle of Kuruksetra the young hero Abhimanyu entered the maze but then was unable to come out of it again, and so was killed at the centre of the maze. It is interesting that he heard about the maze while he was still in the womb. The maze reproduces, in its spiralling forms, the way between womb and tomb — the journey of man from birth to death. Mystically, the maze is itself an image of the womb and the child here entering the maze re-enters as it were the womb.[8] The movement of a person entering a maze is like a foetus in the womb. The way in which a man dies is also somehow prefigured in the womb.

This brings us to the idea of the pilgrim world in constant cyclic motion and the notion of time which underlies the first myth we mentioned where the child and the old sage reveal the mystery of the procession of ants, and the falling hairs. As the circumambulation of the cosmic egg of the stupa was the liturgical reliving of the movement of life, so too was the pilgrimage. We hear that King Asoka, after his conversion to Buddhism, popularized the idea of the great pilgrimage to replace the former worldly custom of the court which went on hunting parties. The great stupas and monasteries which arose in the time of King Asoka, and initiated the course of Indian art and architecture, were in fact to mark this grand procession route. It will be recalled that Buddha advised his followers to build funerary mounds at the crossroads — there again we see the relationship between the stupa and the great journey. In the same way Tantra popularized pilgrimage to the Pithas where according to

< 43 >

tradition the demented Siva had dropped parts of the dismembered body of Sati.[9]

The spiral is a symbol both of life and death and is thus a perfect expression of the villager's understanding of nature and time. The twisting tendrils of the vine which spiral upwards, like the 'thread' of the screw clinging to whatever they can hold on to, are indicative of life's will to grow upwards. But inversely the spiral is also representative of nature returning to its source.

< 44 >

CHAPTER 4

The ecology of symbolic elements and transfiguring energy

< 45 >

[OVERLEAF]

Carved stone figure of the sage Bhagiratha sitting in meditation near his asram — detail of 'The Descent of the River Ganges' at Mahabalipuram

< 46 >

In popular Hindu religion we sometimes have a sense of the closed-ness of the tomb. Everything is cyclical and, like energy itself, nothing is lost, but also (and here is the anxiety) nothing appears to be trans-figured, in the sense of transcended. We feel that we are all the time being dragged back to the cycle. Even our youthful deity, in so far as he is the principle of incarnation, seems to draw us irresistibly back into the closed symbol of the world. The symbol almost stifles, in that it becomes impossible to break its wholeness.

In an essay entitled *Civilized Man's Eight Deadly Sins* Konrad Lorenz suggests that there is an ethology of man's cultural history comparable to the ecology interrelating other biological species. We see clearly in the symbolic process a cyclical harmony in which every symbol is part of a total wholeness. I feel that the connection of symbol with the elemental balance of nature is responsible for this link between the ecology which is the study of nature and the study of the symbolic process in which every part is related to a whole.[1]

There is a constant tension in the human mind between what is symmetrical, static and consequently inorganic, and growth, which implies imbalance, imperfection, in order to reach towards a future which has not yet been realized. In attempting to analyse the trans-formation process in popular Indian thought, I think that it is necessary to see the relationship of symbolic thought to organic life process, and to the total evolutionary effort of nature itself, which, even in its closed cycles, maintains a dialectical struggle for union through separation, creativity through opposition. Perhaps the cycle seems impossible to transcend, and yet it is the transcendent which gives to the cycle its dynamism, its capacity to evolve. The circle of symbolic thought is not a static circle, but an ever evolving circle, like the waves going out from the point where a stone has plunged into a pool of water. It is a circle which expands, taking within its radius ever wider spheres of meaning and relationship. In fact many circles seem to intersect and, like the synchronized wheels of a clock, operate together to create a total order of interpenetrating sym-metries.

To demonstrate what I mean, let me try to take a particular myth, that of Sagara, which I mention later in connection with tree symbol-ism (see p. 155). The myth is given in a number of different forms as it is found both in the Mahabharata, and the Ramayana, and in at least six Puranas. John Dawson, in his *Classical Dictionary of Hindu Mythology*, gives the etymology of the name as sa, 'with' and gara, 'poison'. The name is explained by the fact that his mother, as a result of poison given to her by a rival wife, was unable to give birth to her child, even though it was conceived in her womb, for seven

< 47 >

years. The king had two wives, but was unable to have any children until as a result of a boon one wife had a single child, while the other had sixty thousand children. But we are told that all the children were impious. One myth tells the story as follows:[2]

> King Sagara performed a horse sacrifice, but the horse was stolen by Indra and hidden in the ocean, at that time devoid of water. The king sent his 60,000 sons to find the horse; they dug down into hell, where they saw the horse, but the sage Kapila, who was performing tapasya there, released a flame from his eye, and burnt the sons to ashes. Sagara's one remaining son propitiated Kapila, and obtained the horse, with which the king performed his sacrifice and the ocean became Sagara's son Sagara. Many years later Bhagiratha, the great grandson of Sagara, propitiated Siva and the Ganges. The Ganges fell from heaven (where she is the Milky Way) to earth, flowing over the ashes of the 60,000 sons and reviving them, and Siva received the first torrents of the Ganges upon his head, breaking the fall so that it would not shatter the earth.

Another variant of this myth is given by Zimmer.[3] There we are told that the sons of Sagara were travelling with the horse, as part of the ancient Aryan ritual of letting a consecrated horse free for a year, the journey of the horse being a symbol of the journey of the sun, and the area which the horse covers indicating the domain of the Cakravartin or king. The sons of Sagara were thus an army defending the sacrificial horse. The horse disappears, and the sons dig down at the point where it disappeared, until they reach the underworld where they find the horse near an ascetic who is meditating. This ascetic is Kapila, meaning the 'red one', an epithet both for the sun, and for Siva himself. Kapila burns the sons, all except one, to ashes. We are reminded of Kama who was also burnt to ashes, and was in many myths connected with a tree. In fact the burning of Kama to ashes is probably related to an ancient Indo-Aryan rite wherein a tree was burnt as part of a ritual of renewal, perhaps even relating to certain primitive agricultural practices of burning a forest area before cultivating it. The cosmic tree is called the Asvattha tree, meaning the place where the horse stands. In the myth we have then the following elements:

> *Fire* (burning to ashes) – a creative–destructive element which is necessary in order to temper the body (as in the case of the corpse which is burnt) but which is also renewing.
> *Water* (river pouring down to earth) – also destructive and

< 48 >

creative, destructive in that it floods the land, creative in that it also irrigates the earth.

The horse sacrifice is connected with solar symbolism (Sagara himself belongs to a solar dynasty) and the consecration of the king. In the myth of Sagara, the horse disappears into the earth, and is found near the sun (Kapila). According to one version of the myth, it is stolen by Indra who is the cosmic king, and ruler of all waters (there is no water in the ocean). In some way the descent of the sons to the underworld brings about the ocean Sagara. Bhagiratha, a descendant of Sagara, does the asceticism of the five fires in order to bring down the Ganges from heaven, and revive his ancestors who were burnt to ashes by the fire of Kapila. But how to bring what is above to what is below without destroying the balance of earth? Siva, seated on the mountain (who is himself Kapila, often practising a fiery asceticism immersed in the ocean), allows the heavenly river to fall on his head (from which also fire issues from his third eye, burning to ashes) (see p. 48). Siva thus plays a dual role as destroyer and creator. He is destructive in that he burns, creative in that from his head a life-giving river flows.

Zimmer in his *Myths and Symbols in Indian Art and Civilization* gives further details concerning the myth of the descent of the river Ganges. We are told that Agastya, who was a great yogi famous for the fiery powers of his digestive juices, once swallowed the ocean to get rid of the devils which hid there. This was a noble act in itself, but as a consequence deprived the universe of water. Bhagiratha, who is also thought of as a descendant of Manu, did the penance of fire (tapasya) in order that the heavenly river might descend and give life to the earth. We remember at this point that Sagara was poison, and that at the churning of the cosmic oceans poison came forth from it, which was swallowed by Siva in the same way as Agastya swallowed the ocean in order to get rid of the demons (poisonous elements) that were lurking in the waters. Further, all the sons of Sagara were impious. Here Siva (and also Agastya) were saviour figures. But yet again imbalance ensued, and this could only be corrected by Bhagiratha, himself a descendant of Manu, who survived the cosmic flood, by drawing the river Ganges down upon the head of blue-throated Siva.

We begin now to see a very intricate pattern connecting earth, ocean, fire and sky within a complex system wherein nothing is lost, elements being constantly transformed and inverted in the process of tempering, that is purifying, them. The sons of poison are turned into ashes for their sin, the ocean is swallowed in order to purify it of

< 49 >

evil spirits, what is above is brought down to what is below in order that what has been burnt might be given life again. Some very ancient alchemical notions of transformation in matter – ashes made into agents of fertility, oceans of bitter water made into the sweet water of a river, poison swallowed, etc. are here implicit within the myth. Fire as the transforming agent is the essential motif. Yet to explain the ecology of the myth as merely representing a natural ecology would be simplistic. Certainly the problem of drought as against flood is a perennial problem for the Indian peasant. But for him the myth does not so much explain what happens in nature, as nature explains what is happening in the myth.

EVOLUTION OF ELEMENTAL SYMBOLS TOWARDS THE SYMBOL OF MAN

There seems to be a certain growth in consciousness evolving from the elemental forces of earth, air and water towards the highest symbol of 'person' which is fulfilled in man. Already we may notice a tendency to personify the elemental, so that rivers are seen as feminine figures, and mountains as fatherly presences. Angelic presences give a 'personality' to trees and flowers. The angelic presences (known in India by many names such as Devas or Asuras, of which lesser powers might be called Gandharvas, Apsaras, Yaksas, etc.) are a linking motif showing the connection between apparently inanimate and animate beings, between the inorganic and organic, animal and human.

The Asvins were two very important vedic deities, and could be related (according to Cirlot, *Dictionary of Symbols*) to the Gemini. In Hindu thought they represent the dawn.[4] Like the Gandharvas they were thought to be physicians and were called 'ocean born' and 'sons of the submarine fire'. They were totally benevolent, being known as 'two kings, performers of holy acts'. Many acts of healing are ascribed to them. In their relation to each other they represent the 'whole', being heaven and earth, day and night (hence Sandhya).[5] The Sanskrit name asva (horse) also carries the meaning 'pervader', so the Asvins are thought to pervade everything and are supposed to be young, giving youth to the world, though they are also very ancient. One might speculate in the light of this concerning the horse-riding king and his retinue who are thought in the folklore of Tamil Nadu to guard the village. Groups of horses are set up as symbols of this guardian angel Ayyanar outside many villages of Tamil Nadu. Like the Asvins, Ayyanar is thought of as benevolent, protecting the

< 50 >

The ecology of symbolic elements and transfiguring energy — hero riding on a horse. This is a very popular theme of Indian folk art and in south India, especially in Tamil Nadu, whole groups of such figures made out of clay or plaster can be found on the outskirts of villages

< 51 >

village from thieves, epidemics, evil spirits and natural calamities like cyclones and floods. This horse-riding guardian angel is seen then as a physician of the village, both in the material and physical sense, and also in the spiritual sense of protecting against evil forces.

The horse seems to be related very much to sun symbolism, and by association with the sun, to kings. The horse sacrifice (asva medha) was central to the Hindu notion of the king as Cakravartin, or representative on earth of a solar dynasty. Yet the horse also seems to relate to death and the sea. According to Mircea Eliade, this animal is often related to burial rites of Chthonian cults. The descent of the horse into the ocean is clearly a symbol of the death of the sun in the sea and its constant rebirth.

The symbol of the horse thus represents energy, often in the form of wind or white-crested waves. One might contrast it with the other important animal symbol of India — the cow. The cow is far more domesticated, representing the agricultural civilization of a settled people. Hence in the Indus valley seals it is by far the most represented animal, often depicted in association with ceremonial censers, indicating a very ancient cult worship. The worship of the cow is possibly pre-Aryan, typical of the settled pre-Aryan culture of the Indus valley. The horse on the other hand is much more associated with the nomadic tribes of the Aryans. Subsequently in Indian culture the horse has come to stand for the sun, whereas the cow is connected with the moon.

Sacred animals or birds in Indian thought are thus a stage in the total movement in nature linking natural elements, and finally culminating in man himself. The angelic beings are also a link motif connecting the material–phenomenological, and the conscious, noumenal. To clarify the inter-functioning of these symbolic elements, we might draw the following schematic chart:

man ⟶ noumenal, conscious
↑   ↑
animal, bird, snake ⟶ angelic presence
↑
elemental, fire, water   ↑
air, earth, etc.⟶ phenomenological appearances

THE ANALOGY OF AN ECONOMY IN RELATION TO THE SYMBOL AS TRANSACTION

In a society all forms of exchange are in fact symbolic, and when we are describing the symbolic process, we are in fact describing the way

< 52 >

in which exchange goes on in the society; the image is thus inherently social in that it arises out of a society, and speaks to that society, giving to it its whole value system. The transformation process within the symbolic field is thus closely related to change as it goes on in the society, and in fact changes in the structure of society give rise to transformations in the symbolic process. In this way symbols are used in order to analyse social structures, and also to create dynamic movements in the social structure.

Let us examine more carefully how this exchange system is structured. We see that society is divided into those who buy (receive, store) and those who spend (give, distribute). That is not to say that some people are buyers and others spenders, but that in any transaction these elements are present, so that in order to buy a man must spend, and in order to receive he must give. Further, in any exchange one receives (buys) and the other gives (spends). This applies ultimately speaking to energy itself, for energy expends itself in order to receive the means by which it is restored and renewed.

Erich Fromm in his analysis of personality (*Man for Himself*) shows that even in the psychology of individual types, some are inclined to amass wealth (receptive–hoarding orientation) while others are predisposed to spend and be generous (marketing orientation). These orientations can be both productive and unproductive. The receptive, hoarding orientation can lead to excessive dependency and conservatism, whereas the marketing orientation can easily become exploitative. Societies have at various times given value to either one or the other 'type', saying that either the storing, capitalist type is best, or the spending, generous, pleasure-loving type is preferable.

In Hindu society the two extremes are characterized by the samnyasi and the householder, symbolically the mendicant beggar and king, both roles having a symbolic value in the society as a whole. The samnyasi is thought of as naked and without a house, therefore he does not possess anything (he has spent all that he had). On the other hand the householder has wealth, and this is his dharma, to amass riches. But these roles are very quickly reversible. The samnyasi is a beggar, therefore he receives, whereas the householder must always be generous, especially to guests (he is a giver). Conversely, the samnyasi is an ascetic, and by asceticism the Hindu understands the storing of energy – tapasya. The householder on the other hand is erotic (and eroticism is understood in Indian thought as spending of energy). But then, returning to the initial characteristic of the samnyasi (i.e. his nakedness), he is seen as highly erotic. His very chastity is called 'holding the seed up' or 'lifting the seed up', meaning by that both the storing of sexual energy and also, physically, his

< 53 >

erect penis. (It is interesting that even in English idiom a moralistic, chaste person is referred to as 'upright', i.e. 'erect'.) As far back as in the Indus valley seals we see a representation of an ithyphallic deity, presumed to be a proto-Siva, sitting cross-legged in meditation.

In an elemental world energy is symbolized by fire and wind. Fire is thought of as conserving, tempering, whereas wind is expending, broadcasting. The mountain is vertical, reminding one of the chaste ascetic with his seed held up (the lingam), whereas the river seeks the horizontal and is ultimately erotic (bathing in water is very often equated in Indian thought with sexual play, hence water is both purifying and contaminating). The mountain is the immovable symbol of hoarding, or piling up, whereas water is the symbol of spending or pouring out, eternal flux.

It is necessary to understand this functioning of symbolic exchange, as in an economy where giving and receiving, credit and debit, are the basic motifs. The householder is said, in Hindu social law, to be repaying a debt to the world and society. It is only within the context of the response to the givenness of life that symbolic language can be interpreted within the total mechanics of social exchange.

THE WORLD AS TRANSFORMING SYMBOL

The lingam is perhaps the prime symbol of Hindu culture. From the time of the later Upanisads (Maitrayani, Katha, Svetasvatara) the term lingam seems to be associated with bhutatman, or the subtle body. It is also called retah-sarira, or seed body, and Berriedale Keith in his book on the Samkhya System relates it to the 'psychic apparatus'.[6] Of this psychic apparatus he writes:

> The psychic apparatus, which is incorporeal, and is prior to the conception of time, accompanies the souls throughout transmigration from body to body, in accordance with the rule of causality, playing like an actor various parts, a power which it possesses since it shares in the property of all pervadingness which belongs to nature.

The lingam is believed to emerge of itself (svayambhu murti) from the body of Mother Earth, as an 'automatism' in nature. Everywhere among natural forms we find the lingam in mountains, rocks, ant hills, and so on. On the one hand it seems that the symbol has arisen out of the primal structure of earth itself, but on the other hand it seems to have fallen onto the earth, as a sort of lustre of form shed upon the formless substance of matter.

< 54 >

The two aspects of the symbol, one appearing to arise out of nature, and the other to be impressed on to the material, plastic body of nature, are given mythic expression in the idea of the shed seed of Siva which falls to the earth, or arises out of the earth as his lingam. In both cases the symbol becomes a thing in itself, separating from its origin, and establishing a life of its own.

< 55 >

CHAPTER 5

Symbols of magical power in folklore

< 57 >

[OVERLEAF]

The destructive hand of Siva carrying the curling tongue of flame — symbol of both the destructive and the creative

< 58 >

INCUBATION AND GESTATION – NATURE 'COOKING'

According to myth the child god Skanda, the god of war, is the son of Agni, god of fire. Fire, as we have already seen, is a very important symbol in Indian thought and, like so much else connected with the intuitive language of symbol, it contains within itself many opposites. As pointed out in the preceding chapter, fire is thought of as both creative and destructive. A very elemental understanding of the process of nature has identified the presence of heat, both in the emergence of life (as in the incubation of the egg, or the germination of the seed), and also in decomposition, where rotting organic matter is found to emit heat while destroying its own cellular structure.

Not only is there tension between the fire of creativity and of destruction, but fire is connected both with the seed of Purusa, the archetypal male, and the womb of Prakrti, nature. According to one myth the fiery seed of Brahma or again Siva was so full of energy that nothing could bear to touch it, and so it remained essentially beyond conception. In another myth the feminine principle of the universe is seen to be a creation out of the fusing of all the fires of primal energies which became concretized in the form of the first Mother.[1] Thus woman herself is spoken of as a fire. Gestation in the womb is thought of as a kind of 'cooking'. Based on this idea, intercourse between man and woman is described in terms of a fire offering. Thus in the symbolism of the Indian standing lamp, the lamp itself is the lingam, but the ring of fire is the feminine womb. But in that sense all fire in Indian thought is related to the feminine, especially in its relation to the cycle of organic life. The fire is thus especially related to the Tree of Life, which is an idea also shared by the Jews, whose Manora, or seven-branched candle-stick is meant to be the Tree of Life. Agni is called Vanaspati, or the Lord of Vegetation (a name which is also applied to Ganapati). Certainly the ancient Indian Fire God was probably the hidden energy within growing things (one myth describes him as 'hiding' in a tree) and the Vedic or Aryan fire altar was a pictograph of the world-cosmos which is based upon energy. In this sense the cosmology of Heraclitus which saw the universe as essentially fire is very close to the Hindu concept of the cosmos as arising out of the incubation of a cosmic fire-egg called hiranya garbha, or the golden womb.

FIRE IN THE RG VEDA AS HIGHER BEING

There are many hymns of fire in the Rg Veda. The idea of fire is

< 59 >

connected in Indian thought not only with the primal sacrifice, but with the birth of the boy god, and the emergence of speech and thought. We must recall that Ganapati is also thought of as the manifestation of the essential sound Om, the 'unstruck music' which is both eternal vibration and energy. He is the wisdom which is born out of that germ of life which is seminal as well as mental, permeating all forms as not only the energy of movement and life, but as nascent consciousness itself which at a higher level of being becomes pure self-realization.

CHURNING AS COSMIC TRANSFORMATION

Fire arises out of friction, the rubbing together of matter. On one side matter is seen as the mere coming together of lines of energy which unite to concretize in the ultimate manifestation of word become flesh (an idea to be found, we note, in the sabda yoga of Tantra), but on the other side matter itself is dynamic and therefore generates heat. This is the cycle of the phenomenological world from energy back to energy. There is no place in this concept for the notion of entropy, the gradual depletion of energy along a linear line of movement (for example the rolling ball which ultimately comes to a standstill) because what is static and what is energetic are not opposed to each other as void and substance, but are really only aspects of the same essential reality which is cyclical rather than linear or progressive.

THE BIRTH OF SKANDA, GOD OF WAR

Fire is essentially a god of home and the hearth. It is on this account that he was able to seduce the Mothers, the wives of the sages who are in fact the Pleiades. By giving his seed into the wombs of these noble wives of Brahmin priests, the child god Skanda was conceived and was born with six faces. Skanda is the great god of war. The seed which Agni conveys to the wombs of the Mothers was not his own seed, but came ultimately from the terrible third eye of the transcendental god Siva himself, whose seed was too full of energy in itself to be born by anyone until it had been tempered and in some way transmitted through Agni. The six faces (sanmukha) of the child god are thought to be the bringing together of different deities. As fire itself is the bringing together of many energies, so too the child incorporates within himself different aspects of divinity. He is at once

< 60 >

Agni, Soma (the elixir of life), Indra, Varuna (demiurges of water and wind), Brhaspati (god of wisdom) and hiranya garbha. He is thus at once a symbol of the unity of all natural forces and their conflict, as he is the very essence of war.

THE MAGICAL POWER OF HEAT

The power of fire is thought to be magical. It transforms matter from what is wild and raw into what is cooked and cultured. Constantly in Hindu mythology we get the idea of magical powers derived from long austerities and yogic practice. This intense discipline is called tapasya which is a word deriving from tapa meaning fire. Folklore is very much concerned with the magical. Man is magical in so far as nature is magical. The word maya, applied to nature, is linked to the Indo-Aryan root which is also the origin of the English word magic. Man is not thought of as over and against nature, as in Western scientific thought. Man, as an entity, arises out of the magic of nature. That is why the whole concept of 'person' is not so much thought of as anthropomorphic, but rather as arising out of nature, where forces in nature concentrate, through some unforeseeable coincidence. A stone, tree, river or place is thought of as having a personality, because the same incidence of forces that go to the forming of man as a conscious creature, imbued with feelings and a purpose in life, have arisen here also. There is no very clear notion of where man is distinct from the rest of nature. This may be conveniently labelled 'animism', but the label is dangerous in so far as it supposes some very clear, cut and dried theory about what we can shelve as 'primitive', and therefore somehow not recognize as our own, thinking as we do that we have advanced beyond such unscientific views of the world around us.

The story concerning the creation of Sakti out of the combined energies of the gods, describes how the goddess fights the demon-tyrant Mahisasura who had the form of a water-buffalo bull.[2] This Titan was threatening to destroy the whole universe. The story is interesting because it forms the basis of a very popular festival — Navratri, or the Nine Nights which culminate on the tenth day of Dusehra. The myth is a long one, and is given graphic expression in the wonderful rock carving on this theme to be found in Mahaballipuram, which is one of the greatest southern representations of the Mother. The myth must derive from very ancient Dravidian folklore where the village goddess is associated with the buffalo, as we read repeatedly in Whitehead's *Village Gods of South India.* The battle

< 61 >

between the Mother and the buffalo demon Mahisasura as described in the myth is essentially a magical one. The buffalo demon, using maya or magic power, continually changed his form. This is an extremely common notion of magic. The goddess first nooses the demon with a rope, but he changes into a lion. She then beheads the lion, but the demon changes again into a hero with a sword. The goddess then attacks the new embodiment of the demon with arrows, but the demon then changes into an elephant. The goddess strikes off the trunk of the elephant, whereupon the demon returns to his favourite form as the buffalo. An interlude then takes place while the goddess refreshes herself with an inebriating draught of the life-substance which turns her eyes red. After this she returns to the battle with renewed vigour, and once again strikes at the head of the buffalo demon, sinking her trident into his throat. Once again the demon tries to escape in the form of a hero with a sword, but is caught just as he is emerging, and beheaded at the point when he is half in and half outside the carcass of the buffalo body.

The same theme of constant transformations is to be found in the myths connected with Agni. There Agni is described as constantly changing his forms by entering different things — now a fish, now a frog, then animals, birds, trees, grasses, water. The story is basically his effort to escape from his pursuers. He wishes to hide within things, as their inner being. Thus too Skanda is called Guha, meaning he who was conceived hidden. The child is hidden in the womb (p. 103). Magic has a hidden power, it is subtle in that it is not to be found on the surface of things. The villager assumes a hidden force behind the phenomenological world seen by the senses, which is constantly capable of changing and transforming itself and its environment. This inner power within things is Agni, and is available to experience in the form of feeling, i.e. hidden inner impulses.

We see here the clear roots of the later systems of yoga. Mircea Eliade devotes a chapter in his book on yoga to what he calls the aboriginal sources of certain yogic disciplines. Very important is the idea of the control of breath and the vital fluid of the semen, and also the idea of the magical heat of fire. It is supposed in yoga that the natural energies of man can be introverted so as to give rise to a heightened consciousness. This consciousness is not of some objective phenomenon, but is rather consciousness in the given reality from which the world of objective phenomena is constantly being re-created. It is a passive consciousness intent not on distinguishing, but on unification. The fundamental transformation which yoga aims at is the changing of potentialities in nature, such as seed and heat, into higher levels of consciousness. Energy which in nature is mere

< 62 >

instinctual drive must become, through a process of integration, the source of awareness. We recall that fire and seed are described as springing originally from the third eye of the divine yogi Siva. Ultimately these very energies, motor and sexual, have to be transformed back into pure vision through yogic concentration, 'dhyana'.

Magic heat which acts as creative as well as destructive energy is an impersonal force. And yet everywhere in Indian art we find it represented in the form of a torana or halo of fire around the figures of divine yogis who become central images of Indian iconography (see also p. 131). As it is in the mandala, a ring of fire delineates the inner space of consciousness. Indian art reveals in symbolic form the inner path of the yogi's meditation. It is also magical in that it is in harmony with the processes of nature — the womb–tomb cycle of eternal recreation and decomposition. We try to draw here a link between intuitions of folk culture and the more mature reflections of yoga. What Indian imagery seems to be striving for is a sort of 'Biblia Pauporum' (book for the illiterate poor) of meditational techniques. Through significant symbols folk culture is impregnated with an awareness of conscious process moving inwards to explore the psyche which often is completely lacking in the sophisticated scientifically oriented mind of the so-called educated élite of today.

One of the most perfect expressions of this basic idea of space ringed about with fire is the great creation of southern medieval art, the Siva Nataraja. There we see the Lord dancing in an encircling torana of fire, one foot lifted in a gesture of liberation, the other pressed firmly down upon the back of a child demon, who according to one interpretation is in fact Andhaka, a son of Siva who was born out of his eye. In the myth Parvati playfully closed Siva's eyes with her hands, thus resulting in total darkness of the universe, in which night this blind deity was born out of a tear from Siva's eye shed into the hand of Parvati. As W. Doniger O'Flaherty comments, 'The motif of the eye is central to the myth of Andhaka; just as he is born of Siva's eye, and born blind, and given to a demon named Golden-eye, even so he is destroyed by Siva's eye and finally reborn through it.' The tandava dance is both the destruction of the demon child Andhaka, and also his liberation into a new vision — a vision of the Lord dancing in the space of the cosmos (cidambaram) as its very centre of light and energy.

The most fundamental symbols are the ones which touch on the realities which the villager feels most strongly. One of these basic signs which the man who is close to nature finds manifested in the world around him, is the sky. The sky represents the openness of space, but also the infinite darkness through which the light of

< 63 >

Symbols of magical power in folklore — the Nataraja, Lord of the Dance, the great south Indian icon of Siva

< 64 >

manifestation pours in on the world. The figure of the dark-skinned one, or blue-skinned one, is essentially that of the deity who is clothed in the sky. There is also a difference between the day-time sky and the sky at night. The former is blue and ruled by the sun, while the latter is black and ruled by the moon. The first is associated with the god Visnu, while the second is related to the Great Mother and Siva.

The concept of 'space' is connected with 'consciousness'. Space in Indian thought is itself magical, as is the space within the egg or space of the womb from which life springs. It is through the unity of space that the individual consciousness — the cidakasa, or sky of the heart — is linked with the space of the whole universe. Space is conceived of as built up of a network of lines of force running from north to south, east to west, and the points of intersection of these lines are filled with magical energy. The Hindu temple is built on this idea of space, its construction surrounded by magic rites. The mandala pattern on which the temple plan is based is a grid system of squares, created by intersecting lines of force which cut each other at right angles.[3] These opposing directions of parallel lines are oriented to the cardinal points of the compass thus linking the here and now with a cosmic field of consciousness. This point on which I am standing is not just isolated, a point without meaning or relationship with any other point; on the contrary it has meaning in so far as it is the intersection between the All and the All, a point of sunya at the crossroads of infinitely extended directions.

This idea of consciousness as space probably goes back to a very primal folk sensibility. Thus in some mysterious way the sky of the day and the sky of night communicate to man a state of being within himself. For him the day-time sky with its azure blue and shining glory of the sun is the perfect symbol of consciousness, in which the sun is the radiant intellect, while the blueness of infinite space is the depths of the psyche illumined here by intellect. On the other hand the sky at night fills the villager with a sense of the mysterious and unknown. Midnight on the dark night of the moon (amavasya) is the depth of unconsciousness. It is at this time that the shaman or kodangi of the village religion is commissioned on occasion to go to the dreaded burning ghat outside the village and fetch from there the skull of a dead man. The night is associated with the spirits of the dead who also are a sort of space waiting for a body to house them.

Dark caves bring back to primitive consciousness the memory of the night and the unconscious. There has been considerable speculation why in the art of Buddhism and also Jainism (later Hinduism) there has been a fascination for excavating caves. Many of these caves are totally dark; they have no windows. The richly painted caves of

< 65 >

Ajanta have no provision for natural lighting. In these painted caves we have the clearest symbol of the unconscious — a dark space full of latent images (see pp. 31, 143-4).

The interplay of manifest form emerging out of the matrix of shadowy rock in the great images of Ellora again depicts the movement of consciousness out of the primal mould of the unconscious. The darkness from which structure arises is the mother principle, the womb from which everything is born forth. A name for the Great Mother is Digambara, or 'she who is clothed in space'. Space is essentially that which is without colour — its colour arises out of its conjunction with light. Light vibrates through space, giving rise to the phenomenological world. Light is pure primal energy, and space is the receiving medium of that energy which, in conjunction with light, gives rise to matter.

The burning ghat combines the aspect of space and darkness, which are the locality of death, with transfiguring fire. The figure of Siva Daksinamurti is essentially the figure of the Lord who frequents the burning ground. The south is thought to be the domain of death, and also of the fiery heat of the sun. In the symbol of the burning ghat we have a very deep notion of the magical power of heat, and initiation through death. Often in village festivals an ordeal for the shaman, or those possessed by divine frenzy, is the walking over fire, which clearly has an initiatory meaning. In the 'fire of the idea of nothing', an ancient Buddhist tantric text on ritual tells us, the individual consciousness is obliterated. Space itself is here seen as a fire or 'hiranya garbha', the golden womb, from which, through magical incubation, the soul is born into higher realms of consciousness.

< 66 >

CHAPTER 6
Symbols of authority

< 67 >

[OVERLEAF]

The yogi lost in meditation. His body assumes the still, cone-like form of a mountain. (There are even stories of yogis who get lost inside an ant hill as the termites build their clay castle around the yogi without him noticing.)

< 68 >

The lord Ayyappan is a child deity who enjoys a very great cult in the south, especially in Kerala. Though, through a process of sanskritization, he has been linked up with the pan-Indian system of myth, there is reason to suppose that this deity is in fact a very ancient god. His name is itself something of a mystery. One suggestion is that the name derives from the Sanskrit words Arya Appa. Certainly the term 'appan' suggests the familiar word for 'father' though we must remember that the deity is generally thought of as a child of twelve years of age, and further he is a bramacari as he himself specifically avows when Lila (the divine play) asks to be his consort. Let us proceed, however, to look more carefully into this myth.

The story is that a childless king of Kerala, Rajasekhara, whose kingdom was called Pantalam, greatly longed for an heir. While hunting in the forest he camped with his retinue by the river Pampa. The king, followed by his dewan, went a little distance from the others, and fell into a deep reverie. Suddenly he heard the cry of a new-born child. He looked around and discovered a beautiful baby lying alone and unprotected on a rock by the river. While he stood wondering at this strange occurrence an old Brahmin hermit appeared, and advised him to adopt the babe, adding that the secret of his origin would be revealed after twelve years and that, in the meantime, because of the gold bell he wore round his neck, he should be called Manikantha.

The king adopted the child and brought him up as his heir, but the dewan hated him because, in the absence of an heir, he had hoped to snatch the throne after the king's death. Further, the queen was finally able to have a child of her own, and resented the fact that Manikantha, though a foundling, was designated heir apparent. Together the queen and the dewan devised a plot to get rid of Manikantha. The queen feigned sickness, and the dewan persuaded the court physician to say she could only be cured by a leopard's milk. He guessed that the dutiful Manikantha would at once volunteer to seek the leopard's milk, and hoped that on this dangerous mission he would be killed by the wild beasts of the forest. Manikantha sets out alone, taking with him, at the King's request, a coconut, representing the three eyes of Siva, and a bundle containing food.[1]

At this point the myth digresses to reveal Manikantha's origins. We are told of a marriage of opposites between the angelic couple Datta and Lila. Datta, as Dattatreya Maharsi, would seem to represent cosmic asceticism, and Lila is cosmic play, cosmic eroticism.[2] At first Datta is drawn into the play of Lila, but then renounces her and returns to asceticism. She tries desperately to draw him back, but he curses her to be born as Mahisi, the buffalo-headed demoness, sister of Mahisasura who was killed by the great goddess, variously

< 69 >

called Durga, Camundeswari, or Candika. As Mahisi, Lila performs great austerities in order, by magical power, to avenge her brother against the gods. She obtains the boon that nothing in heaven or earth can overcome her except a child born of two males, who must live as a mortal for twelve years. Having obtained this boon she overthrows the king of the gods and rules the universe with an evil dominion. In order to destroy her Siva goes to Visnu, who in his form of Mohini (which he assumed to distract the Asuras at the dawn of the cosmos from coveting the nectar of life), is both male and female in his masculinity. From the mating of Siva to Mohini is born a child called 'Ayonijatah' (not born of a female organ),[3] who is in fact Ayyappan, or Manikantha as he is called in the world.

When Manikantha returns to the forest to seek leopard's milk, he fulfils the magic condition that a child, born of two males, and having lived a mortal life for twelve years, is able to overthrow the cosmic demoness Mahisi. In a battle he throws her down, and dancing on her buffalo body, liberates the world from her evil rule. He does this on Makara Sankranti, or the Ides of January, known as Pongal in south India. Out of the destroyed body of the buffalo demoness comes forth the liberated goddess Lila, who begs to become the consort of the child god. This he refuses, since he, like Datta, is the incarnation of asceticism. But he assures her that in the next life this marriage will be achieved, though its fulfilment will be the end of this age.

The child hero Manikantha returns to the kingdom of his foster-father accompanied by a multitude of leopards, who are all Devas in disguise. He himself rides a tiger. The king realizes that his foster-child is a divinity, and worships him. Manikantha offers leopard's milk to the queen. The king offers to punish the queen and the dewan, but Manikantha reveals that what they did was pre-destined and no real fault of theirs. He instructs that a temple should be built in the forest on a hill called Sabarimalai, and that an annual pilgrimage should be made to this hill especially at the time of Makara Sankranti.[4] The pilgrims should set off to the forest carrying the coconut and bundle of food (irumudi) even as he had set off to the forest in search of the leopard's milk. Further the pilgrims must observe a very strict asceticism, especially with regard to sex, for a stipulated period, even before the pilgrimage is begun. Anyone who is incontinent is thought to be in danger of being killed on the pilgrimage into the forest — especially by wild beasts.

< 70 >

THE CONCEPT OF AUTHORITY AND KINGSHIP

Let us now see if we can expose certain aspects of the basic structure of the Ayyappan myth. The myth is concerned with kingship both on the world plane and on the cosmic plane. In the world there is a male king whose role is legitimate. But on the cosmic level there is a ruling female-demon, whose position is not legitimate, because she has usurped the throne. Running parallel to this theme of kingship is the whole opposition of asceticism and eroticism, and the marriage between the two. The demoness Mahisi is in fact Lila who has been cursed for her eroticism. On the other hand, the king Rajasekhara is unable to have a child, and though it is not explicitly stated, we recall that the ascetic is also one who renounces having children. But the king wants a child, and Mahisi undergoes severe asceticism in order to avenge her brother. This pattern of strange oppositions and inversions of nature is further developed on yet another dimension – the conflict of the cultured city life of the king in his palace and the wild world of the forest. The king enters into the forest in order to hunt. On the other hand, on the cosmic plane a demoness who is a wild-buffalo usurps the position of ruler of the universe.

The child is found in the forest, where he seems very out of place. It is strange that such a weak and defenceless babe is discovered in a place where dangerous wild beasts roam. His association with an old ascetic reminds us of a theme which we have already encountered – the conjunction of the wise old man and the innocent babe. The king takes the child of the forest back with him into the civilized world of his kingdom. His position in the palace is complicated by the fact that the queen is at last able to have her own child and the whole question of legitimacy, central to the claim of authority, is presented in a dramatic way.

Returning again to the cosmic dimension we are told that the child is born of two males. In the whole myth the feminine is represented on the side of eroticism, and world-involvement. Both the queen and Mahisi seem to be dominated by an irrational longing for power; in the demoness, power over the gods, in the queen, power through her own offspring becoming the future king. The position of ruler is very much related to a need for power. But the child Manikantha does not seem at all ambitious for power.

As the king had to go to the forest to find the heir which he was lacking, the child hero has to return to the forest in order to obtain from there the supposed cure for the queen. According to one popular version, not given in the story as told above, the young hero goes to the forest because he is rejected by many conflicting forces

< 71 >

in the city (typified by the interests of queen and dewan) and finds in the forest a friend who is a tribal king, thought even to be a Muslim, that is a 'king of the forest' who is outside the pale of accepted Hindu civilization.[5]

The climax of the story is the overthrowing of the demoness. As Mahisasura was overthrown by the goddess Durga, this feminine demon has to be overthrown by this ultra-male child god, in whose conception woman has taken no part.

The conclusion of the myth is the return of the child god to a kingdom of the earthly monarch Rajasekhara, but this time the child is revealed for what he is, a divine being and not a mere mortal. Roles are reversed. The king prostrates himself before the child. The wild beasts are Devas in disguise. A cult is instituted whose central pivot is a holy mountain, sabri, to which a pilgrimage has to be made. A temple is ordered which is a microcosm, reflecting the centre of the universe, a sacred capital. But it is situated within the forest. An asceticism is demanded of the pilgrims as they enter the forest, which in so many other ways symbolizes the forces of eroticism. Indeed it is even thought that those who fail to be continent will be punished by wild beasts.

In this way we could outline a certain structure in the myth revealing a few main points of opposition and correspondence.

A kingdom on earth	A kingdom of the whole cosmos
The forest with wild beasts	The cultured palace and kingdom
Eroticism	Asceticism
A childless monarch	A child born of male wedded to male
Legitimate, good rule	Illegitimate, evil rule

The symbol is compounded through the 'throwing together' of these elements and a dramatic story on two very different levels is outlined. We are also able to see how the individual symbol (king, child, forest with wild animals, etc.) interrelates with a total intuitive structure. In fact, this structure extends beyond this particular myth to the whole myth-structure of India because basic themes which we have outlined here are found to underlie the whole framework of Indian symbolic thought. Thus the connection between asceticism and culture and the king's authority, as contrasted with eroticism — wilderness — and the forces of fertility, seems to be a fundamental axial structure of Indian myth and symbol. Asceticism is transforming tapasya, which through magical heat makes the uncooked raw forces of nature cooked — and thus 'cultured' and ultimately 'conscious'.[6] We must appreciate the great civilizing force of asceticism in India, and how the great achievements of Indian consciousness rest

< 72 >

on this essential asceticism. But still, this asceticism is also sterile, and unable to have a son for the future. In some way it has to come to terms with the life forces of the unconscious which are here characterized as erotic and beastly. Authority which arises out of an erotic lust for power and revenge is however not legitimate, and has finally to be overthrown. But again all that is found in the forest is not necessarily contrary to the ascetical ideal — both the old rsi and the child god were found in the forest, the very domain of life-force, the counter kingdom of the tribal, outcaste, other-religion king. And all that is found in the 'civilized' palace is not necessarily different from the raw, erotic power-lust of the forest — the dewan for example who is the alter ego of the king, and the simple-minded but ambitious queen who wants her own son to rule. And yet, for the well-being and ultimate fulfilment and completion of the cosmos, the ascetical youth must be wedded to the erotical maid, however incompatible the relation might appear. Thus according to popular belief, when Ayyappan is at last wedded to Lila, the end of time will come and the final dissolution of the universe will be heralded.

THE SYMBOL OF THE KING

The authority of the king is based on his position at the very navel of the world. The kingdom becomes as it were the image on the earthly plane of the cosmos, whose hub is the throne of dominion. The king is thus a 'symbol' of power invested at the centre of life. In Indian thought he is the Cakravartin, he who commands the wheel of the cosmos. All emperors aspire to a semi-divine role mirroring, through symbolic identity, Indra who is the legitimate ruler of the universe. This idea is inherent in the rites of coronation whereby the king is invested with supernatural powers and functions. In so far as the temple is a microcosm, reflecting on the earthly plane the whole structure of the cosmos, the designer and builder of the temple takes on the role of 'maker of the universe' — Visvakarma or Pantocrator. The rise of temple art in India, as also the concept behind much of Buddhist art, runs parallel to the development of a truly indigenous concept of earth rulership. This idea which seems to have been imported into India from Persia by the early Kushan emperors, and adopted by the Mauryan rulers, had probably its seed in the consciousness of local Dravidian tribal chieftains. The concept emerges naturally out of the human consciousness itself, where, as in the initiation rites connected with the mandala, we find in the individual a self-identification with the creator of the universe.[7] The initiate

< 73 >

believes himself to be sacramentally transfigured into the image of the supernatural being who has ordered the universe, thus discovering himself to be a ruler of the world that he experiences around him. He becomes in this way a king, and realizes this kingship by taking his throne at the heart of the mandala. And so we see the need in the new 'Cakravartin' to create in his kingdom icons of the universe so that he might discover, through ritual enactment of entry into the mandala, his own imperial authority. Asoka discovered his identity through the Buddhist religion. Like the early Christian emperors, such as Constantine, who saw their own enthronement as an icon here below of a heavenly enthronement of Christ, Asoka identified his own imperial power with the universal sway of the Lord Buddha. Ritual connected with imperial enthronement became naturally a part of the worship of the Lord Buddha, very much as the imperial rituals of the Romans became a part of Byzantine liturgy. It was Asoka who developed the ritual of the stupa, which does not seem to have been a part of Buddhist life before the times of Asoka. As far as we can ascertain, the ceremony connected with the stupa derived from ancestor worship. The funerary mound, which seems closely associated with the stone cist tombs of an ancient megalithic culture, was given a cosmological significance. The dome of the mound became symbolic of the dome of the sky (see pp. 39, 79). The ritual procession round the sacred relics, in which the king himself took a leading part, was tantamount to turning the wheel of the law, the establishing on earth of an absolute order. The great processional route demarked by Asoka, around the great stupas commemorating central points in the life of Buddha, was also a turning of this wheel, by ritual identification with the life pilgrimage of a sacred archetype of the self. Thus, too, through the cult of Ayyappan (also known as Dharma Sastha), in which a pilgrimage to a mountain, or journey to the centre of the universe, is an essential feature, man is invited to identify himself through ritual action with an archetypal figure of the self. Every individual who goes on the pilgrimage is, during the period of the pilgrimage, not addressed by any personal name, but as Ayyappan-swamy himself. The symbol thus becomes the locus for a self-discovery through an exemplary event demanding individual effort — in this drama the individual is re-born, because through it he discovers the real world of eternal origin, and meets the author of his own life-destiny.

The need of man to feel that his universe is ordered and governed by a way which is synonymous with a supernatural Law or Word, seems to be archetypal. We find it in the village too, where the agriculturalist sees his work in the fields as part of an effort to create

< 74 >

order in the universe. Thus in the elaborate ritual connected with the planning out of a city, or the delineating of an area on which a temple is to be constructed, we read that the land is first ploughed, with the king himself as ploughman.[8] Auspicious seeds are sown, and allowed to germinate and spring up from the soil, because this first crop is thought to be a good omen for the future construction of buildings which in a sense are seen as growing up out of the ground, like a sort of great organic crop of brick, mortar and stone. In this way the king identifies himself with the aspirations of the villager, taking the plough as a symbol of his power to cultivate the land and change the chaos of the untilled earth into the well-ordered pattern of irrigated and cultivated fields.

The limits of the village are delineated by the creation of 'boundary stones'. These stones which in southern villages take on the function of menhirs, are thought to be possessed by the spirits.[9] In some areas they are thought to have within them the soul of some ancestor king, or tribal leader, founder of the village. Asoka, who seems to have drawn much from folk tradition, giving to this tradition a new dimension borrowed from Persian culture, erected stone pillars to demarcate the boundary of his empire. On these pillars he inscribed his famous edicts. It seems possible that these pillars were not all erected by Asoka — some show evidence of being more ancient. It is possible that Asoka used already existing pillars in certain cases to write his edicts on. Anyway the custom of erecting boundary pillars, and investing them with a sacred significance as symbols of the order or law of an empire, seems to go back to a number of village or tribal traditions where ancestor worship is combined with the drawing out of the limits reached in the process of establishing an ordered society within the prevailing chaos of nature. To this day in folk tradition the dead are put outside the village; cemeteries and burning ghats are on the village boundaries. The ghosts of the dead are given the task of guarding the ordered universe of the living. In the practice of meditating on the mandala we find the same phenomenon; the ghosts of the dead appear at the boundaries of the mandala, and are in fact probably the iconographic prototypes of later dvarpalikas or sivabhutas (see p. 132), guardians of the sacred temenos. Thus Ayyappan is Bhutanatha, or Lord of the Ghosts (Bhutas).

THE MOUNTAIN

A Gandhian worker who is involved with tribals in Gujarat told me recently that when the tribals take an oath they take the name of

< 75 >

'the Lord who lives upon the mountain'. Siva himself seems to have been a pre-Aryan deity of the mountain and, like the Hebrew Jehovah, was probably also associated with thunder. The epithet Rudra meaning the 'howler' is given to Siva. The divine yogi, seated upon the mountain and controlling the elements, is certainly a very ancient Indian figure. It has been suggested that even in the Mohen-jodaro seals we have the prototype of Siva in a seated, cross-legged, apparently horned deity, with a very prominent phallus, and with four heraldic animals representing the four points of the compass, depicted around him (see p. 108).

The mountain brings heaven and earth together — it is like a ladder reaching up from earth to touch the skies. The horned motif appears in later iconography in the form of Siva's knot of hair in which we can see the crescent moon entangled.[10] The mountain is the 'axis mundi' and is thus also associated with phallic symbolism. The relation of temple structure to that of the cosmic mountain is well established.[11] We have only to recall the great Kailasa temple of Ellora, hewn out of the side of a cliff, to illustrate the Indian pre-dilection for mountain forms in temple architecture. It seems that the structure of the sikhara or vimana is made to imitate the form of the cosmic mountain[12] — Mount Kailasa or Mount Meru — which is visualized as the pivotal centre of the universe, the peak of con-sciousness at the spiralling heart of the mandala maze.

Year by year Hindu pilgrims take the long arduous journey up the valley of the river Ganges from Haridwar to Gangotri, to attain to the feet of the mountain of the Lord. One is reminded of the stations of the cross, which also probably go back to very ancient rites of processional ascent to discover the centre of the universe. The figure of the yogi is very much interrelated with this experience of the centre, for he stands or sits lost in contemplation, at the hub of the spinning universal wheel. As such, again like Jehovah, he is a law-giver,[13] because he has been initiated into the order (dharma, cosmos) of the universe, and is thus able to impart to man the word or logos on which the universe is founded.

The journey to the mountain is thus the path to the source of life. In the mandala, we sometimes see depicted the river of life, flowing from the mountain, like the river Ganges flowing down from Siva's knotted hair. As such, the mountain becomes a symbol of the descent of water. The waterfall was a favourite theme of Taoist art, especially in Japanese screen-painting. The waterfall represents the linking of heaven and earth, and the pouring of bounty upon creation. In India this theme is given magnificent imaginative form in the 'descent of the river Ganges' as we see it represented in the great relief at

< 76 >

Symbols of authority — the proto-Siva as we see him hinted at in the Mohenjodaro seals. The figure appears to have three heads, is surrounded by four mythic animals probably representing the four quarters, and is seated in a yogic posture of meditation

< 77 >

Mahaballipuram (see p. 118). There again it is the archetypal yogi, Bhagiratha or Arjuna, who evokes the boon from heaven. For a long time it was not clear to art historians whether the theme of the Mahaballipuram relief was Bhagiratha's penance (for the descent of the River Ganges), or Arjuna's penance (linked with the boon of his weapon the bow). What is given from above is cosmic power, and so there is a close relationship between the descent of the river and the boon of cosmic weapons. In fact the bow has from ancient times been linked with the strength of many waters, being related with the rainbow which is seen to form not only in the clouds but also over the waterfall.

Earthly kings have turned their gaze towards the mountains to seek there resources with which to support and protect their realms. There is a natural desire to command the high places, and build there military camps. Thus the mountain becomes one of the most central symbols of authority. Towering above the plains, the mountain seems to represent the power of the king towering above his vassal peoples.

THE UMBRELLA

Above the mountain is the dome of the sky. This has been symbolized by the umbrella. Umbrella forms are found above the stupa and also the vimana or sikhara in the form of what is known as the Amalaka after the round fruit of the amala tree. The amala tree is worshipped in the north by processional circumambulation on the festival of the sun (see p. 157). The umbrella is clearly related with sun symbolism. If we look at the decorative features of the processional umbrellas we note that symbols of the sun and moon and other astral bodies are employed. Flower and tree symbols also appear, indicative of the connection between the umbrella and the tree.

The important function of the umbrella is to cast a shadow. Thus it is seen to be a symbol of protection.[14] There is a curious intermarriage between symbols of light and shadow. The fact therefore that the umbrella is connected with sun symbolism and yet throws a shadow is by no means thought to be self-contradictory in popular thought.

The dome of the umbrella is held aloft by a vertical handle which becomes identified with the 'axis mundi'. It is carried above an important dignitary, or the image of a deity, to indicate that the person or symbol below the umbrella is in fact the centre of a universe. Umbrellas seem to be especially important in processional rites, being

< 78 >

like mobile temples. In the great car festivals of south India and up the eastern coast to Bengal, whole constellations of umbrellas move in solemn procession. Tiered umbrellas as we see above the stupa, represent the many 'lokas', i.e. the many heavens rising one above the other. As in kundalini yoga, each cakra or umbrella represents a 'station' through which the pilgrim passes on his journey to the centre.

THE PILLAR OR FLAGSTAFF

In the typical temple complex as it developed, especially in south India, we see in front of the garbha grha the flagstaff. This flagstaff is the centre of a yearly temple festival. According to Viraswami Pathar in his book *Temple and its Significance,*[15] the raising of the flag in the temple symbolically re-enacts the rise of the kundalini up the spinal column (see p.161). Thus the thirty-three divisions of the flagstaff are like the vertebrae of the human spine.

The significance of the flagstaff goes back to the pillars or lats set up by Asoka, which in their turn were based on folk tradition. These pillars were primarily magical in purpose. They were often decorated with symbols of the sun and sometimes with signs of the zodiac. The famous Sarnath capital, which has been adopted as a national symbol, derives much from Persian origins. But still there is a truly Indian character about its symbolism which has translated into a Buddhist world-view forms belonging to Iranian art. This world-view, which became central to the Indian concept of earthly rulership, became an enduring feature of Indian symbolic art.

The symbol of the cosmic pillar is related to a myth concerning a magical lake which is meant to lie in the depths of the Himalayas. It is thought that when the sun rises over this lake, which is known as Udaya or Anavatapta, a pillar arises from the centre of the lake and grows upwards until it reaches its greatest height at mid-day, thus becoming a throne on which the sun and the moon rest awhile at their zenith before once again taking their path downwards,[16] a movement which is followed by the pillar itself, which gradually sinks back, absorbed once again into the lake at sunset. From this myth we see the relation of the pillar to the sun at mid-day and the axis of the universe arising out of the cosmic ocean.

We have in the pillar a symbol of man's effort to climb up and take possession of the throne of the sun. From this high point all the points of the compass are commanded. These points of the compass are symbolized by four creatures who support the throne of the sun.

< 79 >

In India, as exemplified in the Sarnath capital, these four beasts are represented as the lion and the elephant, the horse and the bull. In these four beasts, much more than in the four beasts of Western apocalyptic literature (which also owe their form to Persian eschatology), there can be seen a certain balance of elemental forces. The elephant and the bull are related to forces of water and earth, whereas the lion and the horse are related to the forces of fire and air, heat and speed.

The figure of the standing Buddha, and later of Visnu, repeats in anthropomorphic form the same pillar-like structure. Crowned by the sun, which is here represented as the great orb of a halo, the Lord stands erect, himself the very axis of the universe. The erect stance of the body creates the impression of kingly authority. There is a strong relationship to phallic symbolism in this noble figure standing like a pillar. By assuming this pose many ethical qualities are indicated, such as bravery, steadfastness, strength and so on. In the very way the figure stands we are able to understand the character of kingly authority.

THE GESTURES OF THE HAND AND FEET

In Indian art there is a highly developed language of gestures. But perhaps one of the most ancient gestures which is to be found everywhere in Indian imagery is that of the upraised hand, palm facing outwards. This hand is to be found in folk art, imprinted on walls as a magical device to ward off evil.[17] In the art of mudra it is known as the 'abhaya mudra' or the 'do not fear' mudra. Figures of Buddha, Visnu or Siva invariably show this gesture. It could be described as a gesture of blessing, but it also conveys the sense of halting, calling attention, commanding.

In folk tradition we notice that the hands and feet are painted, generally with orange or scarlet, in preparation for marriage. In the north of India the preparation of the bride is an important social function called 'Mehndi'. On this occasion the bride is to sit on a swing while the bride's maids paint her hands and her feet with intricate patterns drawn with the juice of a plant (mehndi) which makes a deep orange stain on the skin. As in so many Indian symbols, the idea of meeting or union is indicated. The hand becomes the ideograph of a man's fate. Both future and past can be read in the lines of the hand. Palmistry is probably a very ancient magical art in India, and certainly a very popular one.

In Islamic art, especially in the iconography distinctive of the Shia

< 80 >

sect, the hand in conjunction with an umbrella is used as a symbol of the authority of the Prophet. In an art which forbids the anthropomorphic representation of spiritually significant beings, the mark of the hand or the feet indicates the presence of prophet or deity. So also in early Buddhist art the Buddha was not represented, but a platform on which the marks of his feet were shown, indicated his throne and his authoritative presence. In Jain art the upright hand, palm facing outwards, and marked at the mystical centre with the word 'ahimsa', has been adopted as a symbol of the faith. Footprints of Tirthankaras indicating their presence are also to be found.

THE THRONE

The various insignia of authority which we have described are all related to the throne that is the seat of authority. This throne in Indian art is the mandapa, or high plinth which in the village is generally situated beneath an important tree at the centre of the village. It is here that the village meeting is held and the village elders preside. It has been suggested in fact that the early temples of the Andhra region (Aihole etc.) owe their structure to such village meeting places, which were sometimes enclosed in some way, and given a roof, thus becoming like open halls where the elders took their seat upon a carpet. In Rajasthan the design of the carpet on which the elders of the village sit is of a special type, and has often a sort of mandala form, having at the centre the pattern of the Indian chessboard, known as chaupad. According to folk tradition in Rajasthan, when the elders sit down on this carpet they must not rise until they have reached a decision. The structure of this village assembly place is developed in imperial courts into the hall for darsana or darbar where the temporal authority sits in state. The king is flanked on either side by servants who hold ceremonial fly whisks, and elaborate precautions are taken to keep off the evil eye. The figure of the king enthroned with attendants becomes a common feature of Buddhist and Jain art and later Hindu iconography, where the deity is given the entourage of temporal authorities, very much as we find Christ depicted as enthroned in the manner that was customary in the Byzantine imperial court.

THE CROWN

Finally we might glance at the form of Indian crown in which many

< 81 >

of the elements which we have already described are brought together.[18] The crown in Indian art is very much like the tall peak of the mythical mount — the sikhara of the northern temple is both the image of the mount Meru, and the crown of the cosmic man Purusa.

The often elaborate motifs which decorate the crown, as we can see in the crown of the magnificent Trimurti of Elephanta, seem to derive from various elements of Indian coronation rites. Thus one might distinguish the forms of vessels overflowing with organic life, as we find depicted on the pillars of temples especially from the late Gupta period and the early Hindu dynasties of northern India. This vessel is probably symbolic of the vessel containing the lustral liquid with which the king's head is anointed at the time of coronation. Also we get the impression of an elaborately piled coif of hair as seen among certain sects of yogis. The Hindu king after coronation did not cut his hair for a year, because it was believed that the lustral liquids of coronation had given the hairs of the head a supernatural power. We recall also the myth of Siva and the descent of the Ganges which he broke by allowing the river to flow through his hair, thereby breaking its supernatural force. Flowing hair, as also in the Siva Tandava, is symbolic of the cosmic lines of force and creativity (see p.105). Krsna himself was born from a hair of Visnu placed in the womb of a maiden, and for this reason he is known as Kesava. Hair had a significance for the Buddhists also, and the piled, almost spiralling, hairdo of the Buddha appears like a sort of crown of snail shell curls. This idea of cosmic life as invested in the hairs of the head, becomes a part of the symbolism of the crown, and we can also distinguish in the decorative features of the crown representations of cosmic bodies like the sun and the moon.

< 82 >

CHAPTER 7
An elemental art

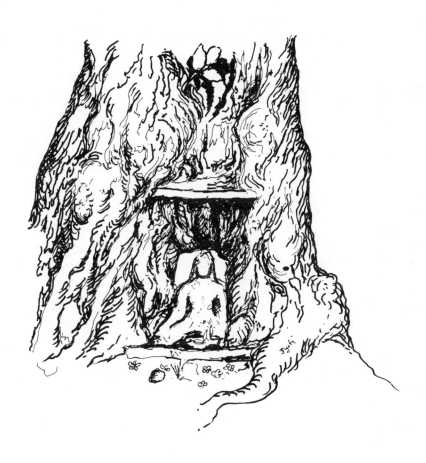

< 83 >

[OVERLEAF]

Small deity carved in stone placed between the roots of a tree

< 84 >

Every day the villager has to contend with nature. But what is this nature? On one hand nature is the real elemental world — the earth, the weather, the sun, water, fire, seed, animals and so on. On the other hand, nature is the concept we have of these things. Kant understood nature as 'the connection of appearances as regards their existence according to necessary rules, that is, according to laws'.[1] Man, contending with nature, tries to understand how it works. He wants to see an overall general plan or 'way' according to which every happening in his life can be seen as a part of a whole, as related to general order, and therefore meaningful. In that sense nature lies beyond the particular phenomena which illustrate it. The Western concept of nature is largely mechanical. For this view of nature we might blame the philosophic movement of the Enlightenment in eighteenth-century Europe, but this world-view can even be traced back perhaps to the notion of nature as put forward in the first chapter of Genesis. There man is described as commanding nature — the whole of nature was put under his control. Thus he, as the high-pinnacle of consciousness, had power to give unconscious and chaotic nature name and function. His relation to nature was comparable to the relation of spirit to body. Nature was seen as an ensemble of forces and things. Man was understood as distinct from nature, as the only 'conscious' being in the world of phenomena, who could understand the 'general laws' governing nature and therefore had power over the very essence of nature.

In India, however, especially among the villagers, we do not find this mechanistic view of nature. Man is not understood as being in control of nature. To understand this different world-view, we must also understand his concept of time. The Indian villager has no sense of 'history' in the sense that Western man might mean when he uses the term. History, like nature, is both the phenomena which comprise it, and a concept of the underlying order beneath the phenomena. When we say that the villager has no sense of history, we do not mean that he does not remember. What we mean to say is that he has not fitted his memories of 'things that have happened' into a general, overall mechanistic order of cause and effect. What we call history is really highly selective (as is memory also). It only remembers what it thinks significant, that is to say, what fits into the general overall plan of things. In that sense history is really only concerned with the 'end' of things — their wholeness. Strangely enough this 'end' is itself outside what history is describing, and can never be a part of it. The events of history are merely descriptive, for the historical process which they illustrate is itself beyond everything which can happen. In this sense history is similar to myth which is also an 'order' that lies beyond the way things happen.

< 85 >

It is essential, however, to see clearly the difference between history and myth. History, though it transcends historical detail, is nevertheless also determined by (or, looked at another way, itself determines) its content. The 'content' of history is clearly empirical facts, which can be verified as having happened. The word 'fact' is itself significant. It comes from the Latin word *facere* — to do. So a fact is anything done. In one sense it is also anything made. Consequently history is interested in achievements, in landmarks, one might call them completed things, processes brought to a certain definitive end. Of course, in life itself there is no such thing as a definitive end. But for the purpose of history, which is concerned with the 'end' of things, the quality of completion is 'invented' in order to give events significance. Thus wars are won or lost, kingdoms rise and fall, lives are born and come to an end. If this were not so, there would be no history, because there would be no facts to report on. The dancer, for the sake of his art, divides up movement (which in a sense has no divisions) into clearly defined movements, having a beginning and an end. It is this clear ordering of movement into conscious gesture, which can be seen to have a beginning and an end, that gives beauty and order and distinguishes dance from other sorts of movement.

When we experience myth, we cannot ever claim that it describes anything that has ever happened, as the historian understands that term. Even the question 'Did it ever happen?' is incomprehensible to one who lives in a mythical world-view, because the question itself is artificial, and pre-supposes an understanding of time as having particular landmarks which are complete in themselves.

THE IMMEDIATE IN VILLAGE RELIGION

I have often been struck by the fact that the villager lives on a very immediate plane of reality. In this way he appears in his thought process to be non-historic, since he is mainly concerned with the immediate present. It is always an important feature of what we might call folk religion that a cyclic notion of time tends to throw into relief the existential experience of the now and here which is thought of not as a fraction of the historical process, but rather as a reflection of an archetypal beginning at which level all action takes place. Thus any work which is begun, is begun from the point of view of this beginning realized in the here and now, which is the only real reference for effort on the personal and phenomenological level of action.

The worship of the villager is a response to the here and now of his

< 86 >

situation. He thus chooses his 'symbols' from the immediate world around him. A lump of rock, a clod of clay, a humble earthen pot of water become for him his 'god' because they are the most immediate, elemental realities of his life. The villager could even be described as iconoclastic in his extreme simplicity which abandons all that is formal, artificial, in preference for the natural. The village shrine is a very crude affair and almost bare within. But this does not mean that the villager has not his richly evocative world of images. It simply means that he has not created his own images, for he has relied on what he has found existing in nature to supply his symbolic needs.[2] For him the knotted trunk of a tree or the suggestive presence of a rock are far more real figures of the divine, or rather numinous, than anything his hands could contrive. This somehow relates also to the villager's feeling that the nature he lives in is not under his control; rather he is controlled by it, because it is greater, more powerful, more holy than he is. In some mysterious way it is even more conscious than he is.

Anthropologists speak of 'momentary gods' — that is to say, the intuition to be found among those who are more in touch with pre-rational mind that things in nature are 'charged' with the supernatural. How a 'thing' becomes 'charged' in this way it is difficult to say. There is no definable class of objects which by its very nature is prone to be charged by the supernatural — all trees are not charged, all stones or pots or even human beings are not charged. But in every class of animals or inanimate objects, this supernatural energy (sakti or whatever you might call it) is capable of taking possession. And, as far as we can observe how these charged objects are recognized as such by man, it seems that the recognition is closely connected with the power which such objects have to evoke remembrance of the supernatural. This remembrance rises out of latent impressions which are like a 'fragrance' clinging mysteriously even to an empty object, and testifying to a super-life substance which has left its nuance of presence, even though it cannot be seen, felt or heard in an empirical way. 'The vasanas have their origin in the memory', says Vyasa in his commentary on the Yoga Sastra (IV.9). This subliminal reflection which the external object creates in the mind of man causes him to remember (which means once again to become a member of) something which had become forgotten even though it was stored away in the categories of the mind. The 'symbol' thus draws up into the conscious mind elements which had got assimilated into the unconscious and therefore forgotten. So an object which itself is rejected (because it cannot be assimilated into the existing categories of the mind, being uncanny, inexplicable, or in some other way indigestible) has

< 87 >

An elemental art — Hanuman, the monkey-faced god, often known in south India as Anjanaya, the son of the wind god Vayu. This god is often connected with the elements, carrying the mountain or spreading fire in the enclosed capital of Lanka

< 88 >

the power to bring up from the unconscious things which have been assimilated, but which are here once again reviewed, remembered, relived, and consequently rediscovered and re-interpreted.

The symbol has the power to create in the mind a state of wonder. This term 'wonder' has two aspects. On the one side, it is a questioning: 'I wonder what this means?' On the other hand, it is awe and reverence. The very questionableness of life is evoked by the symbol.

Walking along a village path in the moonlight, some really elemental emotion arises in one. The half-defined shapes of trees and deep shadows evoke all manner of thoughts and dimly stirring, almost dream-like, recollection. At this time especially nature seems charged with the divine and inexplicable. The heart is filled with wonder and a sense of the mystery of the world. Here then, I feel, is the 'motivation' we are looking for, the 'intention' behind the image. The symbol does not speak in veiled terms of something which is non-symbolic and factual. Rather, it reveals life itself as symbol — the world as symbol. This is surely what is meant by the term 'maya'. We note there are two word-concepts which link with this Sanskrit term, which is so difficult to define philosophically. On the one hand maya is magic — the charge in things which transforms them and makes them powerful, gives them power to evoke new forms. But on the other hand, maya relates to measure, to time and space (which are the instruments of measurement) and to creation which takes place through the process of measuring what is the immeasurable flux of experience. If the former 'meaning' of maya indicates its aboriginal roots in the pre-conscious, the latter 'meaning' of maya already indicates how rationality which is so much connected with systems of measuring is already latent in the symbol. When we say 'the world is symbol' (maya), we state both its pre-conscious and its rational, discursive, coefficients.

< 89 >

CHAPTER 8

Symbols of sacred space and dance in relation to the moon symbol

< 91 >

[OVERLEAF]

The ecstatic dancer. In all folk cultures, including India, the shamanistic cult of inspired dance plays an important role

< 92 >

We have said that for us the symbol is not a thing, but a dynamic milieu in which certain combinations of everyday objects and events become significant. C. G. Jung developed this idea in an essay which he entitled *Synchronicity*.[1] By this he appears to have meant a notion of space and time which is not based on cause and effect, on a mechanistic view of reality, but rather arising out of certain significant coincidences or configurations. In this chapter I want to try to explore this very intuitive idea through the consideration of the symbol of the moon, and the grouping around it of various observable phenomena in the sentient life of the earth.

The relation of the moon to the rising sap in plants, to the ebbing and flowing of the ocean, to the weather and the menstrual cycle of women seems to the intuitive mind a significant coincidence of various observable, often acausal, links between all these phenomena. What mechanistic connection can there be between the phases of the moon, the life of plants, the states of consciousness in the mind and the menstrual cycle in woman? Such intricate configurations can only be treated within the 'logic' of the symbol or myth, not rationally in terms of cause and effect. The moon in its behaviour, its different times of rising in relation to the day, its growing and then fading away, seems to become the very symbol of all that is irrational, mysterious, indefinable. And yet it is clear there is a pattern, a rhythm which seems to underlie the movements of the moon. In his effort to understand this basic rhythm of nature, as intuited in the phases of the moon and their relationship to natural phenomena, man seems to have stumbled on a most fundamental concept of time and space. It seems that all the most ancient of methods of reckoning time are based on the moon rather than on the sun. The mysterious relation of the moon to air, the currents of the wind which seem to be governed by the moon cycle, indicate that the whole of space comprising water, earth and air are somehow meshed through and through with the net-like rhythms of the moon. The symbol 'moon' thus becomes the essence of intuitive order and form (dharma, logos), and upon it the emergent culture of man is seen to depend for its life.

THE CYCLE OF THE MOON AS RELATED TO CULTURE

For the villager or tribal the moon is extremely important. Life in the countryside seems to revolve around the phases of the moon. Much of the cultural life of the country people depends on the moon. The day-time is filled with labour; it is only when the sun has gone

< 93 >

to rest that the life of folk culture can begin. When the moon is dark the villager tends to go to bed early because there is no light to see with, but when the moon is bright he feels inspired. Then is the time for singing, for telling stories and dancing. Thus it is natural that in folk thought the moon is related with all the forms of creative reflection; in fact, the mind itself is thought to be of the same nature as the moon, the word for the mind (manas) being related in many languages to the word for the moon. The power of the mind to reflect is related to the reflective nature of the moon, and disorders of the mind result from the vagrancies of the moon.

There is a great deal of poetic symbolism showing the connection of moon with states of the mind, especially the moods of man. The moon plant is thought to be soma from which the drink of the gods is made. In fact all intoxicating drink, so closely related to the cultural life of the people, is thought to be connected with the moon. Even the quality of the drink is thought to be influenced directly by the position of the moon in relation to the times when fermentation began in the plant juice. The mysterious effect of intoxicating drink upon the mind and moods of man is thought to be a direct result of the influence of the moon over the inner consciousness of the mind.

The creative function of the moon has many cognates. It is related to the cycle of nature and to the forces of fertility. A very ancient belief links the movement of the moon with the menstrual cycle in women and also the vital semen in man. And thus all forms of conception are thought to be conditioned by the position of the moon in relation to nature. For the agriculturalist the 'time' for sowing is determined by the moon. And so a deeply held folk concept of time as the time for planting or reaping, a time of crisis in nature, is based on the moon symbol in relation to time. Going back to the source of time, the moon is believed to have a very primal connection with creation itself, and creation myths all over the world relate the moon to primal man, and the creation of the universe. Here the notion of the cosmic sacrifice of the moon, the perennial birth, growth and final dismembering of the moon is related to the creation process itself. The cosmic serpent Vrtra, according to the Rg Veda, who had power to control the flow of waters, was dismembered by Indra, and from his divided body the universe was made. The myth seems to have an ancient Iranian prototype, going back to the very source of civilization in Sumeria, where it was believed that the cosmic serpent Tiamat was divided by the god Marduk (in India Marut, god of the winds), thus creating heaven and earth. According to the Satapatha Brahmana (I.6,3), Vrtra implored Indra 'Do not strike me, for you

< 94 >

are now that I was once!' He begs to be divided into two parts. From parts containing soma Indra creates the moon, while from parts containing non-soma, that is non-divine elements, he makes the bellies of human beings. This is why there is the saying, 'Vrtra is within us!' Vrtra is apparently the same deity as Varuna, god of the oceans, who rides on the ebbing and flowing of the waves, and governs the rhythms (rtu) of the universe, the very personification of dharma. The sacrifice of the primal serpent of the oceans is the measuring out of time, and the divisioning of space. The chopping up of the primal being as part of an elemental sacrifice is itself the act of creation. Similarly the ritual breaking open of the coconut, the shedding of its inner liquid and the dividing up of its white flesh is in a way an act of sacrifice, a vital act, symbolically re-enacting the dismembering of the first child of the cosmic egg, from whose broken body the whole universe was constructed.

THE MOON AND COSMIC SOUND

Cosmic music has been associated with the moon in many cultures, the very shape of the crescent moon being related to a musical instrument, particularly the harp. In Indian thought the moon has been conceived of as the visible manifestation of the cosmic sound 'Om'. Ganesa himself is thought of as the image of this cosmic sound, the shape of the Sanskrit letter Om being traditionally related to that of the elephant-headed deity. Ganesa is thus the logos, representing both matter, in his relation to the Mother and the grossness of his physical form, but also the manifestation of primal word within matter. He is the beginning of all utterances. This is part of the mystery of the child symbol: on one side he seems so close to matter and to the physical contact with his mother, but on the other he learns to speak and give 'name' to things, and thus is the word arising out of matter.

The movement seems to be a double one. On one side there is matter aspiring to higher consciousness and to the logos, which is the expressed word, but on the other side primal vibration, in a constant process of incarnating itself, is becoming matter. This idea is expressed in tantra, as has been described by the expert on tantric art, Ajit Mukerjee. According to tantric thought, the 'A' component in the cosmic sound Om (or Aum) is associated with the upward-pushing fire and light of the cosmic lingam. The sound U is thought to be the womb of nature, or the cosmic waters (jalahari) and the marriage between the two has been related to the sound 'M'.[2] This 'M' is the

< 95 >

bindu or drop from which creation arises — the star in relation to the crescent moon in Islamic art. Nature is tara, the star. The moon has been connected in many cultures with love, and the light of the moon has been seen as the cosmic semen (sukra). This is because the light of the moon is thought of as creative and impregnating the womb of the earth. The cosmic sound of the moon proceeds on waves of bliss (ananda lahari). In the light of the moon, according to tantra, the word becomes visible, Pasyanti. It is this movement from cosmic sound to the visible that is characterized by the sign of Om which is perhaps the most sacred sign in India. It has been suggested that this sign is itself based on a moon symbol, namely the three mountains above which is the crescent moon, symbolic of the three phases of the moon. The cosmic resonance which emerges as light enters into the womb of space, and concretizes, crystallizing like the diamond into the geometry of matter. This last movement into the physical is characterized in Indian thought as the dance.

SACRED DANCE IN INDIAN ART

Dance has occupied a very central place in Indian plastic art; in fact according to the Silpa Sastras (canonical books concerning the arts, compiled mostly in the Gupta period) dance is the mother of all the arts. Everywhere in Indian iconography you will see dancing figures. In these dancing figures, so sensuous and earthly, it seems as though the cosmic sound symbolized by the moon has entered into matter (this state is known as Vaikhari). Here then we have the total movement from primal pulsating rhythm through manifested energy in fire and light, until matter is created out of space. These are the stages described also in Sabda Yoga. In the great temple of Cidambaram in Tamil Nadu all the one hundred and eight main poses of Bharata's Natya Sastra have been given very material representation in stone. But the central icon of that temple is not the dancing, sensuous figures, but the lingam of space — that is the inner nothingness of the temple which is shaped in the form of the lingam. In the same way, in the temple of Khajuraho, though the exterior crust of the temples is bursting with erotic imagery, the interiors of the temples are surprisingly bare and austere. Out of the tantric understanding of material form emanating from the word came the theory of the yantras which are an important class of images in India. Yantra literally means 'machine' but in conjunction with mantra has come to mean what Berriedale Keith so aptly calls the 'psychic apparatus'. The yantra is an abstract structure which has a certain dynamism. It is capable of expanding, evolving.

< 96 >

Symbols of sacred space and dance in relation to the moon — the theme of Radha and Krsna dancing together in the sacred groves of Vrndavan is very dear to Indian folk art

< 97 >

The point from which the yantra moves, as do the ripples from the centre where a stone has disturbed the still surface of a pool of water, is called the bija or seed. It is also known as the bindu or drop. These abstract patterns of lines and colours are used for yogic contemplation, and are held in great respect as icons by not only Hindus but Buddhists also, for tantric thought was as much Buddhist as Hindu. The bija is generally not represented, being the mystic germ of life, the dot above the crescent moon in the symbol OM, as written in Sanskrit. But this germinal seed or drop of living moisture, is intuited in the heart of the icon. In the Buddhist gnostic schools of the Vajrayana, found in Nepal and Tibet, these yantras have been developed into what are known as mandalas. These mandalas are painted on cloth and involve a complicated liturgy of their own. Representational details of gods and goddesses, flowers and animals, are inserted into an abstract pattern which, in its main structure, is a square with four gates, a sort of garden having four entrances. In this it is a pictograph of the whole cosmos, according to tantric thought. But the setting is that of the classical temple stage, or mandapa, which is to be found near the temple, in its precincts, where ritualistic classical dancing is performed. The dance is here the Lila or play, upon the cosmic stage.

In the centre of the space where the dance is to take place there is very often a great standing lamp. This lamp generally stands at the centre of a kolama pattern. The kolama pattern is basically a mandala, a representation of sacred space. It is possibly related to the maze — in certain areas near Madras it is called a Fort or Kote. In Poona district, I am told, a pattern built up at the time of Divali, on which lights are displayed, is called Killa which again means fortress. This would connect with the idea that the mandala itself is conceived of as a fortified city. An interesting description of the symbolism behind the Kathakali stage is given by Bharata Iyer. According to him, the stage represents the space of a primal act of creation, probably the Maha-purusa mandala which is the basis on which the temple is also constructed. We might note also that, as the mandala is a grid pattern having eight divisions rather like a chessboard, the basic dance steps of classical Indian dancing are built on patterns of eight. The great oil lamp in the centre of the stage has a thick wick, and a thinner wick, representing the sun and the moon, the eternal binomials of creation. The drumming with which the performance begins is meant to symbolize the cosmic deluge and the dawn of a new age. The curtain which is held in front of the principal actors represents Rajani or Tamas, the darkness that divides. The opening song and rhythms of the dance symbolize the creation of language, and the dance is Lila.

< 98 >

THE LORD OF THE DANCE

Siva is called the Lord of the dance. It seems that this white god of the mountain was an old pre-Aryan moon deity. He is especially connected with the bull, which again in many mythologies is related to the moon, for its horns are in fact the horns of the moon. Siva was originally known in the Vedas as Rudra, the howler, and was also called the dancer within the pine forest. As such he seems to have been especially connected with the wind, and his children the Maruts, are in fact different aspects of wind energy — wind speed, wind force, wind-destroyer, wind-circle, wind-flame, wind-seed and wind-disc. These deities are very popular among an agricultural people, being the spirits which govern changes in the weather. The very idea of wind conveys the feeling of movement in space and the essence of dance.

One popular representation of the dancing Siva shows him wrapped in the skin of a great elephant demon, whom he made to dance until finally he was destroyed, and Siva stripped his skin off, and danced, with overflowing destructive frenzy, within the elephant demon's body, wrapping its skin around him like a great mantle. My understanding of this myth is that the elephant demon was in fact gross space itself, and we have here a variant of the theme of Siva's transforming spiritual dance within the space-body of the cosmos. As Siva dances he carries in his hand the little drum which is shaped rather like an hour-glass, and which conveys the idea of the pulsating rhythm of cosmic time. In another hand he holds the spiralling pattern of destructive fire, his hand holding the fire being in the position known as ardha candra mudra, or the half-moon mudra (see p. 200). Here in his dance we see the emblems of pure sound, and its counterpart pure energy. As pure sound brings all things to birth, pure energy receives the universe back, and dissolves it into non-being. The drum is the creative aspect of the dance, its fertility. The shape of the drum is two triangles or cones meeting each other, which in tantric thought symbolizes the act of marriage — the 'hieros gamos', the meaning of heaven and earth. The curling tongue of fire on the other side is the destructive aspect of the dance.

Perhaps the greatest icon of southern Shaivism is the figure of Siva Tandava, which brings into a perfect unity many aspects of sacred space and time. It is a true configuration of many symbolic details, which together convey the mystery of the cosmic dance. In this great image of the Nataraja who is sacred time (Maha Kala) dancing in the sacred space of the universe, of his six limbs (four hands, and two feet) five are on the left side of the icon, that is, the recreative side,

< 99 >

the upward ascending side, in the yin-yang pattern, while only one arm is on the right side, the downward moving side of the yin-yang pattern, and this arm holds the spiral of fire (see p. 105). Despite this apparent unbalance, the whole icon is perfectly resolved, showing how deeply satisfying is this geometry of symbolic time, based on the interrelation of the numbers five and six. Here we have the relation of the two legs (standing and stepping across, stability and movement), the three hands (boon-giving, protecting and beating the drum of life) and the one hand holding the all-consuming, all-embracing fire of the universe.

< 100 >

CHAPTER 9

The symbol of life-further reflections on the significance of the moon

< 101 >

A hanging lamp representing the parrot. The parrot is sometimes connected with myths of Agni, in that it is supposed to watch the love play between Siva and Parvati and then steal the blazing seed of the god in its beak

< 102 >

In Tagore's collection of poems about children *The Crescent Moon*, the child asks in one poem, 'Where have I come from?' The question is a very natural one, and modern well-informed parents who lay much stress on being 'open' with their children launch into a long biological explanation, trying to be as frank and honest as possible. The result is the child is genuinely confused and puzzled. The child is not an empirical scientist, he is far more comfortable with images and symbols. If the villager tried to answer the question 'Where have I come from?' he too would search for a poetic answer, for that is what he is looking for, not the mere 'facts' of life, which he is very aware of, but which don't in any way answer the question. Tagore tries to give expression to a truly Indian answer to this basic question.[1]

> 'Where have I come from, where did you pick me up?', the baby asked its mother.
> She answered, half crying, half laughing, and clasping the baby to her breast, 'You were hidden in my heart as its desire, my darling. You were in the dolls of my childhood's games; and when with clay I made the image of my god every morning, I made and unmade you then. You were enshrined with our household deity, in his worship I worshipped you.

It was in answer to this existential question that Hindu thought conceived of the notion of man as born from the light of the moon (see pp. 94, 113), as it flows down to the earth through the moisture, and is first incarnated in the very sap of plants. In the Satapatha Brahmana (VIII 7,2,16–17) it is stated 'jyotir prajanaman', 'light is procreation'. Mircea Eliade quotes Tibetan tantric sources[2] which believed that at the beginning men were a-sexual, radiating light: 'No moon or sun was there in these days. The light emanating from the body of man lit up the womb of the female, and sex was satisfied by seeing alone.'

The act of bringing a child to birth is the perennial creative process of separating a new being from a primary maternal unity. Parturition is the mystery of making two from one. This is also the process of drawing an image out of matter. The child is in a very deep sense the image or pratima – the reflection on the world of duality of an original unity. Thus C. G. Jung speaks of what he calls the child archetype as 'born out of the womb of the unconscious, begotten out of the depths of human nature, or rather out of living Nature herself', or again 'not a copy of the empirical child, but a symbol clearly recognizable as such'.[3] The child symbol is an image, making visible the invisible, or, as he is known in Hindu myth, 'Guha', born of the 'secret place'.

It is perhaps in this way that the moon is connected to the child

< 103 >

archetype, for it too is a mirror-reflection, an image of the light of the sun. Also it grows, as it were in the womb of the sky; it is born out of the eternal darkness. As we have already seen earlier, and shall again see when speaking of the sun, the child is thought of as itself a manifestation of light (see pp. 125, 201). Light is not only ethereal, without substance, but becomes concrete, crystallizes out of the cosmic flux. One of the central concerns of alchemy, which looked for the transformation of matter into spirit, was the search for the jewel which is life transformed into the hard substance of rock. In certain experiences of shamanism, the mystic finds that he has a crystalline form emerging within him, as the very heart of his body; his body itself ultimately becomes light. In Indian thought, the jiva, or life monad, is adamantine, a hard, jewel-like centre, which is both light and fire, and also stone.

As the jewel has many facets, or the mirror reflects many images, the central life monad in man is seen in different forms. The child symbol is at once the very essence of life in matter, but is also passing, changing, becoming, as the image too is flowing, never 'fixed', that is ultimately 'determined'. On the one hand the image which comes forth from the stone is the very essence of the stone being revealed from where it was hidden, but on the other hand this very image, too, is not definitive, for many images are possible from the same matrix of matter, and each image is itself in the process of being exposed, never completely revealed, but always in the process of showing itself. Again the child has a wholeness, which is the beauty of every stage of its development; it is never incomplete, like a half-finished sentence, only it is never fully realized, that is perfectly understood.

THE MOON AND THE CONCEPT OF WHOLENESS

The phases of the moon have constantly fascinated the mind as a symbol of the perennial search for wholeness. In nature there is perhaps no greater symbol of wholeness than the full moon. I feel that the realization of the symbol of the moon and its relation to the mensuration of time lies at the heart of Hindu symbolic mathematics. The field is a vast one, and I can only touch here on the fascinating concept of sunya and its symbolic meaning in Indian thought.[4] Sunya is both the void and also the fullness, and is characterized by a circle or egg which is white in colour. It is said that India's great contribution to the field of mathematics was the discovery of this symbol. Certainly it seems to lie at the heart of Indian

< 104 >

representations of mythic time and space and is most perfectly characterized by the yantra which was known in the far east as 'yin-yang', but which emerged out of the Buddhist view of fundamental form (see p. 196).

(see p. 196)

THE SPIRAL

By studying attentively the geometry of the yin-yang pattern we begin to discern the rhythms of a spiralling motion. The pattern is created by drawing a circle with, inside, a figure of eight, that is two circles having half the radius of the greater circle, and touching both each other and the larger surrounding circle. This figure of eight, or the two-petalled white lotus, was from ancient time a symbol of eternity. The dividing wall of the yin–yang pattern is made by taking one half of the figure of eight pattern, that is an S-shaped line, whose length is equivalent to exactly half the total circumference of the greater circle. In turn the inner circles of the yin-yang pattern can be broken down into further yin-yang patterns in an endless progression inwards like the path of an inward spiralling pattern. The moon has been related to the spiralling patterns of shells, and the mathematical progression which seems to govern the volutes of growing organic forms.

The spiral has been connected from ancient times with the very force of life – the movement of fluid substances or the growth of cellular structures. The twisting forms of horns which are meant to contain life-force, or the curling patterns of flowing hair, which is also associated with life energy, both follow a spiralling movement.[5] In Islamic art, for example, the spiralling shape of the ram's horn is thought to symbolize the energy of life. In India hair has also been very much associated with vitality, and thus the hair of the yogi is piled above his head in a spiralling topknot, while the dancing Nataraja allows his hair to flow out like streams of cosmic force. The world-denying ascetic cuts off his hair, as Buddha did; but even there in the case of Buddha the hair assumes a magical life of its own, and is described as rising up into the air, and forming as it were a knot of energy in the cosmos. We are reminded again of the sacred hair of the prophet Mohammed which is said to be preserved in various shrines, including a shrine in Kashmir. Kashmir is also a centre of certain sects of the Hindu sakti-cult, comparable in certain respects to Zen Buddhism. After cutting his hair to the length of two finger breadths, the head of the Lord Buddha became crowned with countless shell-like curls of hair, representing the involuting force of his mind power.

< 105 >

In fact one curl of hair between his eyebrows is said to be so full of light that it can illumine the whole universe. This equation of spiralling hair and light and life is probably implicit in the myth which describes how one white and one black hair of Visnu entered the womb of the mother of Krsna, impregnating it with divine life, so that the two sons Balarama and Krsna were born to her, one from the white hair, the other from the black hair. It is for this reason that Krsna is known as Kesava, reminding us that he is born of hair. In Eastern thought the vegetation is referred to as the hair of Mother Earth, again connecting spiralling movement with growth and life.

A certain pattern emerges, which cannot be explained rationally, but which is deeply evocative, showing the configuration of light, spiralling movement and the seed of life. The connection between these is not to be found in the static ideas of light, or life, or the spiral. Rather it is in the relation of these phenomena, the way in which they seem to flow into each other, that the symbol as an ensemble of images emerges. As in the dream, images overlap and complement each other, themselves spiralling towards a hidden meaning. Nothing can be taken merely literally, language is itself never merely descriptive. Always the unspoken remains an indefinable quality, nature manifesting itself through the creative round of the seasons, the spiral which never comes back to exactly where it was but grows towards a wholeness.

THE STAGES OF THE MOON AND THE 'GUNA' SYSTEM

The moon governs the cycles of the seasons and the stages of life and is thus very naturally related to the 'guna' system. This system seems to be very ancient and is a truly indigenous system, affecting many schools of thought. 'Guna' is interpreted as meaning 'a part of a whole', but it is also the quality of a thing.[6] These 'gunas' are applied to the whole of nature, and every aspect of life is seen to fall into place within this total system. Thus the three principal castes, together with the outcaste, each have their characteristic 'gunas'. The three principal colours which we find used in folk art all over the world, namely white, red and black, are associated with the three main strands of the 'guna' system — white is sattva, red is rajas, and black is tamas. These three colours also represent the three stages of the moon, white being the moon in its ascendant phase, red the full moon, connected with the menstrual blood and the fullness of life, and black being the moon in its receding phase. So all-embracing is this guna system that it not only applies to external objective reality

< 106 >

The symbol of light and life — the tree lamp. This design is derived from tree lamps to be found in many parts of India

< 107 >

such as the properties of foods and the castes of the social system, but it also applies to psychological states and the different modes of consciousness. Black and white are the principal poles of our fundamental opposition of light and dark, conscious and unconscious states. The colour red emerges at the point where these two polarities of nature intersect, life and death, emerging and receding movements in nature. Red symbolizes the living sacrifice between all the polarities of life – it is the colour of the Mother, and blood.

TRINITY IN CONNECTION WITH THE MOON

We have mentioned how the phases of the moon are seen in folk tradition to fall within three broad divisions:[7] the rising moon, the full moon and the waning moon which includes the dark of the moon. These three stages seem to have been represented from early times as a three-headed god or goddess. In India there appears to be a prototype of this figure in an Indus Valley seal which depicts a deity seated in the familiar yogic pose known as the lotus posture. He appears to have three heads, and is crowned with a form which looks like two horns with a central fan-like shape giving an overall impression of a trident (see pp. 76-7). The relations of this proto-Siva with a moon deity is seen from his horns, and his association with the bull, which is by far the most represented hieratic animal in the Mohenjodaro seals, often shown together with emblematic censers, indicating worship offered to this beast. The bull is the progenitor, and is also connected with phallic symbolism. In India, as seems to have been the case in all ancient societies, the moon is thought of as masculine, not feminine, and is believed in many tribes to impregnate women who expose themselves to him, especially at the time of the full moon. We see here how once again the theme of the creative power of the moon is linked with human sexuality. It is probably on this account that the light of the moon is thought to be very romantic, and one recalls those deeply emotive pictures of Krsna and the gopies, sporting in the quiet glades of Vrndavan forest, beneath the moist whiteness of a full moon.

< 108 >

Kolama pattern with decorative lamps on either side. The pattern in the centre is meant to represent interlaced mango leaves

< 109 >

CHAPTER 10

The feminine figure in Indian thought

< 111 >

[OVERLEAF]

Sculpture in stone of a dancing girl putting a bindu on her forehead while she is looking in a mirror — drawn from a statue in a small wayside temple south of Madurai

< 112 >

The world-process, known in India as samsara, is thought of as feminine. Between this world-process and the all-transcendent Father there is an eternal dialectic. In the highly developed metaphysics of the later medieval schools, the term adhara, meaning support, container, is supplied to the feminine, as opposed to adheya, meaning that which is to be supported, meaning here the masculine principle. Thus, although the feminine according to one viewpoint is understood as the relative, maya, seen in a different way it is the container of all that can be known, the very substance of all that is (sati).

The concept of the transmigration of souls which is the basis of the Hindu concept of samsara, is thought by some to have entered Hinduism through certain non-Aryan agricultural ways of thought such as are to be found, for example, among Indian tribals. According to R. C. Zaehner, there is no trace of the doctrine of reincarnation either in the Samhitas or Brahmanas, and it only begins to appear in the Upanisads.[1] In the Brhadaranyaka Upanisad (6.2.15–16) two paths are described, one the 'way of the gods', also known as the 'way of the sun', and the other the 'way of the fathers', which is also called the 'way of smoke' or the 'way of the moon'. This latter path is the cycle of samsara, for here the 'fathers', meaning ancestors,[2]

> pass on into smoke, the night, the world of the fathers, and finally into the moon. There they become the food of the gods, but when that passes away from them, they descend into space, from space into air, from air into rain and from rain into the earth. When they reach the earth they become food. Once again they are offered as an oblation in the fire of man, and thence they are born in the fire of a woman. Rising up into the worlds they circle round within them. But those who do not know these ways become worms, moths, and biting serpents.

The way of the sun is the way of moksa, whereas the way of smoke, or the moon, is the path of samsara. This samsara takes man back into the womb of the mother, whereas moksa delivers him from the cycle of rebirth. It is necessary to understand this basic picture of the two paths if we are to realize the significance of the feminine figure, for the feminine figure as she has been depicted in Indian art is the visual representation of the way of smoke into which all those who are to be reborn are to enter.

I have often been surprised by the fact that in Indian art we do not see developed the highly evocative theme of the mother and child which has been so central to Western Christian art. Indian art has concentrated on the relationship of the feminine to the masculine, depicting the many aspects of love play which are so popular in Bhakti

< 113 >

poetry and art. Here the feminine figure is that of the enchantress, Mohini, who playfully draws the masculine into the world-cycle. The perfect feminine figure is therefore a girl of sixteen, halfway herself between childhood and maturity, because her spirit is a perfect intermingling of childish playfulness and sexual maturity. The Indian woman as she is depicted here is both mother and child in one, so that it is not possible to distinguish her from the fruit of her womb. She is herself the principle of incarnation, the eternal womb into which all creation is drawn. She is therefore never contrasted with the child, as Mary is contrasted with Jesus; rather she merges with the child as the gopis did who played with Balakrsna, or as the playful Valli merged with Murugan. She becomes part of the child's own tender fantasy, a projection as it were of his erotic world-involvement.

As the souls of the ancestors descend as space, air, rain and plants, the feminine is all of these. She is clothed in space (digambara). She is the sacred rivers and streams which fill the earth with life. She is the luxuriant plants. Durga, perhaps the most ancient of Hindu mother deities, was probably originally a goddess of the forest and the overflowing life of vegetation. As far back as the Yajur Veda we have the verse: 'Plants, O ye Mothers, I hail ye as goddesses'. These are the yaksinis, otherwise known as the seven mothers (sapta matrka) who became important in the medieval temples of central India. Over these mothers of vegetation the lord Kubera is said to rule and it is this ancient god of wealth who is in many ways the prototype of such child figures as Ganesa (indeed the term Ganapati was originally applied to Kubera). The daughter of Kubera is the famous Minaksi, the fish-eyed goddess, to whom is dedicated the temple of Madurai and who, like the goddess Vasundhara, is depicted as a sixteen-year-old girl at the very prime of her maidenhood.

The Indian feminine figure is depicted with swelling breasts. This again is thought to show her overflowing fertility, rather than her specific relation to a child whom she is feeding. It is almost as if the Indian feminine figure has been abstracted beyond any personal relationship, which is the intention behind the highly personalized depictions of the mother and child images of Christian art. For here the woman is the all-embracing principle of nature, and even the milk that fills her breasts is described as 'the essence of water and of the plants'.

The figure of woman in folk art seems to develop very naturally out of a feeling for the shapes of animals. There is in all truly Indian art a deep empathy for the forms of animals which goes back as far as the art of Mohenjodaro. Though the bodies of animals are often idealized, there is a vitality in the modelling of their limbs which

< 114 >

exhibits an inner understanding of their strength and grace, their power to move beautifully as well as purposefully. It is this inner feeling for the purely natural and almost instinctual that character- izes the treatment of the feminine body. We find that quite frequently the carving or painting of the feminine body is closely associated with, and set off by, an animal representation, or even a bird. The curves of the bird or animal form are carried through and fulfilled in the figure of the woman. A favourite theme is the relation of the feminine body and that of a cow, or herd of cows. In Mahaballipuram in a great panel of high relief carved out of the living rock, we see the favourite theme of Krsna as Giridhara holding up the mountain. Below in the shelter of this mountain is a very tenderly conceived scene of the cowherd's family. A mother cow is licking her calf which is sucking at her udder. Around are a group of girls whose strong yet sensuous bodies perfectly complement the subtle render- ing of the cow's form. The same relation between human and animal is found in the Lepaksi murals, and there again it is the female human form which seems to provide the essential link between man and beast.

This relation of man and beast itself brings us back to our under- lying theme of the child. The child somehow merges with the animal — like the animal it walks on all fours, and seems to live a purely instinctual life. In Ganesa the animal and the child have become fused. The child Buddha is depicted as entering the womb of his mother as a baby elephant. Perhaps an ancient sense of being part of the animal world gave rise to myths where the child hero is brought up by an animal mother. In the Iranian Gilgamesh myth Eabani and Enkidu were brought up in the desert among wild beasts. In India Siva is known as Pasupati (Lord of beasts). As such, he can be com- pared to Orpheus, while Eurydice has much in common with the Hindu idea of Prakrti.

In women the whole of nature finds its perfection. The organic structures of trees and vines are not only to be found by analogy in the lithe limbs of the female form, but they are also in some way fulfilled by woman. It is a very important folk belief that a young beautiful woman spreads fertility to the rest of creation because she is the vessel of nature's over-abundant power.[3] The idea that by physical contact with a young mature woman fruiting trees become more fruitful probably goes back into folk magic. We find as far back as in the reliefs of Bharhut the much-favoured theme of a young maiden swinging on the branch of a fruit tree, one leg lifted in a sensuous gesture of embrace. Perhaps the most perfect realization of this figure is to be found carved on the lintels of the great ceremonial

< 115 >

gates of Sanchi where the relation of playful swinging girl and bending fruit-laden tree fits perfectly as a kind of bracket beneath the
horizontal cross-beams of the gate.

Swing festivals connected with the rainy season as well as the
spring are not only an important feature of the past, but are very
much a part of present-day village culture. The idea is the same, that
by swinging in the branches of trees, especially fruit trees such as the
mango, the fertility of the crop is increased. But there seems to be
another idea too. The ceremonial swinging of a priest is meant to
imitate the swinging of the universe itself. By swinging, a maiden
becomes like a heavenly body — the moon swinging in the great tree
of space. The rhythmic motion marks the beat of time, and is thus
a simulation of the measured beat of the cosmos, and the pendulum
motion of time itself. So this swinging motion of the woman's body
is a very profound icon of the grace (lavanya) of the universe. Her
dancing step sways from side to side, and in fact there is a deep
relation between a swinging movement and the child in the womb,
rocked near the heart of his mother. Swinging becomes a symbol
both of sexual ecstasy, and the fertility of nature's powers. It is also
a symbol of the child's relation to its mother, and by extension the
relation of man to mother nature itself.

There is a desire in Indian art to personify forces of nature. The
figure of woman becomes an icon of some natural force. Water, for
example, in particular rivers, is constantly being personified in the
form of some beautiful young lady. Perhaps this is one of the reasons
why, at least in classical Indian art, the depiction of nature itself is so
minimal — the human form seems to predominate everywhere. Yet
this human form is not seen as distinct from nature but rather as its
most perfect symbol. Thus a group of dancing maidens could very
well be the meeting of rivers and the playing of waves.

A very common feature of the Hindu temple is the depiction on
the pillars of the halls adjoining the central shrine of sacred rivers as
maidens dancing with sensuous gestures. The musical instruments
which these maidens sometimes carry are again symbolic of the sound
of water, and beyond, the music of the spheres. The sacred rivers are
themselves thought to be astral energies brought down to earth. It
will be remembered from the myth concerning the descent of the
river Ganges that it was originally a heavenly element which by the
grace of the deity, was brought down to earth. But the force of this
heavenly river would have destroyed the earth if it had not been for
Siva who sat beneath the descending waterfall and enmeshed the
stream in his abundant matted hair so that by the time it emerged
onto the terrestrial plane is untamed ardour had been quietened.

< 116 >

The feminine figure in Indian thought — beside the door leading into the temple stand feminine figures, often representing the sacred rivers. The motifs of this design have been inspired by sculptured details of the Teli temple in Gwalior Fort (eighth-tenth century)

< 117 >

The theme of the descending of the river Ganges has been magnificently depicted in the rock reliefs of Mahaballipuram (see pp. 76–8). There a whole natural face of rock has been transformed into a mythological pageant, and a natural gorge in the rock has been peopled with water nymphs to represent the downward pouring stream. Water nymphs are generally thought to be serpentine from their breasts downwards and, like the Western mermaid, combine the physique of a cold-blooded creature with that of a beautiful graceful maiden. In many Indian villages, especially in Karnataka, you will see 'nagakals' or 'snake stones' on which reliefs of half-woman half-serpent are carved.

Though Indian art has a very conscious bias towards the depiction of the human form, in general it has never developed an interest in the human nude body as such. This has not been out of any prudery — in fact the sexual significance of the body has been portrayed with a frankness that is shocking to many. But on the whole the body as such is not important because it is divested of its most human characteristic and made into a symbol of what is not particularly human at all. The only figures which approach anywhere near what was the main concern of the western artists when they developed an interest in the nude, are to be found in certain semi-clothed figures of maidens where the body is seen to merge into the natural environment which is shown to contain and embrace them.[4] For example, a favourite theme of the miniature schools is that of the gopis bathing naked in a river pool, and Krsna as the mischievous herdsman climbing up a tree, having stolen the maidens' clothes. But here again the bodies of the girls are almost fish-like, silvery and supple, and the water seems to flow around them like a sort of veil. It is not the nakedness of the women which seems so important to the artist as their complete identification with the principle of water, with all its poetic charm of blossoming lotuses and richly verdant banks. The boy Krsna seems to be a tree-being over and against the feminine which is the genius of the waters.[5] The significance of stealing the clothes of the maidens seems to underline their imprisonment in the water, because without their clothes they cannot come out of the water. The traditional explanation of the story is that before the divine person (Krsna) we are all naked: here nakedness is given a spiritual meaning as it is given also by the digambara sect of the Jains, for nakedness implies freedom from attachments, and hence transcendence of the world-cycle.

This brings us to the treatment of garments in Indian art. Essentially the female body is 'digambara', that is, 'clothed in space'. But this 'space' is symbolized by the ornaments on her body. For example,

< 118 >

in India the art of making garlands has had a very ancient source. Leaves and flowers have been studied for their various medicinal and symbolic properties. In folklore the symbolism attached to a plant is thought to be identical to its magical powers. The fact that the ancient Indian palasa tree (*butea frondosa/butea mono-sperma*, known also as the Flame of the Forest) has three parts to its leaf, links it with the trinity Brahma, Visnu and Siva, and thus adds to its sacredness and consequent sacramental powers. The same is true of the bilva tree, which is sacred both to Durga and Siva. In the Mahabharata the wounds on the body of a brave warrior are described poetically as being like the palasa tree in full blossom. Garlands of flowers endow the body with symbols drawn from a natural lore. The properties of flowers and leaves in garlands are transferred to those who wear them. Above all, the garland is a symbol of the cosmos itself, whose milky way is like a garland of stars.

The same significance is given to garlands of jewels and other ornaments. The purpose of such fineries is to give to the body a supernatural beauty. Every particular article of jewellery is made into a microcosm in which the macrocosm is mirrored forth. This is the meaning of woman as the archetype of all that is precious, and clothed in riches. It would be easy to see a mere glorification of materialism in the figure of woman as in Laksmi, for example. But this feminine figure of wealth is like everything else in Indian iconography, at once the most literal glorification of the immediate world of the senses, and yet also the icon of what is essentially beyond direct perception – the very epitome of the universe as the eternal jewel, the adamantine reality which is perfectly resilient with a fire that burns from within.

It is this confusion of the most carnal with the most exalted conception of the nature of reality beyond the senses that characterizes the Indian concept of femininity. Woman becomes inward-looking like nature itself, almost to the point of worshipping herself. She is the essence of pleasure-seeking. In art she is exalted not so much for her self-sacrifice, or self-effacement, as for her sublime self-consciousness. She enjoys her own beauty. She looks at herself in a mirror. The woman at her toilet is a favourite theme of art in all nations. The theme seems to capture woman at her most artful, and therefore somehow at her most instinctive. And yet, though in Western art this self-adulation of the woman at her toilet seems to aspire to little beyond a playful narcissism, in Indian art we might rightly suspect a deeper meaning. Woman looking at herself in a mirror, affixing to her forehead the bindu, carefully formed at the centre of the eyebrows, at the point of the third eye, is nature looking into herself to discover her own centre. She becomes the perfectly reflective one, herself

< 119 >

like the mirror of still water, or like the moon reflecting the sun. Her gazing upon herself is her looking into herself — her looking out in order to look in, her returning upon herself like the cosmic wheel returning to its point of origin.

The figure of the woman contemplating herself in a mirror is also woman enjoying her own sexual potency. The mirror in Indian art takes on the meaning of the yoni, the feminine organ. Sex in India is itself far more than the merely biological — it is the energy of the universe wishing to unite, longing to discover a higher dimension of being through union. This is why in Hindu thought the very essence of samsara is Kama, the youthful god of love, because it is through him that all creatures long for union (samadhi). The woman looking at herself is already preparing for her lover — she wants to unite with herself, and hence, through a unity in herself, she seeks duality in her image, in order to discover the meaning of union. Indian woman is Sarasvati, that is 'she who flows out', she who wants to go beyond herself in ecstasy, in order to discover the union of all things in love.

The very basic values of male and female are not seen as in any way particularly human. Rather they are cosmological. Male and female are forces in the universe, manifesting themselves in plants, in animals, and also in the human dimension. The very fact that mankind also is divided into male and female, shows that man is but a part of the rest of the universe. Thus sex is not specifically a human activity. It is essentially an activity of the universe in which man is caught up. Teilhard de Chardin speaks boldly of love as an energy to be found in matter itself,[6] perhaps its primal seed of consciousness contained as a sort of 'interiority' within substance. It is the longing for unity which seems to be a drive coextensive with life itself, a drive which seems already prefigured in the behaviour of molecular structure.

This capacity to unite is not only the cause of the world-cycle, driven by the twin energies of attachment, Kama and Mara, but it is also mysteriously the moment of release (samadhi) because the eternal feminine is delivered from her fascination for her own image at the point when she surrenders herself to the masculine.

< 120 >

A kolama pattern very likely influenced by the basic structure of the Hindu temple

< 121 >

CHAPTER 11
The symbol of the sun

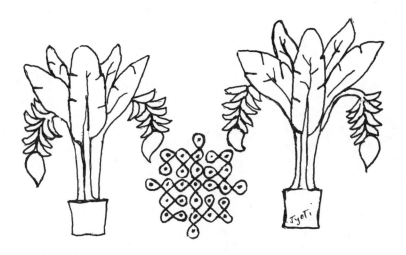

< 123 >

[OVERLEAF]

A kolama pattern placed before the door, on either side banana plant decorations — a traditional folk design

< 124 >

In mythology, Hindu as elsewhere, the sun is seen either as the father or the son. However, there is a considerable body of legend which understands the sun as a youthful deity. There is, as everywhere in myth-making, a constant process of identifying polarities within the one whole, so here also the sun is both the most ancient father and the most youthful son — the two aspects become fused together in the one composite image of father and son. In Hindu thought the sun (Surya) is sometimes called Martanda, that is, 'born of the lifeless egg'.[1] According to one myth, it is an eighth part of the original golden egg from which all energy sprang, and which was the blazing universe. The sun as he appears as the divine child is more generally identified with the cycle of the year or seasons. The following is a description of the birth of the Lord Buddha, which is a favourite theme of Buddhist iconography:[2]

> Mahamaya, wife of Suddhodana, of Kapila Vastu, dreamt one night of a white elephant entering her womb. She became pregnant and her womb became transparent like a crystal casket. She felt an urge to withdraw for meditation to the forest and there, while beneath a Sal tree, she gave birth from her side. The child was born in full awareness and looking like a young sun; he leapt on to the ground and where he touched it there sprang up a lotus. He looked on the four cardinal points, to the four half points above and below, and saw deities and men acknowledging his superiority. He made seven steps northwards, a lotus appearing at each footfall. His birth was greeted by Asita, a sage from the Himalayas who likened him to Skanda or Kumara.

Writing about the birth of Skanda, Wendy Doniger O'Flaherty comments, 'Astronomical factors are central to this myth which may represent the birth of the year (skanda) with its six seasons (six heads) during the new moon of the spring equinox when the sun is in the Pleiades.'[3]

In the same way Manu, the primal man, born from the mind ('man') of his father the sun, is the founder of a new aeon of 4320000 years, known as Manvantara and also as the Mahayuga. Sanat Kumara, who is represented as the eldest of eight brothers is described as born from the sun in the Harivamsa. There Markandeya relates the epiphany of Sanat Kumara: 'I saw the divine Aditya (the sun) and an effulgent being, bright as fire itself, and small as a finger.'[4]

This effulgent child deity is described in popular myth as coming out of the mind (man) of his father. This mind is symbolized by the fiery third eye of Siva, from which the child springs as from a womb.

< 125 >

Thus, according to one tradition, Ganesa is also born of the mind of Siva. 'Siva, while immersed in profound thought, a great brilliance emanated from his forehead, and there sprang to existence a wondrous being . . .'⁵ To understand the nativity of the child god we must understand that on one hand he was born of the mind of the father via the eye (which is another epithet for the sun); but on the other hand he was born of the virgin mother, who is also the queen of the waters of regeneration.

THE WAY OF THE SUN

The villager has seen a close relation between the sun and life in creation around him. Without the light and warmth of the sun, nothing could flourish and be fruitful here on earth. And yet again the sun by itself has a consuming fire. It is only in conjunction with water that it is truly life-giving. Thus in the villager's view there is a continual inter-play between the fiery splendour of the sun and the waters of the depths. It is thought that every dawn the sun rises from the waters, and the whole day it seems that the waters of earth are drawn up into the arms of the sun.

But the path of the sun is not only seen as a cyclical one. Very important to man's consciousness of the symbol of the sun is the idea of its height. It seems to him that the sun is like a door leading up to a reality beyond the cycles of nature. It is like a window through which man glimpses an escape from the ever recurring rhythms of birth and death. Perhaps the circular path of the sun is only an illusion — so it seems from man's viewpoint, caged as he is in his own rounded cell. At noon-time it almost seems that a ladder reaches between earth and sky pointing upwards to a reality beyond the circling horizon. At that time everything seems like a cone reaching upwards to a point of escape from the hour-glass of the world.

THE SYMBOL OF THE DOOR

Arising out of this view of the sun and its significance, from very ancient times the door has been invested with solar symbolism.⁶ In the door of the home or temple we have an image of the meeting of inner and outer, of high and low, darkness and light. Further, by passing through the door, man has a sense of the inner meaning of initiation. The door seems to him to hold a mystery, and so he tries

< 126 >

to decorate the door with figures and forms that remind him of the connection between his lowly home and the whole macrocosm.

I have often been impressed by the way the Indian villager instinctively respects the fundamental symbols of life. Around the door of his home he will very naturally place simple symbols, which indicate his intuition of the inner significance of the door. Especially in south India, the woman of the household will take great care to clean the doorstep and decorate it with patterns, often very intricately drawn in white powder, and known as kolamas. At the side of the door they will often paint symbols with coloured powder paint. Above the door a small figure or framed picture is placed. At festival times a torana, or archway of leaves and flowers, is put over the door. These symbols, simple though they are, have a wealth of meaning which also appears to be very ancient, for in early examples of Buddhist art, in Bharhut and also later in temples of the Gupta dynasty, we find in the decorative features of ceremonial gateways, and doors into the inner sanctum, all these elements which are so easily discernible in folk tradition. But in classical art these motifs are rendered through a highly sophisticated art into stone and metal.

THE DOOR AS A SYMBOL OF THE MOVEMENT OF THE SUN[7]

The ordinary door which is rectangular in shape consists of three sides which are clearly visible above the ground, the fourth side being part of the doorstep, and thus the ground itself. Thus we see the door as arising on one side out of the ground, reaching a zenith in the architrave over the door whose central stone exemplifies the vertical axis of the door at its highest point. Finally the door seems to descend back into the earth. The 'arch' of the door is clearly divided into three parts which remind one of the three times of the day, morning, mid-day and evening, that is, the movement of the Sun god.

This circular movement of the door is symbolized by the swastika, an ancient sun symbol which is often to be found over the door. This symbol clearly goes back as far as the Mohenjodaro civilization, as it is found in terra-cotta seals of that period, but probably it is even older than that. It is thought that the form relates to ancient fortification plans or mazes. As such it is very prominent in the kolama patterns which decorate the doorstep, and which, as recorded near Madras, are called 'forts' by local tradition. These patterns on the doorstep are nearly all circular, and possibly represent the cosmos as it is pictured in mandala form.

< 127 >

The symbol of the door is the entry into death and final dissolution into the source of being, but it is also the exit into life. All life owes its origin to the movement of the sun, and so we find in the sun temple of Konarka and elsewhere in middle India the depiction of erotic couples engaged in physical union. These couples (called Mithuna figures) are often to be found at the side of doors. The door itself becomes a symbol of union, and thus is decorated with a profusion of fruiting plants and flowers, especially the banana plant, at the time of marriages. Dramatic entry through the door is part of marriage ceremonies all over the world in folk culture. Erotic signs are to be found in conjunction with the pillars near the door in tribal art, as described by Verrier Elwin in connection with the Muria Ghotul.[8]

PLANT DECORATION AROUND THE DOOR

The most common decoration to be found around the door is connected with organic life. This symbolizes the earth cycle and links the door with the tree of life. The magical heat of the sun's light brings all things to birth. Around the doorway into the garbha grha of the temple are little niches for lights, forming generally a complete archway of flame, especially on festival days. But even in simple homes a niche for light above the door or sometimes on either side of the door, is a common feature. The tree of life is also the tree of the universe, and thus the luminaries of the firmament are connected with the flowers and fruits of the tree. A winding, clinging trellis around the door, in which many flowers and fruits are to be found, becomes a very common feature of Indian decorative art and is often executed with great beauty and feeling for growing forms. It also becomes a symbol of the inter-relatedness of living forms which seem to melt into each other, and get lost in the tangle of existence. The same symbolism is found in Mithuna couples which are described poetically in organic terms. Thus woman is said to cling to man like a creeper, and her rounded breasts are like fruits, and her legs like the smooth stems of the banana tree. Garlands hang over the door, again connecting the door with the chain of stars which are likened to a great garland of lights, and also the underlying theme of union, for the garland is an important symbol of marriage.

Fertility and birth, which the tree forms around the door exemplify, are personified in the figures of Yaksis or tree nymphs which are meant to represent the rising sap and life in plants. These sensuous feminine figures are a common motif in Buddhist and later Gupta

< 128 >

art in relation to ceremonial gateways and temple doors. The same figures appear in the later gopurams of south India. In connection with the door, we find the very ancient figure of the lord of the tree spirits, Ganapati. He is above all the remover of obstacles, and with his elephant trunk he can root up the tree of samsara which holds back the soul from liberation. But he is also the baby, combining in his strange form, the head of the elephant with the body of a human baby. Here we might see the characteristic of the door as the opening of the womb, the way by which the world is born forth. We recall from myth that it was while guarding the door to his mother's mysteries that Ganesa confronted the fury of Siva (the heat of the sun), who cut off the head of his own child for daring to prevent him from entering into the inner sanctum of the mother.

SYMBOLS OF WATER AND THE DOOR

Water is connected with the door in its aspect of initiation.[9] Nearly all initiations involve a ritual dying and entry into water to wash away the past. In this sense water has two aspects, firstly as a source of life, and secondly as a source of cleansing. Spatially it is represented as either descending in the form of rain, or heavenly streams like the Ganga and Yamuna, which come down upon earth in order to renew the earth and wash away its guilt. Or again water is represented as springing up from the earth as a principle of life in the soil and the sap within plants.

The descending, cleansing waters of the heavenly rivers are personified, and represented by feminine figures. Generally the Yamuna and Ganga are represented on either side of the door. This was particularly a common feature in the art of Gupta times. Decorative pots with overflowing foliage, lustral vases depicted above the door, are also common motifs. Carved on the door lintel we might see Laksmi rising from the waters, standing on the lotus, her body washed by streams of water poured upon her by elephants on either side of her. Symbols of elephants are a common feature of decoration near doors.

THE DOOR AND THE RAINBOW-HALOES AROUND DEITIES

The circle of fire representative of the movement of the sun, and also the entry of fiery light into the watery darkness, gradually developed in Indian art beyond the usual forms of ceremonial gates and doors

< 129 >

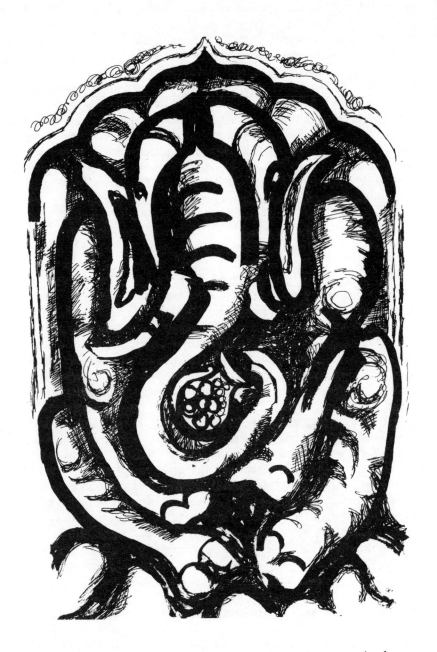

Symbol of the sun and the door — the god Ganesa is the guardian of the door

< 130 >

into the inner sanctuary. Niches and blind windows, such as the so-called caitya windows typical of Ajanta and Ellora, are almost drop-like in form, or like an orb rising from the ocean, part of which still lies hidden beyond the horizon. This archway seems to spring from the gaping mouth of a makara, which is a mythical sea monster, and returns to be swallowed back again by another makara depicted on the opposite side. This symbolic doorway, which was now more like a window than a door, became an image of the space of the cosmos or cidambaram. It is in this arch that Siva as Nataraja is depicted as dancing with fiery splendour. In this way the arch becomes not only a space through which man must pass, but is also the frame through which the divine reveals himself to man in and through nature.

The frame of the door is slowly converted into the halo, or aura, around a figure of the deity. Sometimes this aura encloses the whole body but sometimes it simply arises out of the shoulder and encircles the head of the divinity. Haloes, as we know them in Western Christian art, are probably of Eastern origin.

This idea of the window already seems to presume an ascent. The halo appears to crown the figure of the Lord — it is the door of the heavens opening up above man. In the northern sikhara, as also in the southern gopurams, we see these ceremonial windows like portholes opening out to the four points of the compass. It is thought that the sikhara evolved naturally out of the idea of successive layers of cakras piled up one on top of the other, each level with its windows facing out to the points of the compass. The gopuram or ceremonial gate of the later Dravidian temple, is composed, in the same way, of a series of floors, each with its own windows, crowded with figures of deities, who look out in various directions on to the points of the compass which they are supposed to command. These various layers which make up the great gate of the universe are meant to symbolize the different layers of consciousness such as waking, sleeping and deep sleep, or again the different realms of the gods, the seven planets, or the thirty-three divisions of the gods, which are also represented by the thirty-three sections of the flagstaff in the temple. In this way the door becomes like a ladder. In fact, we can see a relationship (especially in the northern temples, such as those of Khajuraho) between the steps leading up to the door, and above the door the tall crown of the vimana. The main door of the temple in this way becomes itself a step between the steps and the architecture above leading up higher to the crown of the sikhara whose final peak is a many petalled lotus which represents the opening into the sun. The elevation of the temple reminds one of the cakras of kundalini yoga, the lower reaches of which are the earthly levels of the purely

< 131 >

emotive, and the centre (corresponding with the main floor of the temple) is the cave of the heart, and above, crowning the sikhara, is the many petalled lotus of supramental consciousness.

THE GUARDIANS OF THE DOOR

As we can see from the whole structure of the Hindu temple, what is being depicted is the mandala of the universe. The doors of the temple are thus the points of the compass leading into the heart of the temple which is like the centre of a maze. This idea is most developed in the later Dravidian temples such as at Madurai. The devotee must find his way into the heart of the temple. He thus mystically re-enacts the path of the sun which finds its way into the womb of nature (the garbha grha of the temple) only to emerge again along the never ending way of being and becoming. Man is initiated into this path of the sun, so that he might discover his own centre.

In order to set about this journey man has to surrender himself. The rituals of initiation into the mandala all entail a testing of the neophite. The mandala is guarded. The very arches which crown the gentle beings who shower blessings on mankind, have a fearful aspect, a kirti mukha. The windows that face out onto the points of the compass have gargoyles. The doors through which the initiate has to pass are both welcoming and forbidding. Thus we have dvarpalikas or guardians of the door. These appear to be very ancient figures: we find the awe-inspiring figure of Kubera, lord of Yaksas (the forest figures) guarding the entrance to the stupa in Bharhut. The dvarpalikas become a feature of the first really indigenous school of art centring around Mathura and the ancient capital of Pataliputra. They show unmistakable evidence of belonging originally to an ancient pre-Aryan folk art, their ponderous forms, instinct with some titanic energy, are to be contrasted with the almost effeminate mannerisms of Gandharan art. They seem to presage the later perfect sense of glowing volume which was to characterize the plastic forms of art during the Gupta dynasty.

< 132 >

A detail from a carved door-frame of a small wayside temple near Mysore. The motif is a typical one and represents the Indian magical bird, the Hamsa, which is connected with the sacred tree

< 133 >

CHAPTER 12
Living symbolism

< 135 >

[OVERLEAF]

Stones piled into a votive shrine on the hill above Banner-gatta temple, near Bangalore

< 136 >

In Indian classical art we see the sometimes exaggerated effort to transform matter into what almost appears contrary to the nature of stone or wood. Endless effort is expended by the craftsman on the intricate working, polishing and perfecting of his image, so that one can see a maximum of energy devoted to the transforming of a natural substance into the image.

The need to polish everything and smooth over any natural roughness is, I feel, particularly significant, because it shows an inherent effort in Indian thought to civilize, almost make urbane, the merely physical, so that like the polished jewel it shines with a spiritual fire. We pointed out in the Introduction that the artist, having released from matter the image that has lain hidden within, stands back to contemplate what has been done. In this way he is both Prakrti, involved in the mother-life of matter, and Purusa, the eternal male, or lingam which is perhaps the most elemental 'symbol' of Indian thought. Within the total action of image-making we get the yoga which consists of the interaction of Purusa and Prakrti, contemplative insight, and active matter.[1]

This living symbolism is also discovered in the act of worship itself — the 'puja' as it is popularly known, deriving from the Dravidian word pusa, meaning to anoint. The lingam, that is the symbol, which is also often spoken of as svayambhu murti, is image arising out of nature of its own accord. It is anointed by the worshipper, who imparts to it a certain radiance, or shine, which is itself symbolic of the transforming power of symbol. These svayambhu murtis are drawn from nature by popular religion, and may be a natural lump of rock, tree-trunk, ant hill or great lump of ice up in the Himalayas, which in some way seem charged with life force that makes them supernatural.

The villager feels that the image or symbol emerges out of its own potentiality from nature, and then, like all living things, the symbol itself follows a course of emergence, maturation and then final dissolution. The symbol of the deity is a dangerous entity in itself, because in it are focused all the forces of nature. It is drawn from nature in answer to an immediate need, is worshipped, and then allowed to dissolve back into nature, the womb, as it were of all that is sacred. To keep the image of a god on the anthropomorphic level of the shrine is to invest the human sphere with an energizing divinity, whose influence might be too much for the villager to bear at such close proximity all the time. The villager has a reluctance to worship a god unless a specific need to do so arises. He does not want too clear a configuration of the supernatural realities; he would prefer to call forth the deities when he is ready to offer them his prayers, and

< 137 >

for the rest of the time leave them to merge into the wilderness or kadu of nature. In the same way he is not anxious to pay too much attention to the memorials of the spirits of the dead, restricting the building up and decorating of their physical houses for such occasions as require the particular worship of their presence. The burial ground, or burning ghat, is a deserted place, not because such places are thought to be unimportant, but because the villager feels a great awe for them.

The villager makes the form or house of his god when he has need for him and then, the immediate occasion over, he allows the form to disintegrate back into nature.[2] This enables the villager to under-stand perhaps more deeply and intuitively than the urban Hindu with his many elaborate deities wrought out of permanent materials and enshrined in ancient temples, that the spiritual is distinct from the physical, energizing beyond the level of rituals and forms. Obviously the villager does not believe that his gods or goddesses cease to exist the moment he neglects to worship them. Rather, they exist without a very clearly defined body, in the total nexus of nature, from which the villager draws them from time to time to give them an objectivity in response to his own worship.

The image is thus like a child born out of the womb of nature. As in the myth of Ayyappan we note that the child deity was found in the forest, in the womb as it were of wild nature, so the Bhagavan is the Lord born of a nature's womb (bhaga). Nature is the source of life and vitality, and from it the symbol derives its own life. When the villager begins some new enterprise, be it building, or agriculture, he makes an image of Pillaiyar, the remover of obstacles.[3] This noble child, Pillaiyar, is himself compounded out of the form of a baby, and the head of an elephant, demonstrating, like the Centaurs of Greek mythology, how the genius of the world forest (the elephant) is joined on to the noble child, who is a king, a creator of the new cosmos of culture. Pillaiyar is thus thought of as the god of culture and learning, the 'word' who is to be worshipped at the beginning. Pillaiyar is made by the villager out of a lump of plastic mud which is very crudely 'pinched' into the form of the elephant god. Some-times the villagers do not even bother to give the god this physical semblance, being content with a round lump of clay pure and simple. In the home Pillaiyar is sometimes fashioned out of a paste of turmeric. The worship of him consists in offering obeisance, flowers, coconuts, and other fruits. The worship over, the god is either allowed to disintegrate naturally into the soil, or, as in the case when he has been made by the village potter and fired into a terra-cotta image, he is carried to the local tank or the sea, where he is allowed to be

< 138 >

washed away into the waters. That is, he is re-absorbed back into the womb of nature.

THE DHULI-CITRA CATEGORY OF ART WORKS[4]

We find in rural India, and in the festivals which undoubtedly go back to very ancient sources, that this pattern of creating and destroying an image in the process of Upasana, or worship, is preserved. In Karnataka, to give an example, there is a tradition in certain rural areas of carving images of the goddess of smallpox, Mariamma, which are carried through the village and left on the border of the next village. In turn the next village carries the images through its limits and passes them on, in a sort of relay. Finally the images are carried to a river where they are thrown in, having taken upon themselves all the diseases of the countryside through which they have been carried. Again, in Durga puja in the Dusehra festivities, images of the mother are made and adorned and then thrown into a tank. In the ritual of the home there are many indications of the same pattern. The kolama patterns[5] of south India are made each morning in front of the main door into the house, later to be obliterated with a fresh coating of cow dung. Many other similar examples could be given of a folk tradition of impermanent images which are, as it were, ritualistically destroyed. Such ritualistic destruction might well have been the fate of many images during the formative period so notably absent in the archaeological remains of ancient Indian art between the Mohenjodaro civilization and the flowering of Buddhist art under the Mauryan kings.[6] We are so used to the idea of a permanent art that it seems strange to us to think that there can be an art which is consciously made not to last — though certain schools of modern art are returning to this approach in the types of so-called 'process art', where the aesthetic experience is captured in a momentary 'happening', like the momentary gods of ancient religion. This organic approach to art, is, I feel, typical of folk art as opposed to the more developed forms of art which aim at permanence. Originally temples were almost certainly made out of wood, or were often living trees (see chapter 13) because stone, being inorganic, was thought to be the house of the dead (see chapter 3). In folk culture village 'stones' are thought to be inhabited by the ghosts of the dead. The fact that we have the seals of Mohenjodaro to testify to their great culture is to an extent a coincidence. They were not made to last. There is no temple in Mohenjodaro with statues wrought out of durable materials. This is itself extraordinary

< 139 >

Living symbolism — earth as mandala filled with living streams, after traditional patterns

< 140 >

in a people who so obviously possessed a very creative plastic sensibility. The sudden flowering of Buddhist art we owe to the new idea of the emperor, or Cakravartin (see chapter 6). Edicts were engraved on stones as a perpetual reminder. Gradually permanent temples were built out of stone, unlike the earlier organic temples which were subject, like everything else in nature, to decay.

It is necessary, I feel, to understand the folk sources of Indian art if we are to grasp fully the later achievements of classical art. Not sufficient research has been done in the so-called 'dhuli-citra' category of Indian art which is mentioned as the last of the categories of visual images in such classical theoretical works as the Manasollasa or Abhilasitartha-Cintamani. This category is commonly interpreted as the 'brightly coloured' and is applied to all those household or village culture art forms which are the foundations for the more cultured art. We might postulate that before carving or modelling came into its own as a highly cultured art, the unsophisticated Indian chose rocks and stones on which he smeared colour as a sign of their being 'holy'. He even did this to trees. We tend to think of painting as something distinct from sculpture but we must remember that all the great sculptures of India were originally almost certainly painted.[7] The installing of an image into a sacred precinct is done by what is known as the 'eye-painting ceremony', whereby the carved image has its eyes painted on at the final moment of consecration, accompanied by mantras, that is ritualistic prayers, thus endowing the image with life and potency. Only after the image was painted could it be thought of as inhabited. The art of painting was a natural adjunct of the art of sculpture, rather as the art of make-up or the wearing of the painted mask is thought of as the natural adjunct of dancing. In fact, the Kathakali dancer, before appearing on the stage, goes through a long ritualistic make-up ceremony in which symbolic colours are painted on his face. It is during this make-up that the artist becomes possessed, ceases to be his ordinary self, and becomes the character whom he is to impersonate.

PLAY AS THE BASIS OF SYMBOLIC THINKING

I have for long been convinced that it is impossible to understand the way in which symbolic thinking proceeds, unless we understand it as basically play. But what is play? What is a child doing when he plays? It is impossible to enter here into the many theories concerning the nature of play. An important modern theorist on the subject of the child's thinking process is Piaget. Piaget began his career as a zoologist,

< 141 >

and so he borrows terms from the biological organic system to explain certain processes in the growth of the human mind. The two fundamental 'processes' on which growth in the organic body depends are 'assimilation accommodation' and 'rejection'. The body 'assimilates' or adjusts to new material. In the case of food, if the body does not accommodate it, it simply brings it up, that is rejects it from the system.[8] According to Piaget, if adaptation or adjustment predominates in a mental process imitation ensues. But if, on the other hand, assimilation predominates, then the mental activity is called play. This understanding of play is helpful in that it shows the relation of play to that organic process which in biological systems is called 'digestion'. We tried to show in our analysis of the symbolizing process the relation of assimilation or adjustment complexes to the whole motivation process which we call 'evocation' and which we also term 'recollection' or 'remembrance'. This will perhaps connect with Piaget's theory of imitation in so far as memory is central to it.

Already in our Introduction we have related 'play' with the activity of discovering the nature of matter, and releasing its inherent qualities and possibilities. It is fundamentally experimental and transforming. For play is essentially the activity of mind–energy entering into the womb of matter and transforming it from within. Erotic play is directed towards entry into the womb and experiments with the living structure of the physical and its relation to spiritual energy. The play forms of children seem to relate to this primal touching of the physical, and seem particularly close to feeling experience.[9] Touch is perhaps one of the earliest and most basic sense impressions, being most closely associated with an experimental involvement with matter.

Too often we have forgotten how to enter into the world blind and naked, and so we do not 'see' the world, because we have not first 'felt' it, explored the inner significance of matter with sensitive hands. I remember seeing a blind man feeling a piece of Indian sculpture, and I could almost envy him his blindness. I felt intuitively that what he sensed through touch of that sculpture was something far more powerful and fundamental than what I could see of it. The symbol is ultimately something which is felt — words are unable to describe that feeling. What the body feels cannot actually ever be communicated. It is unique, and silent. It is an experience which only the body knows. One could almost say that this is the indestructible loneliness of the body, its experience within itself, its own incommunicable act of contemplation. Out of this feeling of the body, out of the experimental play of the child, there arises a vision, a way of seeing. First the child feels, and then out of his feeling-sensation (as also with smell-sensation) a new order of experience is

< 142 >

evoked. Here the constant interaction of play and imitation, experimentation and evocation, digestion and 'bringing up' reveals the process of symbolizing. In the very act of playing memories arise, and experimentation slips into imitation; from absorbing or 'swallowing' the world, the person who plays 'evokes' or 'brings up' a new world.

THE IMAGINATION STIMULATED BY SUGGESTIVE FORMS

If we understand painting in the classical Indian period as arising out of the same concern for tactile form as the sculpture of the same period, we can appreciate better the preference for mural painting. Mural art has always come closest to sculpture, because it is concerned with the organization of architectonic space, howbeit in the flat. It does not have the limitation of a restricted frame. Though the surface of the painting might be flat, its context is three-dimensional. This sense of the intermingling of sculpture, painting and architecture is most marked in the cave painting of Ajanta (see pp. 31, 65–6). A strange aspect of these cave paintings is that they were designed to be looked at with the very poor light of little oil lamps, because the caves have no provision for natural lighting. Here one might conjecture in general concerning ill-lit tactile surfaces such as we find in roughly hewn caves. Did pre-historic man people the walls of the dark caves in which he lived with creatures of his suggestible imagination? How much did the irregularities of the cave wall surface which would have cast curious shadows in the flickering flame light, influence the imagination of the cave-dweller? In other words, did the cave man not so much inflict upon the wall surface a pre-determined scheme of imagery, as merely outline the forms which he felt were already somehow magically present there? Recent experiments show how much man is affected by the suggestiveness of natural forms, their tendency to go through a metamorphosis on account of the altering consciousness of the observer, thus mingling objective reality with the subjective imagination. Art arises, according to Hindu aesthetics precisely at the point of this mingling. When the mind is unsure whether this particular object is a tree or a goblin, whether this stone is an objective concrete reality or merely the appearance of an indwelling immanent living presence, then art begins, and the symbol emerges.

As we earlier noted, the cave is connected with ancient ceremonies of the dead, and is clearly a womb-space within the earth. Consequently in the cave art of the dawning of Indian imagery, we have

< 143 >

the visible symbol evolving out of the blindly tactile. This marriage of image to darkness or obscurity is maintained even in the later Hindu examples of art, such as we find at the great temple of Tanjore. There, in a poorly lit circumambulatory path around the holy of holies, are executed the most delicate and yet monumental of mural paintings to be left to us in the south. The technique is unsurpassed, the tenuous yet firm and flowing lines drawn in pure fresco technique on a very strong lime polished surface. The very delicacy of the classical tradition of mural art, its almost porcelain-like glazes and gentle colouring, seems to stress that these figures are not the creations of man, but rather phantasmal images wrought, as it were, in moments of deep ecstasy, captured like moth wings from the shades of night. The true genius of Indian art avoids the explicit, resting on the immense reservoirs of suggestiveness.

I have felt the same reliance on natural forms in a remarkable sculpture of Pancanana Siva in the Panchavaktra temple of Mandi (Himachal region), which was probably carved in the fourteenth century. Here a great lump of rock which was probably held to be sacred long before it was carved, inspired the artist to see in its uneven and curious form the presence of the five aspects of Siva. These he brought out with the minimum of chisel work, so as to make his vision more explicit, but still maintaining the genius of the stone. The heads of the divine beings emerge from the stone at unexpected angles, as the stone, not man, dictated. One head is facing upwards, while two heads facing to the left and to the right are not symmetrically placed but emerge organically like great knots from the trunk of a tree. The massive yet tense form of Siva, with Parvati on his lap, reminds one of the half revealed forms of rock. In fact this dark stone has been painted white to represent the snow-clad mountains, all except the figure of Parvati, which is left in the original blackish stone, polished, one suspects, by worshipping hands fondling her serpentine form through the centuries. The general surrealist effect of the image is further heightened by the red-painted eyes like masks with a black hole in the centre. The whole work, a composite of sculptured form and colour (the three primary colours of the Varna system being used — that is white, red, and black), appeals to a very elemental depth of human sensibility, and on that account has a power which defies the vagaries of time and changing styles and tastes.[10]

THE SYMBOL AND GROWTH

The image-symbol is not something which has fixed limits, coming

< 144 >

into existence in its completed form, and never altering after that. Rather it is constantly growing and evolving. This growth of the image is subjective–objective. That is to say, it evolves out of a physical objective process rather like a tree grows up putting out new branches, following an internal organic necessity of its own. In addition, our understanding of the image grows, as we look back and contemplate it, exploring its possibilities through ever-widening concentric circles, or spiralling consciousness. The symbol has a life of its own, which seems to develop quite independently of the human effort to guide or determine it. The image as it grows often develops quite unexpectedly, in a way that the image-maker himself had never imagined; yet once it has grown that way, it seems inevitable that it should have happened like that. This is perhaps because the image draws on sources of life which lie beyond the controlling powers of civilizing human rationality, in the very heart of the jungle of man's subconscious. The conscious artist can only watch the image grow up from the depths of his own being, spiralling up slowly through complex after complex of the imagination, following a logic of its own. Man, however, cannot just observe the imagination in a detached way. He cannot just contemplate the symbol as something external which has no power to change him. Looking at the symbol, the image worshipper discovers that it is entering into his very individuality and taking possession of his life. The symbol not only 'points', it appoints. Whereas the individual cannot claim to have control over the symbol, symbols have control over him. They govern the way in which life develops. Actually, nobody. can talk about symbols in an abstract way, and say anything really important about them. Symbolism, though it rises from the collective unconscious, is only impersonal in its source. Rising thence it always configurates around the centre of an individual consciousness.[11]

As symbols are living, they also symbolize life. In the last group of symbols which I wish to study, the life process itself becomes the content of symbolism.[12] In the symbol of the tree we have the eternal reminder of all that evolves out of the earth, a structure which is interconnectedness and also movement upwards and downwards. It is a symbol of life as extensive, reaching out beyond itself. In contrast the symbol of the serpent is life at its most intensive and vital, and almost turning in on itself to discover its own centre. We are conscious that this life flows into the symbol from the most raw and elemental areas of being. The tree and the serpent are nature in its most instinctive form, both capable, however, of a truly miraculous transformation and regeneration. In these symbols life and death seem to be most closely interlocked. Finally, in the symbol of the

< 145 >

overflowing pot, the crucible of a truly alchemical process, heat, growth and consciousness are brought together in a primal symbol of the womb of the universe.

< 146 >

CHAPTER 13

The tree at the centre of the garden of innocence

< 147 >

The tree at the centre of the garden of innocence

[OVERLEAF]

The leaf of the bodhi tree, or Indian fig tree (ficus religiosa)

< 148 >

In many mythic systems of belief the story is told of how man fell
from an original innocence. Childhood is idealized and put on a completely different plane of experience from the rest of life. Though
from the point of view of time the years of childhood are all too
brief, they retain in the memory a quality which seems timeless, and
therefore imbued with the beauty of eternity. It has been suggested
that this primal myth of man's coming of age has something to do
with a new step forward in consciousness which possibly occurred
with neolithic man, bringing about far-reaching changes in man's
social order. From being a wandering food gatherer in the primeval
forests, man settled down to an agricultural way of life. Thus Joseph
Campbell argues[1] that the mandala, or geometric pattern, as a form
in art, only emerges in neolithic art and is a definite step forward, in
the same way as organized geometric designs are an important leap
forward in the individual self-expression of a child. The creation of
mandalas (see p. 98), which are organized patterns often based on
structures of four or multiples of four, indicate an organized view
of reality, which also reflects a new ordering of social relationships,
and man's understanding of his place in the universe. This is interesting because many mandalas depict an ideal garden or paradise, at
whose centre there is often a tree under which is depicted a figure of
the deity. This figure is either that of the teacher, the divine guru (he
who enlightens men concerning life's secret) or it is the youthful
Lord (Guha, he who has been born from the secret place of life). The
picture is that of a sacred space or ashrama, in which man discovers
once again a primal wholeness and innocence.

Myths concerning the ancient Dravidian child god Murugan speak
of his joyful sport in the forest glades, in playful dalliance with his
youthful love Valli. In the same way in the Krsna myths, the youthful deity has a ranga-mandala, or magical bridal chamber amid the
trees, where he consorts with village maidens and dances his ranga-
lila with them.[2] Richard Lannoy suggests[3] that the two institutions
of traditional Hindu life, known as the Asramas of Brahmacarya
and Vanaprastha, stress a return to the forest ideal of tribal culture,
because this remained in many senses a store-house of Hindu wisdom
and vitality. It is this perennial longing for the forest that provided
traditional Hindu life and institutions with a vital counterpoint, an
'alter ego'.

Krsna is popularly depicted as standing with his beloved beneath
the kadamba tree. This tree is here the centre of the universe, the
'axis mundi'. As a youth Krsna, like certain other heroes of folklore,
is described as climbing up the kadamba tree. The tree thus becomes
a ladder to higher planes of consciousness. It was from the branches

< 149 >

of this tree that he leapt into the pool in which the terrible serpent king Kaliya held his poisonous court. Again, when Krsna wanted to tease the girls who were bathing in a pool of the river, it was up this tree that Krsna climbed carrying their clothes.

THE LOSS OF INNOCENCE IN CONNECTION WITH THE TREE

When Krsna stole the clothes of the girls, they were filled with confusion. They were conscious enough to realize that they had reached sexual maturity, and so were afraid to come out of the water and show their nakedness to the young Krsna. In the end they emerged, having no other choice, but covering their private parts with their hands. But Krsna who was in the high branches of the tree refused to return their clothes until they had lifted their hands above their heads, in a total gesture of self-offering, revealing their entire nakedness. Such an erotic story is itself part of an ancient folk tradition to be found with slight variations all over the world. The trickster hero deprives the maidens of their innocence by stealing their clothes. In this dramatic situation the innocent girls become conscious of their nakedness, and are thus drawn out of their paradise into the adventure of life which is ambivalent. They are drawn by a sort of inner necessity to recover part of themselves, for they have a new sense of incompleteness. They reach not only for their clothes, but for Krsna himself, who fulfils their deep longing for union with him.

The tree is thus a symbol or focus for that newly awakened sense of 'order' and 'growth' which is also the point of man's confrontation with the ambivalent forces of good and evil, light and dark, male and female. According to one version of the Kaliya myth, it is said that Krsna while playing with a ball, loses it in the pool in which the serpent lives, and so he leaps into the water to recover his lost ball, and is thus confronted by the abysmal forces of evil into whose centre he has, almost inadvertently, jumped. The motif of the lost ball is again a favourite theme of fairy stories, and symbolizes the loss of wholeness itself, which is the special grace of childhood.

Can that world of childhood be regained? Or do the forces of life itself drive man, through historical necessity, beyond the paradise of innocence to experience the ambivalences of a world no longer whole? The tree symbolizes a historical process of growth wherein through a structured evolution a new wholeness is attempted, a wholeness which comes to terms with the negative forces of creation, achieving a new synthesis at a higher differentiated level of consciousness. It

< 150 >

is this round tree which becomes a symbol of a new cosmos, a structured cosmos into which man has now to be reborn.

THE THEME OF REBIRTH AND ENLIGHTENMENT

The tree is a symbol in Indian thought of birth. The mother of Buddha, Maya, goes to meditate under a tree when she becomes pregnant, and the child is born from her side. Later the Lord Buddha himself sits under the forest tree in order to be reborn into a higher mode of life. The tree symbolizes the force of mother life. An ancient theme is that of a being coming out of a tree like a child from the womb. In a small village shrine in Karnataka there is a great tree which has naturally developed an opening at its roots rather like the opening of the womb. Inside this opening you can see the figure of a crudely carved deity. It looks like a foetus about to be born out of the mother tree. Many village shrines at the base of a tree look like openings into the bowels of the tree. Clefts or forks in the tree seem to be natural openings into the womb of the tree. We have a representation in the seals of Mohenjodaro of what appears to be a female deity standing in a split tree. Another seal shows a woman from whose womb a plant is growing. This female figure is presumably the Earth Mother. According to Tucci,[4] Durga, who he thinks is a mother goddess originating in the Vindyas, is the 'vivifying force of the forest'. He quotes the Atharva Veda:

> I awaken thee in the Bilva tree
> until the worship is accomplished.

Apparently this Earth Mother was worshipped with nine leaves (navapatrika)[5] which were arranged in a mandala, one in the centre, and eight around it, representing the eight directions of space. No temple was needed for her worship except nine leaves, and she was summoned into a branch of the bilva tree. She is here a goddess of all that grows.

The trees grouped in sacred groves, under which snake stones (nagakals) have been erected, are centres of fertility. Childless women and men worship at such shrines, praying for offspring. The tree, growing from a seed placed in the earth, is itself a figure of birth and growth. The sap within the tree is like blood and the seminal liquid in man, or milk in the woman. It is the essence of life. Thus soma, the Vedic offering of intoxicating drink, and coefficient with Agni in the Vedic yajna or sacrifice, is represented as a plant. From the distilled liquor of the tree of life, man is brought into the

< 151 >

ecstatic kingdom of the gods. The god of love (Madan) is himself deeply imbued with tree symbolism.[6] His sacred tree is the indigenous mango tree. His bow is the sugar-cane, and his arrows are tipped with flowers from sacred trees. There is an erotic beauty in the forms of trees. At the time of swing festivals the fertility of nature is celebrated, when everything is reborn.[7]

THE TREE AS A SYMBOL OF MARRIAGE

Each stage in the Buddhist journey to enlightenment is described as a 'hieros gamos', a sacred wedding or kalyanam. Each moment of the yogi's victory over temptation brings yet another shower of petals from the tree which rejoices in his attainments. It is almost as though Buddha and the tree under which he sits are one. As he becomes resplendent with the light of an inner germinal fire the tree also seems to break forth into a new splendour. It is told that when a devotee, Sujata's maidservant, came and saw Buddha sitting under the holy tree, she mistook the muni for a manifestation of the tree spirit.[8]

The word 'muni' is itself interesting. In village religion in the south of India many of the gods related to trees are called 'muniappas'. Perhaps the word comes from the Sanskrit root meaning the 'silent one'. But still there is certainly the belief that this muni, like the yogic figure to be found represented on the Indus valley seals, is himself filled with phallic power. In certain folk beliefs, if a village girl is unable to have a child she prays before a sacred tree to the forces of fertility, hangs maybe a toy cradle from its branches, and even, if necessary, gets impregnated by a local 'muni' who is willing to act on behalf of the spirits in this way. In certain tribal areas, according to Henry Prestler,[9] a girl is first married to a tree. Only in this way will she be fruitful in her marriage to a man. This is because the spirits which are to enter into the womb of women are first in trees (having come there from the moon). The ancestor spirit enters into the girl who is married to the tree and is thus able later to re-enter the world when she conceives. The marriage between a young woman and a tree is frequently depicted in early Buddhist art. Not only are trees supposed to be married to human maidens, but they even marry each other. Two trees interlocked as though in marriage are looked upon with awe. In the centre of the village two trees, generally the pipal (*ficus religiosa*) and the neem are planted next to each other. In this way it is thought that the forces of fertility will be increased and the ancestors will return more easily to life. Little children are

< 152 >

warned against the spirits of trees (bhutas, etc.), because these spirits are antithetical to life and youth, being the yet unborn and therefore hungry. This is why also sacrifices have to be made to these trees to appease their dangerous hunger for life.

These then are the spirits of the trees, whose very virility is linked with their capacity to destroy. For the tree, like every other important symbol, is a meeting of opposites. On one side it is the place where the dead haunt with hungry spirits, demanding the sacrifice of life, but on the other it is the very essence of life itself. The central meaning of the tree is rebirth. And this rebirth requires also a dying. Asceticism and eroticism are one in the process of being reborn.

SELF-SACRIFICE OF THE MOTHER

The sacrificial significance of the tree has been realized in many religious traditions. As the tree stands at the intersection of life and death, and is a symbol of the cosmic structure, myths concerning the self-immolation of a cosmic man or woman have come to be connected with the tree. This immolation is, we must remember, basically creative, because to die in this context means to be born again. Also creation itself is understood as an act of sacrifice whereby through a process of division the manifold world of phenomena arises out of the cosmic unity. The tree in the very act of growing is apparently dividing itself into more and more branches.

It is interesting that there seems to be a basic Indian tradition concerning the immolation of a woman (the Earth Mother) in connection with the tree. We are familiar with the myth concerning Sati who passes through ritual suicide in fire to Muneswara, lord of munis, who is Siva. Siva himself in his original form is a forest god, or wild huntsman, Rudra. The muni practises tapas, which is a word deriving from the root tap, meaning fire. Thus the Earth Mother comes to him by setting herself ablaze. There seems to be some deep feeling of awe for a woman who commits suicide. Many of the village goddesses are village girls who have committed suicide and have been buried under a tree. In this way they have become identified with Earth Mother. According to a Puranic story there was a king, Jalandhara, who obtained a boon to the effect that he could not be overcome so long as his wife Vrnda remained chaste. Whilst Jalandhara was battling with Indra, Indra appeared to Vrnda in the form of her husband and sported with her, with the result that Jalandhara was killed. Vrnda committed sati and from her remains a plant grew which is the tulsi tree, held to be the most sacred of

< 153 >

plants, and worshipped by every Hindu woman. This plant is often to be found in the central courtyard of the home, and symbolizes the total self-sacrificing virtue of the Hindu woman ideal.[10]

THE TREES OF KNOWLEDGE, AND THE
WISH-FULFILLING TREES

The sacred trees give to man whatever he feels in need of. In this way we see the tree as related to the whole folk idea of nature itself. Jainism, which is probably the most ancient religion in India, has a great veneration for trees. One legend describes how the holy trees ceased to give man their fruits:[11]

> In deep antiquity human beings received all that was necessary for life from the godly trees. All people were equal. Happiness reigned everywhere. But the trees gradually started giving less and less fruits and humanity was threatened with ruin. At this time the first Tirthankara Rabha appeared. Having given laws, knowledge, sword, agriculture, trade, cattle breeding and ink, he saved the people. He created books on sciences and religions, but the language of these books was forgotten. They are, however, retold in various languages.

It seems we have here a story of a fall when man was no longer able to get his needs from the wish-fulfilling trees of an earlier paradise. It was consequently necessary for an enlightened yogi, who knew the wisdom of the trees, to hand down to man what he had lost. But the memory of the wish-fulfilling tree continued with man.

Above all, the holy tree was a tree of life and wisdom and seated under it the yogi could discover enlightenment. The relation of the tree with visionary light is almost universal.

TREE AND SUN SYMBOLISM

It has been suggested that the Hindu temple grew out of the worship of trees which was adopted by certain kings during the period of the great Hindu dynasties. The symbolism connected with the sacred trees was very much a part of an agricultural religion. It was thought that the tree spirits had to be placated, and this included the offering of sacrifices before trees. Human sacrifices were above all appreciated by the deities of the grove, and so, according to Tucci, petty kings made it the excuse for military campaigns against neighbouring

< 154 >

kingdoms, for the captures they made during these raids would be sacrificed in their sacred groves. Presumably the gods of the grove were thought to assist in these military campaigns and so the rituals attendant on tree worship became intimately linked with the warlike ambitions of the kings, and their desire to become emperors. Interestingly, the horse sacrifice with its attendant rituals which seems to be linked with many ancient Indian dynasties, was also related to tree worship. I have already described in chapter 4 the myth of the Cakravartin called Sagara[12] whose sons pursued the sacrificial horse into the underworld where it was found standing near a tree under which the sage Kapila was meditating. Angry that they ignored him, Kapila opened one eye and burnt Sagara's sons to ashes. I mention the legend because the yogi is generally associated with a tree, under which he is thought to sit in meditation. But the cosmic tree is called asvattha which is explained as asvasthana, or the place where the horse stands. It will be recalled that the horse sacrifice included letting the horse wander for a year wherever it pleased, followed by armed warriors who laid claim to all the territory which the horse covered as part of the kingdom of their ruler. Wherever the horse stopped they erected a pillar, or tree, which became a symbol of the horse's journey and hence marked the boundary of the kingdom. Such trees or pillars were also erected in front of towns and villages and became symbols of victory and were decorated and worshipped by circumambulation. This symbolism of the tree as emblem of dominion probably lies at the back of the reference to the universe as a tree. We might note too in the ensemble of connected ideas related to the tree, the evidence of solar symbolism. Zimmer points out that the mythic yogi burning the ardent youths in search of their horse indicates solar power which the yogi possesses. 'Kapila' means the 'Red one' and is an epithet for the sun. Again the idea of the asvattha with its 'root above, and branches below' (Bhagavad Gita) is thought to relate to the sun which is the root of the cosmic tree — the branches being the rays of the sun coming down to earth. The sacrificial horse was clearly a sun symbol, and it is probably by way of sun symbolism that we are to link it with the tree.

THE TEMPLE ARISING FROM TREE WORSHIP

The hypaethral temple from which the structural temple developed[13] was a sacred tree with the surrounding sacred space marked out originally by an enclosure or platform beneath the tree. Later this space around the tree was further defined with a wall and a series of

< 155 >

The symbol of the tree — the worship of a sacred tree, probably the asoka. The design is inspired by a low relief carved in the red sandstone stupa railing of Bharhut

< 156 >

small shrines facing inwards towards the tree, each shrine dedicated to spirits of the neighbourhood. A number of southern temples, for example at Kanjipuram and Tiruchirapally, are called 'Ekambara' temples, meaning temples of a single tree. This presumably was to distinguish temples built around one tree from temples associated with groves of trees. It has been pointed out that certain groves of trees attached to temples are extremely ancient and sometimes contain species of trees which were once numerous in the Indian forests, but are now hard to come upon. Recently attention was drawn to a sacred grove at the village of Gani in the Kolaba district of Konkan, which was fifteen hectares in extent, and in which there were supposed to be medicinal plants, used in ancient folk lore.

One of the trees which is worshipped in popular religion is the amla tree (*phyllauthus embilica/embilica officinalis*) (see p. 78). An eye-witness described to me how a group of women worshipped an amala tree in the month of Kartik on Gwalior Fort. Here there is an ancient water tank dedicated to the Sun called Surya Kunda (an annual mela connected with this tank is conducted on the last Sunday of Kartika, and has been celebrated.in this way, it is believed, for the last 1500 years). A group of women, dressed in their best saris, lit incense sticks at the base of the tree and marked it with sandur and haldi. They then marked each other with tilaka on the forehead. Then they performed arati (the offering of fire) to the tree and prostrated themselves. After this they took handfuls of rice from covered thalis which they had brought and began to circumambulate the tree in a clockwise direction singing as they went, and throwing a few grains of rice at the base of the tree each time they completed a circle. This continued until they had used up all the rice. Then all in turn embraced the tree as if it were a person, with a ceremonial embrace. They then squatted again round the base of the tree and marked it once more with haldi and sandur, again prostrating themselves before it. After this they fetched water from a near-by tap in lotas which they had brought, uncovered their thalis and, sitting in a circle round the tree, had a sort of holy picnic.

Elements are seen in this description which relate to temple worship. It is thought that circumambulation around the tree in a clockwise fashion was a basic rite of tree worship. The worshipper exposes to the tree his right shoulder, which he or she leaves bare. This is why the Buddhist samnyasi (as seen in images of Buddha himself) has the right shoulder bare. A figure clothed in this way, presumed to be a priest, was found belonging to the Mohenjodaro civilization. Generally the worshipper even touches the tree (and later the pillar or garbha grha) with his right hand while circumambulating. Offerings

< 157 >

are made to the tree spirits of food. Sacrifices were carried out in front of the tree, and blood sprinkled at the base of the tree to be drunk by the tree spirits. Stones erected near the tree, or before the tree, were anointed with oil and water — hence the name 'puja' meaning 'to anoint'. Also the embracing of the tree by women, as if it were a husband, is very ancient and is depicted in many examples of early Buddhist art, for example in Bharhut which belongs to the Sangha period. The offering of fire (arati) also seems very ancient and, according to Dubois (*Hindu Manners and Customs*), this cere-mony is intended to keep off the evil eye. When one remembers how Kapila and Siva (both yogis sitting under trees) reduced people to ashes with a glance of their eye, we respect the concern of the wor-shipper to keep off the evil eye. Finally, an 'agape' in the company of the tree is probably the basis of the temple prasada.[14]

< 158 >

CHAPTER 14
Symbol of the serpent

< 159 >

[OVERLEAF]

A small village shrine interior, showing snake stones and various articles used in puja

< 160 >

According to the Visnu Purana (I. 5. 26–48), the hairs of Brahma's head became serpents. These were called serpents because they glided (sarpana), and snakes (ahi) because they departed (hina). Whatever the justification for such etymology, it is clear that an important aspect of the serpent symbol is its movement. Its connection with hair also seems very ancient. This is probably partly on account of the linear quality of hair, also its tendency to curl and to spiral. But hair has deeper unconscious connections. It seems to represent life and vitality itself.

According to kundalini yoga, the serpent power at the base of the spinal column could be compared with what Freud called the 'libido'.[1] It is the vital energy in man. The process of man's growth is a process of moving this energy up from the base of the column to higher nodes of consciousness. The movement is described as a spiralling movement; in fact it is supposed that the serpent makes three and a half turns around the central column, which itself is divided into thirty-three divisions.

The whole of man's development from childhood to old age is also pictured in terms of a spiralling movement. Time itself is a spiral whereby a line of movement tends to return upon itself, rather like a snake biting its own tail, or the child Krsna sucking his own toe. In the same way as a wave-like line cuts across a circle dividing it into two equal sections which resemble two pear or mango-like drops locked together in perpetually cyclic motion (the yin–yang pattern, see p. 196), so time flows through the wholeness of life dividing it into an upward and downward movement, a movement of birth and death. This wave-like coiling motion is the great serpent who is so often represented like a many-headed wave curving and bending over the sleeping figure of the Lord upon the cosmic oceans.

Among those figures which seem to appear in every culture, and which, despite certain differences of interpretation, retain a certain common perennial meaning, we find the figure of the serpent. Perhaps no other symbol, except for the tree, demonstrates so well the truth of a collective unconscious;[2] the collective unconscious itself is symbolized by the serpent. The serpent is the foundation of the universe. Coiled around the navel of the cosmos, it appears to be the dynamic centre of time and space.[3] The serpent seems always to be moving and yet always still, like the oceans whose waves seem in perpetual turmoil and unrest, but whose boundaries remain fixed, and whose depths are eternal.

In a beautiful carving of a naga from Badami (sixth century), we see the great coils of the serpent deity, four in number, in a spiralling pattern. Rising from the centre of the coil is the bust of the naga, his

< 161 >

The symbol of the serpent — village snake stones in Karnataka. The stone on the extreme left represents the guardian snake deity; in the centre is the serpent mother, with two baby serpents in her arms, and a suggestion of wings; on the right is the symbol of intertwined snakes, or snakes in sexual congress which is a symbol of fertility. The symbol between the heads of the snakes and, on the other side under the hood of the snake, is the lingam

< 162 >

crowned head hooded with five serpent forms. His face is deeply gentle and grave. Around the whirling pattern of his coiled body is an exquisite array of lotuses, intertwining tendrils, and other blossoms, carved in low relief. This is indeed a wonderful symbol of time, and also the spiralling path of the starry way, twisting into the great ocean of space. Here is Sesa who is both 'the endless one' and the Milky Way. His four coils probably represent the four yugas, each yuga becoming more and more telescoped in duration, as it reaches closer and closer to the dark centre of titanic force.

The symbol of the serpent is found in connection with the tree, which is thought to stand at the navel of external space in the same way as the spinal column is rooted near the navel of the human body. On the nagakals which are found at the base of sacred trees, the serpent is represented as ascending a staff, intertwining with another snake. This figure is exactly the same as we find in the west connected with the Greek god of healing, Aesculapius. So the serpent is thought of not only as coiled on the horizontal level, but as ascending and descending the tree of life. Here two popular notions of life and time, one cyclic or spiralling along a single path, the other dividing into branches in the process of growth, are integrated into the one image.

MYTH OF THE RAPE OF MOTHER EARTH

Repeatedly in folk culture we have the legend of the serpent king or prince who tries to capture a human maiden and carry her away into his subterranean kingdom, because he needs her warmth. If she will but love him, and kiss him, he is transfigured and is released from his own cold nature. Shedding his coils he becomes a beautiful prince. This longing to draw down the warmth of creation in order that he might be delivered from his own cold nature is the basis of the extremely ancient myth of the rape of mother earth.

There are two myths concerning the rape of the earth. The first tells of how the mother herself was taken down into the depth of the cosmic ocean and wrapped in the coils of the serpent. To free her, Visnu had to appear as the boar avatara,[4] and dive deep into the waters of chaos in order to rescue and draw her up once again. Another myth describes how the gentle elephant is ensnared by the cosmic serpent, as he goes to swim among the lotuses. Once again Visnu has to come to the aid of the gentle genius of the forest, appearing in the form of Gajendra, or the god of the elephant. This theme has been beautifully depicted in the temple carvings of Halebid

< 163 >

which belongs to the Hoysala dynasty of Karnataka. The serpent represents maya, which is the energy of matter, that is to say its gravity. It naturally pulls the earth mother downwards. The avatara on the other hand is characterized by fire, coming down in order to lift up mother earth from the navel of the universe.[5]

THE CHILD GOD IDENTIFIED WITH GARUDA

The serpent is depicted as encircling the world egg. In a sense it steals this egg, or at least encases it within its coils. This perhaps relates in an intuitive manner to the age-old tension between the serpent and the cosmic bird often represented as Garuda, the golden eagle. The tension is elemental, between fire and water, heaven and earth. Garuda is the twice-born, for the egg is first born from the primal mother, and then when it opens, the being within it is reborn. The 'twice born' is a term applied to the initiated — the child hero himself is 'twice born'. The myth in the Bhagavata Purana concerning the battle of Balakrsna with Kaliya, relates the child god in a way with the cosmic bird:

> At the beginning of each month all the serpents used to receive an offering under a tree, to prevent unpleasantness; this was agreed long ago by the people in the realm of the snakes. And each of the serpents, to protect himself, would give a portion of this offering to the noble Suparna at the beginning of each lunar fortnight. But Kaliya, the son of Kadru, was full of pride because of the virulence of his poison and he disregarded Garuda and himself ate that offering.

It is important to understand the function of the avatara — he has come into the world-process in order to restore the balance; that is to say when evil, which seems naturally to predominate according to Hindu myth, increases beyond the set balance or 'good gestalt' of creation, the avatara is born. And so Krsna enters into the domain of the poisonous Kaliya in order to re-establish the set order of things. His purpose is not to destroy Kaliya — that itself would cause an imbalance. The child symbolizes wholeness, which means also polarity. So he represents the forces of fire and light in a situation which is grave. That is to say the gravity of matter is always downward moving by its very nature — the child by descending into matter and dancing his fiery dance upon the head of the king of the depths, delivers the serpent from its own overbearing gravity. A miniature showing the many-headed serpent with the child dancing upon it,

< 164 >

depicts Kaliya with hood raised, from which scores of heads unfold reminding one strangely of a tree, whose heads are in fact its roots. Here the serpent itself becomes the inverted tree of the cosmos whose roots are, as it were, the footstool of the fiery sun, and whose nether regions are the phenomenological world as we observe it with our senses. The world as we see it around us is at the tail end of the cosmic serpent.

THE GREAT SIN – THE KILLING OF SERPENTS

It is an ancient story that man, in order to overcome the wilderness (kadu) and make it orderly and cultivated (nadu), has to injure the serpent, or at least pin its head. Many ceremonies concerned with building relate to this mythic piercing of the dragon. We will remember that the Christian figure of St George piercing the dragon's head with a lance is in type not dissimilar to the boy Krsna dancing on the head of Kaliya. Many village folk, however, will avoid killing snakes, especially near their homes. A dead snake is either cremated or it is thrown beyond the habitations of man back into the wilderness from which it came. To leave it near the houses of man, or on the cultivated land, is inauspicious. Concerning this sin against the serpent there is a popular legend which is the background of the Nagapancmi festival, which is much observed in the countryside. According to this story a Brahmin, ignorant of the festival of Nagapancmi, ploughed his field on that day, and in the process killed the family of a snake which was in the earth. When the mother snake came home and found her offspring killed, she took revenge by first of all finding out the house of the Brahmin farmer (which she did by noticing the blood of her offspring on his plough blade) and then killing him and all his children. She wanted to wipe out the whole race of this particular farmer. She remembered that one of the daughters of the farmer had been married into another village, so she went to that village also to kill the daughter and her family. But there she found that the daughter had made all preparations to do the appropriate serpent worship, and had drawn images of nagas on her wall near the door, and had put out milk, sweets and flowers for serpents, so that the mother serpent was mollified. She told the daughter that she had really come to kill her, but as she had fulfilled all the proper observances for serpent worship, she had relented. The snake also told the daughter that she had killed the girl's father and his family. The village daughter then begged the serpent to tell her the remedy for her snake bite, so that she might bring her father and his family

< 165 >

back to life. This the serpent did. Ever since then no ploughing is done on Nagapancmi.

Probably we have in this legend a lesson to be taught to Brahmins who ignore the aboriginal folk traditions of the non-Brahmin indigenes. Reversely the piercing or subduing of serpents represents the overthrowing of pre-Aryan serpent worship. This is one of the interpretations of Krsna's battle with the serpent tribe that inhabited the holy river near Vrndavan. The serpent deity, however, seems to be a precursor to a personal god, being the residing genius of field or home, or the very inner psyche of man, a sort of elemental, natural, indwelling lord. Perhaps all religions which have evolved the concept of a really personal god (a Bhagavan) have imerged out of a tradition in which serpents have been extremely important symbols of the supernatural.

SERPENTS AS PROTECTORS AND HEALERS

The serpent is the 'vastu sarpa' or household snake. It is thus thought to guard the home, and is represented on either side of the door. The yaksas, or forest deities, who became the dvarpalikas (door-keepers) of the Buddhist art which developed around Mathura, were probably often serpent deities. Certainly Ganesa, who became a favourite household deity — represented often above the door — is much connected with serpent cult.[6] In fact, generally the belt around his wide stomach (which, from an esoteric point of view, is the universe itself) is the serpent. This is not surprising when we recall that his heavenly father Siva was no less associated with snakes — indeed snakes hang around him like garlands, and his hair, streaming out in the cosmic dance, is an interlocking mass of serpents. Subrahmanya, also known in the south as Murugan, who, like Ganesa, is sometimes represented near the door as a guardian deity, is connected too with tree and serpent folk traditions. His mount (vahana), which is the peacock, is proverbially associated with the snake, with which it has a love–hate relationship. I have seen an image in a southern temple of Subrahmanya riding the peacock in whose beak is a snake, almost entwining the peacock's neck, rather as Nietzsche's Zarathustra saw the eagle and the snake in loving embrace, symbol of the joining of heaven and earth.

Wholeness is impossible without integration with the serpent. Homeopathy, in its aboriginal origins, is the belief that poison can be cured by poison, which is connected with a mythic understanding of the good serpent (nala pambhu), who is both poisonous and healing.[7]

< 166 >

Various parts of the snake are thought to cure ailments in village and tribal folklore, and in fact the serpent itself is the guarantee of wholeness and consequently health. We might recall that the sign of snakes in sexual congress, to be found represented all over Karnataka on the snake-stones beneath trees, is not only a fertility symbol, but is, as we remarked earlier, the same sign as was used in the cult of Aesculapius, Greek god of healing, and is still employed as a symbol of medicine. The figure of the serpent which was raised in the desert by Moses was to cure the Hebrews of snake-bite, and thus a holy serpent.

THE SERPENT AS A SYMBOL OF PERENNIAL RENEWAL

The popular festival Nagapancmi occurs in the Hindu month of Sravana on the 5th, 9th or 11th day of the lunar part of the month. This month is the month of the rainy season when the whole of nature is renewing itself. Also in this month the snake sheds its skin, which it does every year. According to folk belief, the shedding of the serpent's skin is accompanied by a new lease of life. This is the secret of the snake's apparent perpetual youthfulness. And yet there does seem to be a certain anxiety, a feeling that the snake does need to be renewed. This yearly effort at self-rejuvenation is at the cost of a cosmic effort which amounts to a cosmic sacrifice. Thus serpent worship is accompanied with a belief that the serpent is constantly in need of a sacrifice — the offering of blood or milk being acceptable.[8] Women go and place offerings of milk near the habitations of snakes. In more ancient religions blood was offered them. Wherever snakes are worshipped, a tradition of sacrifices to serpents has been found. These sacrifices in primitive societies even entailed human sacrifices. Many are the tales of dragons who demanded young men and women to be sacrificed to them. In India certain naga tribes (that is, tribes worshipping snakes) were head-hunters. In this cult the serpent is once again the symbol of time itself, which requires the offering of the fruits of youth in order that it might itself remain youthful. The death of the serpent is the death of the aeon, and all that is vital in the cosmos. To renew the world which had grown old and tired, a human sacrifice had to be made. Death and life are the binomials of the serpent cult — the upward and downward tendencies of cyclic nature.

< 167 >

CHAPTER 15
Symbol of cosmic vitality

< 169 >

Symbol of cosmic vitality

[OVERLEAF]

The imprint of the hand decorated with various symbols

< 170 >

Life is a mysterious force — it is energy, but energy endowed with a certain consciousness. We have, with our scientific mind, tried to draw nice distinctions between animate and inanimate bodies and also between thinking creatures, and creatures which are only living and growing. Less rational man, who is closer to what Zen calls the 'original mind', or Cassirer terms 'pre-rational mentality', feels that everything, even apparently inanimate (i.e. non-moving, non-growing) things, has life and mind. There is a legend concerning a sage who was discovered sleeping on the ground with his feet on a lingam. The sage was accused of disrespect for the sublime symbol of Siva, but he retorted by demonstrating that wherever man puts his foot there is a lingam — it is impossible to avoid stepping on it. The lingam, in other words, is an upward-pushing force of life which is immanent every-where in nature — like the termite hills which emerge from the earth all over the countryside.[1] The symbol has an unconscious automatic dynamism of its own. I have seen a temple space in which hundreds of lingams have been carved as sprouting out of the earth, each rising from its own yoni. The impression which I got of this composite symbol was rather like what a farmer might feel seeing his field sprouting with many shoots — a deep elemental sense of the fertility of earth.

There is a story concerning a huntsman by the name of Kanappa (kan being the word for 'eye'), who was sitting in a tree in the forest one day looking out for game. The tree happened to be a bilva tree, sacred to both Siva and Durga, being a tree with leaves grouped together in threes, symbolizing the three eyes of Siva.

As the ignorant, outcaste huntsman was sitting in the tree, he idly plucked leaves from it and allowed them to fall to the ground. Now from the ground, unnoticed by him, a lingam emerged, and the leaves which he plucked fell upon this lingam. When Kanappa discovered this fact he was moved by the numinous, and realized that uncon-sciously he had been directed to an act of worship. And so every day he continued to offer leaves from the bilva tree to the mysterious lingam symbol of earth's life-force. Then he noticed that the lingam had three eyes, and he felt that the divinity was watching him. One day he found that from one of the eyes of the lingam blood was pouring, and it seemed diseased. He was very upset, and felt that he had to do something. The only thing he could think of doing was to offer the lingam one of his own eyes, which were so precious to him as a huntsman. He did this immediately by gouging out one of his eyes with an arrow. As soon as he had offered his eye to the lingam he saw that the eye of the lingam stopped bleeding and became whole again. But then, to his horror, he found that the other eye of

< 171 >

the lingam began to emit blood. Once again he decided that he had to offer his own eye, in order that the divine eye might become whole again. Placing his hand on the lingam, so he knew where it was by touch, he cut out his remaining eye and offered it to the lingam. It is said that when he had done this Kanappa, though an outcaste and a mere forest hunter, achieved moksa.[2]

We might interpret this story by understanding the eye as consciousness, and the need to sacrifice this is the need to enter into that very blind unreasoning life-force from which the lingam itself had emerged, in order to achieve a higher form of vision.

THE POT

The pot, which is held to be sacred, is generally the spherical village pot which does not have much of a neck. Like the coconut it is a symbol both of the head and the womb. An interesting folk symbolism links the pot, the head and the womb, in the figure of a young woman carrying a pot full of some liquid on her head. In village festivals you will often see young village girls dancing with pots balanced on their heads — the climax of the dance is often a feat of considerable skill whereby the girl has to bend down and pick something from the ground with her mouth, without dropping the pot which is balanced on her head. We know that the deity is often thought to reside in the pot in the form of water or grain, or sometimes even an earthenware lamp which is balanced on the pot. The pot containing water or seed is a symbol of the fertile womb, and all that is stable and protective in nature which 'holds' the force of life. The woman is like the vessel which has to carry this life-force without spilling it. Like the pregnant woman, she has a precious burden which has to be supported and protected. In this way woman is seen as the principal conservative element in nature. But it is in and through this conservation of life that woman is filled with her greatest joy. She dances, while yet conserving — this is the tension of her dance. The dance of man is different in that he breaks beyond the bonds of nature. But woman conserves nature in her dance. Even in her terrible aspect of the devouring mother (Kali or Durga), the feminine deity is never the Tandava, that is, he who steps beyond the world-cycle. She is nature's forces imploding upon itself, the negative direction in nature which draws back her children into herself in order to bring them forth again in the inevitable cycle of birth and death.

< 172 >

THE OVERFLOWING POT, OR PURNA KUMBHAM

The need for water is a fundamental need — especially so for the villager. There are certain symbols, of which water is one, which belong to what one might call the biological world, and are therefore elementary in the field of symbolism.

There is a pictograph of the world-view developed in Jainism (but general to Indian gnosticism) which shows the earth as a circle irrigated by a complex of canals or rivers. This pattern is universal enough. The globular earthen pot in which water is contained, is thus the earth in which water is abundant, the Punya Bhumi of folk thought. In tantric ritual (derived from fundamental patterns of folk religion) the liquid within the ordinary household pot is the potent body whose covering of cloth tied on with threads and painted with daubed colour are the flesh, nerves and skin. This pot is an image of primal man, and by breaking it and spilling its contents over the pillar (a rite which is called abhiseka), the womb is symbolically pierced, thus enacting a sacrifice which is both destructive and recreative.[3]

The overflowing pot is nature itself in its abundance. It is the golden vessel which came up from the cosmic oceans, containing amrt, the ambrosia of life. The ancient institution of Kumbha Mela commemorates this archetypal womb of life by a seasonal pilgrimage to the sacred river. In the festival of Pongal the pot boiling over with rice is again nature overflowing with goodness through contact with fire. Heat, we recall, is itself the magical and sacrificial force which brings the emotive world boiling up through the body of the yogi, till it boils over, and he passes into samadhi. Here we have a truly indigenous symbol of evolution (parinama) and the creation of a natural surplus.

THE POT AS A MOTIF IN INDIAN ART

Perhaps because the pot belongs so much to the realm of essential form, we find it implicit in many Indian forms (such as for example in the pot belly of Ganesa), but the symbolism of the vessel is implicit, rather than explicit. Ganesa in perhaps his most original icon carries the kalasam full of laddoos (round sweets), or round cakes (modaka), or the fruits of the bel tree (also round), which are supposed to symbolize the universe containing the life monads. The pot form is often confused with other forms — for example the form of the budding lotus. The crowning finial of the Hindu temple is the kalasam,

< 173 >

The *purna kumbham,* or *full vessel, symbol of plenty, used often during marriage ceremonies and festivals such as Sankranti or Pongul*

< 174 >

or the pot of elixir, which is often also given the form of a budding lotus. This structural element of the Hindu temple probably goes back to ancient folk magic whereby a pot was put on the top of an important building or shrine, to attract the rain. Rain magic is of course essential to the agriculturalist, and the pot has the effect through sympathetic magic of enhancing, or calling forth, the essential abundance of nature. In this way it is also used as a symbol of fertility. From Gupta times onwards we find a pot overflowing with life as a much favoured decorative motif incorporated into the design of pillars. In temple architecture ornamented pillars have the bulging shape reminiscent of pots piled one on top of the other comparable to the stems of Gothic pillars which are slightly bulging, and which signify the life-force brimming up within the pillar. The capitals of pillars often have pot motifs also, connecting them again with folk symbolism, where pots are broken on pillars of stone, that is menhirs or boundary stones, as an act of 'anointing' the pillar and hence giving life. Images of Laksmi depict elephants pouring water on the goddess from pots and in a carving of this theme from the Bharhut railings, even the lotus pedestals on which the figures stand have the form of buds or fruits reminding one of vessels. The figure of woman herself is based on the rounded forms of the pot — her globular breasts being symbols of her fertility. Wherever the pot figures, it seems to convey the idea of the abundant life and fertility of the universe.

THE SYMBOL OF THE EYE IN RELATION TO THE POT

In the world of pure form, the intersection of two globes or circles produces a structure which is fascinating to the artist and mathematician alike. Euclid devotes his first geometric proposition to the analysis of this form which was known in the West as the mandorla.[4] This symbol emerges naturally out of the curvilinear, and the opening or splitting of rounded forms. It is thus the form of the opening into the womb, the yoni, and has been worshipped as a symbol of fertility from very ancient times. Through a natural homology which is intrinsic to symbolic thinking, this form has been found in the fish, as also in the eye. One name for the goddess in India brings these two corresponding symbols into what looks like a metaphor — Minaksi, or the fish-eyed.

There is great importance given to eyes in Indian art. Dancing, from which, according to the Silpa Sastras, all the arts derive, also puts tremendous stress on eye-movement and inflections. No other

< 175 >

classical dance-form has been so conscious of the all-powerful significance of the eye. Everybody knows about the third eye of Hindu
yoga, and its representation on the images of Hindu and Buddhist
deities alike. It has become, one might almost say, the special sign of
the Hindu, the red or black spot between the eye-brows, marking the
point of the third eye. We have already mentioned that the image was
not thought of as living until its eyes were painted in. It seems that
the concept of the third eye emerged first in Buddhist art, but not in
its later form between the other two anthropomorphic eyes at the
centre of the forehead. Rather it appeared first in the hand, and it
is suggested by some scholars as a development of the bhumi-
parsamudra or 'earth-witnessing gesture'. One of the most important
iconographic forms of the Lord Buddha is of him sitting in meditation, with one hand touching the earth, which is meant to indicate
that the whole of nature (prakrti) was witnessing to the reality of his
enlightenment. Certainly many Buddha figures were later represented
as having eyes in their hands, like a sort of stigmata, and not only in
their hands but in their feet and all over their body too. The idea of
the thousand-eyed one is found in epic literature too, where we are
told that Indra, on account of his attempt to seduce Ahilya, the wife
of a yogi, was cursed by that yogi so that his whole body was covered
by the imprint of the female organ, yoni. For this reason Indra (the
god of the cosmic waters) is sometimes called Sayoni. But Indra,
through his yogic power, was able to change those yoni marks into
eyes, thus stressing a curious link between feminine sexual power
and the power of seeing. We find that in the sex-play between
feminine nature (prakrti) and masculine (purusa) the play of eyes is
essential.[5] Repeatedly in Hindu love poetry the meeting of the eyes
is spoken of as a sort of sexual contact. Thus the downcast eyes of
the woman stresses the form of the yoni, while the open staring
eyes of the man represents the lingam.

Perhaps the most primal form of two-dimensional image to be
found in India is the stamp of the hand or the foot upon the plain
surface of wall or floor to make a pattern. This tradition is to be
found in many tribal areas too. Near the doors of a village shrine
you might see on the white-washed walls, the imprint of hands
made by dipping the hands in red earth, and then stamping the
palm of the hand against the wall surface. The Buddha in the early
art of Sanchi and Amravati is never represented in his anthropomorphic form but simply by the imprint of his feet upon the ground.
Where he trod, we are told, lotuses sprang from the ground. I am
told, moreover, that in central India women who were about to com-
mit sati also imprinted their hands on a wall or stone, and thus the

< 176 >

print of hands near to a village shrine sometimes indicates that the woman deity or village goddess committed ritual suicide there.[6] If one imprints one's hand or foot on a flat surface, one finds that the centre of the hand or of the foot does not print, leaving a space. This is because in the centre of the hand and the foot is a hollow. In the image this hollow space gives the impression of an eye. Also biologists tell us that the centres of the hand and of the foot, are the most sensitive localities in the body, having the largest number of nerve endings per unit of skin surface, and it is for this reason that we receive the most vivid impressions of touch through them.

This links up with the fact that Indian art is essentially derived from an art oriented to touch as the most immediate form of aesthetic experience. Certainly, even in the child, a feeling for tactile experience precedes a development of the visual or aural senses. Generally one finds that villagers not only look at Indian temples, but feel them — the instinct to feel the deity, especially the feet, is very strong. Fertility deities show indications that the breasts and sex of the mother were objects of reverent touch. I noticed in Mahabilli-puram that many of the mother figures showed, by the wearing down and polishing of the stone, that through the centuries people have touched their sexual parts. Here again we see the connection between the hand, and touching, and sexual contact in general.

The impression of many eyes is given in those nascent experiences of semi-darkness which one might describe as the basic foundation of rock-art. All natural depressions, or fissures in the rock surface, are imagined to be eyes in an anthropomorphic folk view of in-sentient matter. Thus the body of a rock, or venerable tree, is con-ceived of as full of eyes. These eyes tend to be seen in the flat, that is, as two-dimensional. The representation of eyes in Indian art is always two-dimensional. Even where the convention is to represent the face from a three-quarter angle, as was the case in the long tradi-tion of Jain art, and also in the Hindu art of Andhra, the eyes were always represented as though looked at from the front, giving rise to the odd convention of representing one eye, the further eye, sticking out into the air beyond the limit of the face.

THE MAGIC POWER OF THE EYE

In the folk mind there is no anxiety greater than a fear of the evil eye. We are familiar with the myths concerning the magical heat which emanates from the eye of Siva. This has been explained as being related to sun symbolism and the belief that the eye has, through a

<177>

process of magical correspondences, the power which the sun had to burn or pierce what it gazes at. Thus the Buddha's gaze of infinite compassion has the power to change the angry elephant into a peaceful one. In reverse, a look of anger or jealousy has the power to destroy. In folk religion elaborate precautions are taken against the evil eye. A typical one is the placing of an earthen pot near the object (house or crop) which has to be protected from the evil eye. The pot is generally painted white, and black or red dots are put all over it. These, it is believed, attract the 'eye' in the same way that the dots of the kolama pattern are believed to attract the 'eye' of the ghosts. This 'attraction' is itself on account of a natural attraction between corresponding forms. An eye is attracted to another eye. Also, because of the correspondence between the eye and the seminal drop of seed, the point or bindu naturally draws the eye to itself, because of an inherent tendency in the eye to focus, or to become 'one pointed'. By thus absorbing the gaze of the eye, its destructive power is dissolved. Furthermore we see here once again the relation of the eye to the pot. The eye represents evolved consciousness, emergence, and the pot represents the substance of emotive nature, the eternally nascent. The eye is the dividing power in man to distinguish vision through division, and this power is absorbed back into the unitive experience of being.

THE POT AS A SYMBOL OF BEING

I was told recently about a set of bhutas (energies of Siva) which were carved out of wood, and stood in a temple in coastal Karnataka. These village gods were several centuries old, naturally preserved by the salty air of the sea coast. The Government Design Centre of Bangalore wanted to acquire these village deities to put them into a museum of folk art, but the problem was that the villagers were worshipping them. However, the village priest said that it was possible to put the deities into other forms, and the government agreed to substitute the old wooden sculptures with exact modern replicas. This, however, could not be done immediately, so the spirits of these village gods had to be summoned out of their old wooden images and kept as it were in cold storage until the new images had been made. This could only be done by a village shaman who, in a state of trance, drew the spirits (bhutas) out of the wooden statues and placed them in water pots. As in the case of the spirits whom Christ put into a herd of swine which then drowned themselves in the lake, the natural 'home' of these energies was in fact water.

< 178 >

TWO NOTIONS OF TIME

I feel that in the symbols of eye and water pot we have two basic notions of the universe. The water pot symbolizes nature as a unity, and in the figure of boiling liquid it also symbolizes the cyclical motion of time. The energizing heat operative in nature creates the revolving motion of boiling liquid which is an endless process of heating and cooling; but the eye is a manifestation of nature in its particularity. It therefore becomes a symbol of the person endowed with the faculty to perceive. It is the focus or centre of experience, but it is dividing in so far as it is discriminating. In time it is the here and now, the nimesa (or blink of an eye) which is the smallest unit of time, and yet also the only point of time where revelation and liberation take place. In a nimesa the milk boils over. In a nimesa the Buddha realizes himself, and sees the world as it is. No amount of cyclical time can bring about this release from illusion. Wisdom is like a drop, a bindu, a fractional moment of time. Gnosis takes place ultimately outside of all process, all cause and effect, all cycles of birth and death.

A crude drawing seen on the wall of a village shrine showing a schematic representation of lingam. The phallic form is given a face and symbols of sun and moon are placed on either side

< 179 >

CHAPTER 16
Complementary symbols and the idea of wholeness

< 181 >

[OVERLEAF]

Complementary symbols and the idea of wholeness — the ceremonial pot as a central folk symbol of wholeness

< 182 >

The word 'symbol' comes from the Greek root *symballein,* that is to throw together, or put together (see p. 18). The image which is sometimes given is that of the broken pot, of which some parts are missing. The man who tries to assemble the pot, putting its parts together, is able to 'visualize' the missing parts by reconstructing an image of the whole pot in his mind, of which the parts he has are, as it were, 'symbols'. We must understand that what is symbolized is a 'whole', and the symbol as a manifest part of it has already inherent in it the pattern of the missing parts, of the 'unseen' part. The seen symbol is concrete, and therefore very much an object but its rela-tion with the unseen, which gives it meaning, is extremely difficult to define. While concluding our study of popular Indian symbols it is important, I feel, to define more precisely what lies beyond the immediate concrete image – in the unfathomable reaches of all that is symbolized.

SEEN AND UNSEEN

First of all we might compare the symbol to the tip of an iceberg. It is what is seen; but there is, below or beyond the concrete image of the symbol, a vast world which it is not possible to see. This unseen world is not just 'empty' in the sense of non-existent. What is unseen is ultimately linked to what we see, in the same way as the roots of a tree which we cannot see are extremely important to the whole organic structure of the tree which we see with our eyes. There are several ways in which we can understand this 'unseen' element of the symbol.

First of all it can be understood in the sense that we have already given it when introducing the idea of the broken vessel. The unseen part is the missing part which we are looking for when we are putting the pot together. Cassirer has said that the symbol does not repre-sent a thing, it is the thing.[1] In this way he seems to cut across those schools of interpretation who seek to explain the symbol not in terms of its concrete presence but rather in terms of what is signified, which is a reality beyond the immediate one. This would seem in contrast to the statement of the Taoist sage who said that the finger pointing to the moon is not the moon, Cassirer would perhaps insist that the symbol is something in itself and that this is very much con-nected with what it is symbolizing. To return to the image of the pot – the parts which the archaeologist is able to excavate and assemble of an ancient vessel are very important in themselves, and they are definitely parts of the whole ancient vessel. Though the reassembled

< 183 >

vessel is incomplete because some parts are missing, still the parts which we do have are real clues, and indicate in themselves the nature of the whole, so that by reconstructing them we can arrive in our mind at a concept of the whole.

The second understanding of the unseen element of the symbol is more related to our image of the tree. Here the unseen element is not simply 'missing'; it is an essential part of what is there; it is the ground from which what is visible emerges. The Taoists, expressing the true genius of the East, were more able to understand this than the Greeks. Thus we read in the *Tao Te Ching* of Lao Tzu:

> Knead clay in order to make a vessel. Adapt the nothing therein to the purpose in hand, and you will have the use of the vessel. Cut out doors and windows in order to make a room. Adapt the nothing therein to the purpose in hand, and you will have the use of the room. Thus what we gain is Something, yet it is by virtue of Nothing that this can be put to use. [XI]

Again we read in the same book

> Thus Something and Nothing produce each other. The difficult and the easy complement each other. [II]

Here Nothing is the inner space which gives use, or life, to that which is. The image which is visible has a meaning because of what is invisible. Ultimately speaking no amount of hunting will find the missing part, because what is missing cannot be put into visible tangible form. Here the invisible and the visible are seen to be complementary. The one is viewed as the substance, or inner reality of the other.

THE WHOLE

This brings us to the question of the 'whole' which includes both what is visible and obvious, and what is invisible and subtle. The 'whole' pot is not only what we can see and touch, it is also the missing part of the pot, what in Taoist terms might be compared to the emptiness inside the pot. The whole to which every symbol points is therefore the sum of all that it is concretely, and also all that it is not; the container and the contained, the formed and the formless.

Confusion over this has given rise to a number of misunderstandings I feel. Freud, who seemed to see the symbol (as in dream) in terms of a complicated code system, showed however that a dream (or symbol) could very often be 'about' something which it concretely

< 184 >

never described. This hidden meaning of the dream is expressed, according to him, in a kind of secret language so as to avoid the censoring control of the conscious mind.[2] An example is given of a dream concerning nakedness. 'Nakedness' is itself never represented, but anxieties concerning clothes, or the lack of them, serve as an indirect code language, denoting underlying repressed anxieties about the naked body. A priest might feel 'naked' without his cassock, or an army man might feel 'naked' without some item of uniform. Confusion arises if we assume that the manifest detail of the dream which can be described as constituting the subject of the dream (in the given example, clothing) is felt to be merely a code for something which is never explicit, but only implicit (such as, in our example, anxiety over the natural body). If we take the symbol to be a secret language, the explicit content of the symbolic image is only understood as a disguise for its implicit meaning. But the meaning of the dream, the whole feeling-tone of the dreamer's mind which gave rise to the dream, cannot in this way be separated from the manifest detail of the dream. The dream cannot in this way be stripped naked, any more than on the deepest level of meaning a man can strip himself of all his clothing, for in the last analysis, the body itself is a form of clothing, veiling something which is beyond the body. We see therefore that clothing not only obscures the body, but also adequately symbolizes the body, symbolizes what the mind understands the body to be, a veil covering the real man. Anxieties concerning the body are at root anxieties concerning the reality of the inner man. Images which are truly symbolical are therefore not merely ways of hiding statements but are in fact real statements in themselves — every detail of such an image is significant, and reveals a truth, though it might appear to be hiding it.

Another confusion may appear if we attempt to understand the symbol as merely allegory. By allegory we mean the description of one thing under the image of another. An example is given in the book written jointly by Jung and Kerenyi, called *The Science of Mythology,* in which the rising sun is compared to the primordial child. Kerenyi at one point seems to suggest that we have here an allegory of the primordial child in terms of the dawn, but goes on to say, 'A symbol is not an allegory, not just another way of speaking: it is an image presented or rather represented, by the world itself.'[3] Here we have two images — the image of the child, and the image of the dawn, and the one is superimposed upon the other. Subject and object in the case of superimposed images are brought disconcertingly face to face in a figure in which memory is implicated. To remember is to reconstitute. The image of a dear one is used to remember the

< 185 >

person whom it represents. But then again, going further back to the magical intent of all ancient ritual, the very act of bringing together the elements of an image, as in a ritual sacrifice, is to make present a reality which is otherwise thought to be absent, or at least not wholly present. This introduces the notion of *pars pro toto* which is basic to all magical thought, and is also to be found in the root concept of the metaphor as described by Cassirer.

According to Cassirer, metaphor is the very basis of the process of thinking and consequently of language itself. Metaphor is defined as 'the circumlocution of one idea in terms of another', and Cassirer points out its magical origin, where the part is made to represent the whole.[4] In magic a hair, tooth, or other object connected with a person or thing, can be really thought to be that person or thing, so that what is done to the part is done also to the whole, by magical effect.

The problem we are confronted with is essentially the problem of relating the fragmentary world of which our senses can form impressions, to the whole world of our intuition. Our empirical conscious experience is inevitably partial — but our inner experience always aspires to the universal. Erich Fromm, in his book *The Forgotten Language,* tries to show how in fact the inner universal experience complements our external empirical awareness of reality. In this way Fromm seems to attempt a bridge between a Freudian analysis and a Jungian one. Freud seemed to understand the symbol only in terms of the empirical partial experience of the individual subject, the dream being merely a way of working over repressed anxieties which have built up in the conscious waking state of the individual. For Jung there was a message in the dream which lay beyond the individual's conscious and wholly personal experience, and was in fact a way in which the universal, or world, communicated itself to the understanding of the individual, being on occasion a real revelation, and an enlargement of his psyche. In the symbol man realizes the universal or archetypal which is the primordial pattern of all individual experience. Here the message comes from outside man, and is not simply a code message for something that lies hidden in him, in his merely personal experience.

In my understanding of the functioning of symbol I would like to stress this dynamic of complementary functions, one intuitional and universal, the other empirical and particular. The symbol is itself a particular created object in a limited environment in answer to the distinctive needs of a society which has engendered it. Yet it is not something isolated, but is the very medium for relationship; man relates to man through symbols, that is why we speak of symbolic

< 186 >

language. Symbols, in that they aspire to wholeness, lead man to an integration through shared experience with fellow man. In this way we can understand symbol not as static, but as dynamic. It is not just a *thing,* but is rather an *event,* having its context in the lives of people for whom symbols are important occasions in their experience. In this sense one could speak of the symbol as a celebration. Man is drawn together with man in the symbol, which both transcends the individual, and expresses the need of the individual to discover a higher personal identity. This is why the symbol is both universal, belonging to a shared experience, and also deeply personal.

Symbols are not merely objects of thought; they take on a personality of their own. That is why from ancient times symbols were thought to be alive, to be beings in themselves. But we must realize that the personality of the symbol is nothing other than the extended personality of man in his longing for unity and wholeness. The world that speaks through the symbol is not extraneous to the reality of man, a sort of gnostic world spirit, but is man at the point of his highest consciousness speaking to all that is within him, and related to him. The symbol is the outpouring of an integral vision in which all that is most conscious in man touches and communicates with all that is most unconscious. In light we have many colours which, as Goethe poetically put it, are the joys and sufferings of light, and yet light itself is a primal unity beyond all its mutations. The same is true of the symbol. The objective symbol, which is always partial, is the creation of man's personal joy and sorrow, but this image which he has created symbolizes that wholeness which transcends all accidents as white light transcends all the colours which it evokes from nature.

COMPLEMENTARY COLOURS AND THEIR RELATION
·TO THE SYMBOLIC PROCESS

To clarify this general principle on which my analysis of symbol and symbolism rests, let me take the example of the colour spectrum. The colours of the spectrum (comprising all the colours that exist) can be arranged in a colour circle. This circle when spun, gives the impression not of a colour, but whiteness. This 'whiteness' is not achieved if the colours represented on the circle are not in the correct proportion to each other, that is the proportion of all colours that exist in the world to the whole colour field as such. But it can be demonstrated that instead of representing all the colours, a minimum of two colours can be painted together on a colour circle, and

< 187 >

Complementary symbols — battle of mother goddess against buffalo demon, after a relief at Mahaballipuram

< 188 >

these two colours when spun can also achieve white light. For example, a green and a red, painted in the right proportion on a colour circle, when spun together create white light, similarly blue and orange, purple and yellow. These colour combinations represent, or correspond to, all the colours, and that is why they can make white light when spun together.

Complementary colours are thus defined as colours which when spun together create the whole (that is white light). Let us examine what we have.

green/red   —   white light
blue/orange   —   white light
purple/yellow —   white light

Green is not red, nor can it symbolize red, but in white light there is green and red. Similarly with the other pairs. The products of green and red dynamically involved together, and of blue and orange dynamically involved together, both create the same result (white light) and not different results. Symbolic 'opposites' are treated, like the opposites of the colour circle, as complementary and therefore a part of a whole.

Let us take a group of complementary symbols which represent a whole:

tree   serpent
pillar (lingam)   pot (garbha)
mountain   wheel
hand   eye

Many other examples of complementary symbols could be taken in this way. Returning to our basic analogy of the colour circle, tree-serpent is in some way an opposition which together represents a whole. This totality is the wholeness of reality. In the same way pillar (lingam)–pot (garbha) also represents the wholeness of reality. This wholeness of reality is not different from the wholeness of reality which tree–serpent figures. In other words, all symbolic dynamisms, particular and limited though they are, configurate the same whole reality. Within these very complementary symbols there is a structural patterning between individual symbols. We could, for the sake of a closer analysis, arrange the above complementary symbols into a sort of hop-scotch pattern which is itself a familiar pattern in village thought, and see how individual symbols begin to relate to each other dynamically.

< 189 >

material   spiritual
↑   ↑
masculine   feminine
↑   ↑

hand / action	eye / consciousness	human — rational sphere
pillar / lingam	pot / garbha	sexual — emotive sphere
mountain / vertical	wheel / horizontal / points of / the compass	centrality — spatial sphere
tree / evolution	serpent / involution	movement — kinetic sphere

↑   ↑
masculine   feminine
↑   ↑
spiritual   material

Horizontally these symbols work as complementary oppositions which delineate also planes of functions or dynamism (human, sexual, centrality, movement). But the symbols also work vertically, giving meaning-links, or perspectives. Thus there is a pointing movement serpent-wheel-pot-eye, where feminine symbols pass through a process of spiritualization, from unconscious instinctual life (serpent) through spatial relationship (the wheel, world) to sexuality (the womb) and finally consciousness (the eye, mandorla, opening of the womb). Similarly on the other side, there is a movement in the individual symbols from the spiritual to the gross within a group, which can be called in this context 'masculine' figures. Tree, the 'axis mundi', the living, organic cosmos itself, relates to the mountain which is static, inorganic and therefore more earth-bound, to the pillar which is the sexual potentiality in matter, and finally to the hand which is the active agent, touching matter, and transforming it through direct action.

These patterns are not logical–discursive, and therefore defined and irreversible in a mechanistic process of cause–effect. Rather they

< 190 >

are intuitive, constantly capable of being inverted, because every symbol, itself treated as a whole, has opposites within it (hot–cold, male–female, cultured–natural) in the same way as symbols themselves combine as opposites to create other wholes, within the total symbolizing process.

In the process of harnessing nature man has lost the sense of the world as symbol — for him it is only a collection of 'facts'. The result of this is a tremendous threat to ecology. Man is in danger of destroying the very world which he wants to control; not only the external 'natural' world, but his own inner world of experience. Even language and meaning, the greatest creations of civilization, are in danger. Originally it was only through symbol that man was able to transform matter. Science, which itself aims at 'transforming' man's environment, can only hope to do so if it realizes its inner basis of symbolic thinking. The world is not a thing which can be exploited endlessly. The world has a symbolic relation to man, for man is not over and against the world, but is himself the highest symbol of the world-process.

The world-process in its raw, unrealized, vital being has been symbolized by the serpent. It is a dangerous, poisonous potentiality. And yet it is capable of being transformed. Man has been appointed not as the controller and abuser of nature, but as its transformer. The child lord, the dharma sastha, or body of dharma, is born in order to put the serpent in his appointed place, to dance upon him his death-dealing dance, in order ultimately to liberate him from his own evil. The child plays with the serpent — a dangerous play. He and the serpent represent an eternal effort at renewal and wholeness. They complement each other and transform each other. Without the serpent how could there be vitality in creation, which would bring things to life? And without the child, how would the world-process ever be transformed and transcended?

< 191 >

NOTES

Introduction

1. To this day it is believed in India that a man who dies childless will become a ghost, for a son is responsible for the ceremonies upon which the peace of his dead ancestors depend
   (W. D. O'Flaherty, *Asceticism and Eroticism in the Mythology of Siva*, 68). Householders have need of a son, and wealth; for them a wife is necessary for the sake of a son, and sons are necessary to give the oblations to the ancestors (Brhaddharma 2.60).
2. The child god as described in Hindu myth is not historical in the sense that the child Jesus was historical. That is, he does not represent a particular moment in the historical process. However, history is made out of the stuff of 'birth' in that without things coming to birth, there could be no history. The idea of birth, and its reality, is the foundation of all history. Even in the birth of Christ, although we are told that he was born at this place, under this king, there are nevertheless evidently non-historical aspects to the narrative of the events – the coming of the Magi, the witness of the angels, etc. In this sense one might speak of the intersection of history and eternity, for history not only in its 'end' but in its 'beginning' is founded on a reality which cannot be confined to the merely historical. Ultimately speaking, as Goethe puts it, 'Everything that exists is an analogy of Existence itself.' Hindu stories concerning the birth of a child god are analogues in this way of existence itself, in that they expose the essence of history. For the deep human intuition of deity incarnated in matter is at the heart of man's hopes about history, but is beyond what can be empirically ascertained.
3. The relation of technique to inspiration is a very complex one. As I have tried to stress in various places, the way something is expressed is certainly essential in determining the experience of discovery, and therefore of the very inspiration itself. The way a great artist paints, that is, his technique, cannot be divorced from the way he sees, and beyond that his 'knowing' in the intuitional sense. When Picasso states that he does not paint what he sees, but what he knows, we are not to assume that this knowledge is a pre-conceived 'idea', but rather is his very experience of the artistic process itself, dynamically in the act of doing. When I speak of 'skill' I am not referring to technique (even a child has a technique) in the broad sense of the word as a grasping of the structure of material things which are the means for expression. Technique in that sense is an experimental knowledge of the physical way in which expression takes place, which cannot be divorced

< 193 >

from the inspiration latent in all expression. In that intuitional sense technique and knowledge are inseparable from the actualized experience. But technique and knowledge in the limited sense of skill, that is control over the means of expression, lies on a different level from that on which inspiration takes place, because it is incapable of surprise, and consequently of grace. We must always carefully distinguish between the knowledge which is rational and controlling, and the knowledge which is intuitional and participating. When man says he 'knows' woman (as we are told he knows her in the Book of Genesis) he obviously knows her intuitionally by participating in her life. In that sense every great artist paints not what he sees, but what he knows. This knowledge is not something which he has seen before (as an interior mental conception) and which now he puts into effect. Seeing in this sense is non-involved, and therefore uncommitted and objective. It is the sort of seeing which a scientist is capable of, which is better described as observing, and noting facts. The artist knows in that he immerses himself into the experience, and so his knowledge is a pure engagement in the actualized reality. This actualized reality comes to him in the very act of his trying to express it creatively. In and through painting the artist begins to discover what he is painting.

4. A. K. Coomaraswamy, *Christian and Oriental Philosophy of Art*, p. 61. As he points out, superstition can also mean what is 'left over', that is a mere sediment or accretion which is 'left over' after the initial experience or insight has been drained away, being itself a merely unconscious deposit of tradition.

Chapter 1: The dynamism of the symbolizing process

1. According to Christian bestiaries, which often draw on ancient oriental folklore, the peacock is a symbol of life; see George Fergusson, *Signs and Symbols in Christian Art*, Oxford University Press (New York, 1954). In Roman coins it is often associated with the feminine figure; see J. E. Cirlot, *Dictionary of Symbols*. A motif probably going back to Persia shows two peacocks on either side of the Tree of Life. Peacocks are also sometimes shown drinking at the fountain of life.

   In an interesting monograph entitled *Bones of St. Thomas and the Antique Casket of Mylapore, Madras*, by B. A. Figredo, published by the Christian Literature Society, in a section entitled *Hindu Motifs*, we are told of a legend that Parvati in the form of Mayil or Peacock worshipped Siva as the Lingam. The temple commemorating this was a shore temple of Mayilapuri or 'Peacock town', the modern Mylapore. Thus the motif of the two peacocks on either side of the lingam depicted as a frieze around the temple can be seen as a variant of the Western peacock with tree or fountain of life, the important point being the peacock's association with the source of fertility.

2. Lévi-Strauss, *The Savage Mind*. In the first chapter he compares the myth-making activity to 'bricolage'.

< 194 >

3. For critical analysis of Lévi-Strauss, see G. S. Kirk, *Myth: Its Meaning and Functions in Ancient and Other Cultures*; see also Dan Sperber, *Rethinking Symbolism*, chapter 3.
4. The story of the churning of the cosmic ocean, and the poison emerging from it which Siva swallowed, is given in one of its oldest forms in the Mahabharata. See W. D. O'Flaherty, *Hindu Myths*, pp. 273–80.

Chapter 2: Symbols of opposition

1. See W. D. O'Flaherty, *Hindu Myths*, p. 218.
2. Ganesa is essentially the god of obstacles — the jinx of nature. He is playful — hence his childhood nature, — but also clever in an uncanny way. He could be called a trickster.
3. Janus — a symbol of wholeness (J. E. Cirlot, *Dictionary of Symbols*) and equivalent to the myth of the Gemini, who, like Janus, represents the union of opposites in its dynamic aspect. Marius Schneider traces the Gemini myth to Megalithic culture. He suggests that Janus was possibly identified with the two-peaked Mountain of Mars, and we might recall in this connection that Kartikeya is Skanda, god of war, i.e. also related to Mars. There is a network here of very ancient thought on the union of opposites.
4. See *Man and his Symbols* (ed. by Jung), pp. 160 ff.
5. The person is very much connected with the symbol. The symbol is personal, that is, each individual fits the symbol into his personal experience, which interprets, and is also interpreted by, the symbol. Like the symbol, the person is dynamic not static. It grows, and evolves, pointing to a wholeness which lies beyond itself (the Atman). The process of discovering personhood is a symbolic process in that the realization of the emergence of symbols in an individual life is precisely what we mean when we say he finds his personality. When an individual speaks of his personality, he is speaking of himself as a symbol, and as part of a total symbolic system. Personhood is a living symbol, which throws considerable light on the idea of God as Person. God as Person is God as Symbol.
6. Cf. Getty, *Ganesa — A Monograph on the Elephant-faced God.*
7. A manifestation of the terrible aspect of the god, whose function it is to ward off the impious and to protect the devotee. In the myth concerning Ganesa and the moon, Ganesa assumes the aspect of Rahu, who is the ancient enemy of the moon: it is he who month by month tries to consume the moon. The 'face of glory' is essentially the face of Rahu, who is a face without a body, because, he was beheaded in the act of stealing the elixir of life, *soma,* which is also identified with the moon. As a result, only his head is immortal, and eternally thirsty for more of the elixir. It is this face that one sees popularly over doors, or buildings which are just being constructed, because like the gothic gargoyle it is the evil face that is supposed to frighten away the forces of evil. Cf. Heinrich Zimmer, *Myths and Symbols in Indian Art and Civilization.*
8. The epithet Vanaspati is also applied to Siva.

< 195 >

Chapter 3: Womb–tomb symbols

1. The concept of yin and yang in Chinese Buddhism goes back probably to the Chinese Book of Changes, the *I Ching*. This book probably goes back to methods of divination used in the Hsia dynasty (2205–1766 BC). It is very mathematical in its form, using both binary and tertiary systems. The binary concept of yin and yang, or moon and sun, also seems extremely ancient, though it was later developed by the Taoist Schools. The concept of change which lies behind the yin–yang symbol entails the idea of what is fixed and permanent, which could be compared with the Hindu idea of dharma. In the West, change implies the opposite of what is fixed, but the Chinese idea is that change is the foundation of the universe, for nothing is so permanent as change itself. In India the idea of dharma as the 'firm' has been stressed more than its aspect as the moving, but the basic oriental view of reality which lies behind both Taoism and Hindu notions of dharma is essentially the same, being the polarity which generates transformation as a life principle.

2. Cf. Mortimer Wheeler, *Civilization of the Indus Valley and Beyond*, chapter 6.
3. Cf. A. Volwahsen, *Living Architecture: Indian*, p. 88; see also K. R. Srinivasan, *Temples of South India*, pp. 14–15.
4. Descriptions of such rites can be found in H. Whitehead's *Village Gods of South India*. I have also seen such rites myself.
5. A. Volwahsen, *Living Architecture*, chapter entitled 'City and Temple Layout'. See also V. Pathar, *Temple and its Significance*.
6. The myth concerning the rise of the tree of life from the navel probably goes back to an ancient symbolism with pre-Aryan deities known as Yaksas (cf. Coomaraswamy, *Yaksas*). According to the Atharva Veda, the germ of life 'rose like a tree from the navel of the unborn', which in the oldest passage is Varuna.
7. H. Whitehead, op. cit., p. 126.
8. Maze patterns represent the problem of entering an enclosed space, and coming out of it again. Psychically (as one can see from myths concerning mazes) this effort to master the path into and out of an enclosed space is

< 196 >

connected with initiatory rites of rebirth, thus simulating the trauma of a babe within the womb. The path of the maze, which moves now clockwise, now anti-clockwise, in an apparently meaningless yet controlled symmetry, reminds one of the movement of the foetus in the womb prior to birth. In fact the ball of 'string' which was part of the ritual unravelling of the mystery of the maze in Greek mythology, for it was to be followed by the initiate when retracing his steps after exploring the maze, is probably a symbol of the umbilical cord. According to mythic thought, man retains a deep memory of his birth trauma, which not only affects his whole attitude towards life, but also prefigures mysteriously his path out of life (which again is a rebirth) in the last struggles of death. It was Freud who, because of findings in the course of his clinical work, first postulated the existence of a 'birth trauma' even in modern man, and this has since been corroborated by other depth psychologists and some gynaecologists.

9. The earliest form of the myth concerning Sati is probably to be found in the Mahabharata, and also the Brahma Purana, later elaborated in many puranas and in the Kumara Sambhavam of Kalidasa. In the medieval period her legend was joined to the tantric rituals of the pithas, or holy seats, where it was believed that parts of the dismembered body of Sati were held as relics and worshipped.

Chapter 4: The ecology of symbolic elements and transfiguring energy

1. Konrad Lorenz, *Civilized Man's Eight Deadly Sins*, p. 1 and pp. 46-8. A similar viewpoint is to be found in the anthropology of Malinowski and Radcliff-Brown, who felt that a culture should be studied as a 'functioning and integrated whole analogous to an organism'. This approach was known as particularism, in that it tried to view a culture as a unity, rather than as an ensemble of various items borrowed from other surrounding cultures.
2. O'Flaherty, *Asceticism and Eroticism in the Mythology of Siva*, p. 230.
3. Zimmer, *Philosophies of India*, p. 230.
4. The heavenly Gandharva of the Veda was a deity who knew and revealed the secrets of heaven and divine truths in general. The Gandharva are supposed to live in the sky, and their office is to prepare the sacred soma juice for the gods. They also have a mystic power over women, and are the traditional lovers of the Apsaras. They are also thought to be skilled in healing like the Asvins, probably on account of their association with the Amrt. The Gandharvas are singers and musicians at the banquet of the gods. According to the Visnu Purana, they were born of Brahma, imbibing melody, drinking of the goddess of speech, and it is from this that they get their name. According to the Mahabharata, there seems to have also been a race of people living in the forested hills who were known as Gandharvas. G. S. Kirk, in his book *Myth: Its Meaning and Functions in Ancient and Other Cultures*, relates the Gandharvas to the Greek Centaurs, who he says were spirits of the mountain torrents. Though the association of Gandharvas with

< 197 >

Indra and the Asvins indicates some connection also with horse symbolism, there is not, as far as I know, any tradition that the Gandharvas were half horse like the Centaurs, though in India mixtures of man and beast are not unknown. The Gandharvas are, however, represented as interfering in human love affairs (as in the famous Vedic legend of Puraravas and Urvasi), and are also thought to be the mythic progenitors of the human race, as in the story of Yama and Yami.

5. Sandhya means twilight — personified as the daughter of Brahma and wife of Siva. In the Siva Purana it is stated that when Brahma attempted to do violence to his daughter Sandhya, she changed herself into a deer. See W. D. O'Flaherty, *Hindu Myths,* p. 34.

6. According to Berriedale Keith, *The Samkhya System,* the term 'lingam' appears beside 'mind', and the suggestion to treat it as meaning 'psychic apparatus' presents itself. Bhutatman is the migrating psychic apparatus which is also lingam.

Chapter 5: Symbols of magical power in folklore

1. Cf. Siva Dharmasamhita, 10, 132–50.
2. Myth of creation of Sakti, see Heinrich Zimmer, *Myths and Symbols in Indian Art and Civilization,* p. 130.
3. See Tucci, *The Theory and Practice of the Mandala,* pp. 12–13.

Chapter 6: Symbols of authority

1. This version of the myth is given in *Lord Ayyappan — The Dharma Sastha,* by P. Pyyappan. As with all Indian myths there are a number of variants. In *Sabarimalai and its Sastha,* by P. T. Thomas, we read that according to a version of the myth known to Professor P. K. Parameswaran Nair, Ayyappan is supposed to have been born to the son of a pujari whose temple had been robbed, and a princess who had been carried away by robbers. The child was born on Makara Sankranti (the ides of January) and was found by Rajasekhara lying in the forest near to a yogi who was in deep meditation (presumably his father). In the popular film on Ayyappan the yogi father is seen covered with leaves, so that he appears to be just a conical mountain, very similar to the Sukanya myth (see p. 208) where the sage has gone into such deep meditation that he has been completely covered by an ant hill. The ascetical mountain-like figure of the yogi, near to whom the babe is found, is also a very significant figure, linking the child with the forces of asceticism.

2. This tension between asceticism and eroticism is very much the theme of W. D. O'Flaherty's book *Asceticism and Eroticism in the Mythology of Siva,* where versions of the Mahisasuri myth are also given. For detailed descriptions of the myth of Mahisasura, Mahisi's brother, see p. 62.

3. The child is born of all opposites. According to Sri Raman Menon, Ayyappan

< 198 >

is probably a pre-Aryan god (he notes the fact that even in Kerala, very few of the major Brahmanical temples have important cult worship of Ayyappan, even though he is a very popular deity). It is suggested that the monism of Sankaracarya is based on a piety which believes in the unity of all opposites, which is very much a part of the Ayyappan myth. It was precisely on account of his doctrine of the unity of all opposites that Sankara was expelled from the orthodox Brahmin community, where there was continual tension between adherents of Siva and Visnu. Ayyappan is the child of both Visnu and Siva, and is thus the symbolic unity between them. This sense of unity is also demonstrated by the Vaver episode (Vaver being the legendary Muslim tribal hero who helped Ayyappan) and to this day pilgrims to Sabarimalai visit the mosque of Vaver at Erumeli, and Muslims also go to the Sastha temple and make offering there. It is even proposed that Ayyappan is in fact Buddha, because the image of Ayyappan seems to have many iconographic details in common with that of Buddha.

4. There is a story behind the name of the hill Sabarimalai. Sabari, according to the Valmiki Ramayana, was in fact a tribal woman belonging to the Sabara or Veda tribe, who anxiously waited for Rama to pass through her country on his way to find Sita, and give to her moksa. It is possible she was some ancient tribal goddess who has in this way got absorbed into the Hindu epic.

5. Vaver-tribal king of the forest. According to one story, Vaver was in fact a pirate who became converted to Ayyappan and subsequently became his trusted follower.

6. Cf. Lévi-Strauss, *The Raw and the Cooked*, from whom the idea of the relation between nature and culture as that of the raw and the cooked has been drawn.

7. Cf. Mircea Eliade, *Yoga: Immortality and Freedom* — section on initiatory rites.

8. It will be recalled that, according to the Ramayana, it was precisely when King Janak was ploughing the land that he found the baby in the furrow, known later as Janaki or Sita ('Sita' being the Sanskrit word for 'furrow').

9. Cf. K. R. Srinivasan, *Temples of South India*, p. 25.

10. Cf. Verrier Elwin, *The Murias and their Ghotul*, chapter on the marriage festivals of the Muria.

11. Cf. E. B. Havell, *The Himalayas in Indian Art*, chapters 1, 2, 3.

12. Sikhara means a crown, and is the spire above the north Indian type of temple. It seems to me that the crowns of gods and goddesses are basically the same towering form, often incorporating the motif of an overflowing vessel at the top, which in the architectural sikhara is the finial, often pot-like in form, being the golden vessel of amrt, and probably going back to ancient rain-making magic, whereby vessels were placed on the tops of important or sacred buildings to encourage the rain, and bring fertility to the land (see p. 175). The vimana is more especially the tower of the southern temple, but can also refer to the whole shrine, including its base. The south Indian vimana is meant to relate to the whole structure of the heavens, being like the vault of the heavens, whereas the northern sikhara

< 199 >

is meant to represent the peak of Mount Meru (cf. Havell, op. cit., pp. 31-5).

13. Attention may be drawn to the typical gesture of the Buddha in Buddhist iconography. With his two hands he 'enumerates the points of the Law' — the dharma cakra mudra, or mudra of the turning of the wheel of the law.

14. The umbrella is also very much connected with marriage. At a recent Christian village marriage which I attended, I noticed that as the bride and bridegroom came out of the church, an umbrella was immediately opened over them, and the umbrella was covered with a sari to make it look more festive. This is obviously related to prevalent customs relating to marriage processions.

15. The gesture known as the abhaya mudra in Hindu iconography is in fact called 'pataka' in dance terminology, meaning the flag of the temple. Here clearly we see the relationship between the temple flag, authority, and the directive 'do not fear' which accompanies the gesture.

16. Reference might be made to the great standing lamp which is lit before every performance of Kathakali dance, and which is supposed to have two wicks, one a thick wick, and the other a thin one, representing the sun and the moon, which are here symbolized as resting upon the pillar of the universe.

17. *Mudra* — a term which has a special meaning in tantra, more commonly means 'gesture' in Indian dance. These gestures have been highly classified in the various schools of Indian classical dance, and are found also in Indian sculpture, but in a more simplified form. Important gestures are, for example, the abhaya mudra, meaning the gesture 'do not fear' which is a very natural and authoritative gesture of the hand lifted up in assurance. Another important gesture, found especially in Buddhist art is the dharma-cakra mudra, or teaching gesture, which again is derived from a very natural position of the hands of a teacher enumerating on his fingers the points of the law. (Does the fact that in the Judaic-Christian religion there are ten commandments relate to the fact that there are ten fingers, and a teacher would naturally enumerate the ten laws by pointing to each finger?) Another mudra is the dhyana or samadhi mudra, which, like other gestures of yoga, might relate to an ancient system found in pranayama in which positions of the hands are found to exert an influence on the whole nervous system by means of a sort of remote control. The mudras, beginning thus in purely natural gestures arising out of inner moods, have been stylized into a very intricate language, rather like that used by deaf and dumb people. Those who can understand this language can in fact communicate quite complex messages or stories through the mere manipulation of the hands.

18. Crown forms can also be related to the head-dresses to be found in such dance styles as Kathakali and Yaksagana.

Chapter 7: An elemental art

1. Cf. Kant, *Critique of Pure Reason*, trans. N. K. Smith, Macmillan, 1929, p. 237.

< 200 >

2. There is thus an important category of Indian images called 'svayambhu murti'. These are forms in nature — rock, tree trunks, ant hills, even great lumps of ice in the Himalayas — which represent some form of deity, generally the archetypal lingam.

Chapter 8: Symbols of sacred space and dance in relation to the moon symbol

1. C. G. Jung, *Synchronicity.*
2. Swami H. Saraswati, *The Inner Significance of Lingam Worship.*

Chapter 9: The symbol of life — further reflections on the significance of the moon

1. Tagore, *The Crescent Moon (Collected Poems)*, poem entitled 'The Beginning'.
2. Mircea Eliade, *Two and the One,* chapter entitled 'Experiences of the Mystic Light'. Eliade deals with the whole relationship between light and birth. In an essay printed in *History of Religions,* entitled 'Spirit, Light, and Seed' (University of Chicago, vol. 11, no. 1, August 1971) Eliade develops the idea of the relation between light and seminal seed. Rebirth is very much connected with enlightenment, and thus the child deity is often thought of as a sun God. The world itself is thought of as an emanation of light, thus Coomaraswamy associates the Sanskrit word lila with the root lelay — to flame, to sparkle, to shine (Coomaraswamy, 'Lila', *Journal of American Oriental Society,* 1941). The primordial void, or egg, called the hiranya garbha, is in fact an oval of light from whose sphere all is born.

   It is in connection with virile semen as light that the birth of saviours is associated with light — 'in the night in which Mahavira was born there was one great divine, godly lustre' (Akaranga sutra). 'At the birth of a Buddha five cosmic lights shine' (Mircea Eliade, op. cit.). He shows the concept to be Indo-Iranian, and writes: 'three nights before Zarathustra's birth his mother was so radiant that the entire village was illuminated. Thinking that a great fire had broken out, many inhabitants hurriedly left the village. Coming back later on, they found that a boy full of brilliance had been born' (the source of this story, he says, is a ninth-century Pahalavi book). Further, he shows that the sun is the solar seed (Rg Veda, X; Adharva Veda, X) 'Light is progenitive power' (Taittiriya Samhita).
3. Jung, 'The Psychology of the Child Archetype', in Kerenyi and Jung, *Introduction to a Science of Mythology,* p. 111, especially note 19, and pp. 123–4.
4. Cf. C. G. Jung's Foreword to *An Introduction to Zen Buddhism,* by D. T. Suzuki, in which he deals with the Buddhist concept of sunya as an opening of the conscious mind to the unconscious.
5. Cf. Heinrich Zimmer, *Myths and Symbols in Indian Art and Civilization,* pp. 160–3. See also p. 44 of this book.

< 201 >

6. The Indian guna system, which sees nature as arising out of *quality,* is opposed to the binary system, being in basis a tertiary system. For reference to the *I Ching,* which employs both the binary and tertiary systems, see p. 196. See also Danielou, *Hindu Polytheism,* p. 24, for guna defined as part of a whole.
7. Cf. M. E. Harding, *Woman's Mysteries,* pp. 162, 216–23.

Chapter 10: The feminine figure in Indian thought

1. R. C. Zaehner, *Hinduism,* pp. 78, 208.
2. Ibid., p. 77.
3. The connection of woman with the fertility of the whole of nature is an important concept of Indian folklore, commented on by both Havell in 'The Feminine Ideal' in *The Ideals of Indian Art,* and Coomaraswamy in vol. 1 of *Yaksas.* The favourite motif of a woman bending the branch of a tree is, according to Coomaraswamy, a Yaksi-dryad theme, and he notes in connection with Malavika's performance of the ceremony whereby the Asoka tree is made to flower by the touch of a woman's foot that 'the scene takes place beside a slab of rock under the Asoka tree, and this shows that the tree itself was a sacred tree haunted by a spirit.' Havell points out that the whole of the third act of Kalidasa's play, *Malavikagnimitra,* is based on the idea of woman's power to awaken the fertility of nature (*Ideals of Indian Art,* p. 163).
4. Cf. Kenneth Clarke in *The Nude* (Penguin, 1956) on the relationship of the body of the nude figure to its clothing. Flowing draperies were used by Renaissance and post-Renaissance artists to convey the mood of the body rather as the miniature artists of India used the landscape setting to indicate the inner feeling of the picture.
5. The young hero who captures the clothes of water-maidens is an old Indo-Germanic fairy tale according to Penzer (*The Ocean of Story,* Delhi, 1968, vol. 8, pp. 213 ff.). In this way the hero gains control over the fairy women, through possession of their clothes (or in the case of bird-maidens, their plumage). The fairy bride cannot get free from the spell of the hero lover until she can get back her clothes. In the myth of Pururavas and Urvasi (Rg Veda, X, 95) the mortal king loses his apsara wife when he sees her naked, thus breaking the spell which brought her under his power. We thus see in mythic thought a magical significance attached both to clothing and to nakedness; the possession of another's clothes or nakedness being a power over their lives, that is, over their secret reality.
6. Cf. Teilhard de Chardin, *The Phenomenon of Man,* pp. 264–8.

Chapter 11: The symbol of the sun

1. An epithet for the sun, so-called either because the sun is 'the bird in the sky', and a bird is 'born of an (apparently) lifeless egg', or because when the

< 202 >

sun was dwelling in the womb of his mother, Aditi, she performed such severe asceticism that her husband, Kashyapa, feared that the egg in her womb would be destroyed. See W. D. O'Flaherty, *Hindu Myths*, p. 348.
2. See V. Ions, *Indian Mythology*, p. 128.
3. O'Flaherty, op. cit., p. 104.
4. Cf. Heras, Introduction to *The Problem of Ganapati.*
5. Cf. A. Getty, *Ganesa – A Monograph on the Elephant-faced God.*
6. Cf. A. K. Coomaraswamy, *Christian and Oriental Philosophy of Art*, pp. 21, 32 – 'holes in the roof' as reminders of the door-god. In this connection one might suppose that Santa Claus who comes down the chimney is another aspect of the door-god, for, as we have noted, the sun-god is both a child and a very old man. On the same pages Coomaraswamy speaks of the home as a miniature cosmos out of which one breaks through the door or hole in the roof as if breaking out of the universe in the experience of initiation. In this connection one might refer to Lévi-Strauss's idea (*The Savage Mind*, chapter 1) that all art originates in the miniature, which is inherently artful, in that man tries through the miniature to make a microcosm of the macrocosm. In that sense a house or a door are in fact 'miniatures' of the whole empyrean.
7. Attending a village religious ceremony, I noted a villager touch the architrave of the door as a sign of respect to the door. I think this is very much an Indian gesture. Village doors are often very low. One explanation for this is that it makes the person entering it stoop, which is a sign of respect, comparable to the action of leaving his shoes outside the threshold.
8. Verrier Elwin, *The Murias and their Ghotul*, pp. 330–50.
9. In front of the Southern temple we have the great temple tanks which relate bathing to the significance of entering into the temple. In these tanks, on ceremonial occasions, the images of the deities are also bathed, and sometimes even totally immersed.

Chapter 12: Living symbolism

1. Maritain writes in his book *Art and Scholasticism*, 'The mind rejoices in the beautiful because in the beautiful it finds itself again, recognizes itself, and comes into contact with its very own light.' The scholastics thus spoke of Beauty as the 'radiance of form'. They understand man as using his 'wits' and projecting on to matter the light of his inner reason, thus giving to matter the clarity which belongs to the truth of the inner mind. It is thus man who gives, through his art, the radiance of intelligibility to natural substance. One might compare this idea with that of samkhya philosophy, which sees the essential life principle in man (which is also mind, manas) as jewel-like, and in opposition to the rough matter of the physical world.
2. The worship of gods who are allowed to go back into nature applies only to a certain group of gods, not all gods. Belonging to this group would be Ganesa, and various gods who would be termed 'bhutas' or spirits, or gods (mainly mother-goddesses) of sickness, or again various gods of implements,

< 203 >

which are in a sense personified powers, connected with actions, which could be agricultural, domestic, or instruments of some craft. The gods of the Aryan-Hindu pantheon tend on the other hand to have more fixed abodes, and fixed images which are not destroyed, together with regular forms of worship.

3. Pillaiyar means 'noble child', and is a name given to Ganapati, or Ganesa, or Vinayaka (he is known by all these names). The main festival of this god is Ganesa Chaturti (i.e. the birthday of Ganesa), when clay images of Ganesa are put in the home for eight days and then thrown into a tank, or into the sea.

4. Cf. D. N. Shukla, *Hindu Canons of Iconography and Painting*, pp. 387-8. The Manasollasa, or Abhilasitartha–Cintamani, classifies painting into five types, of which the Dhuli-Citra is the last category. In the author's comments on these five categories we read:

> The Rasa Citra and the Dhuli Citra go together. The Dhuli Citra is the Tamil Kolam, done with white flour on the floor and in front of our houses. In the month of Margasirsa, Tamil girls vie with each other in the villages to draw the biggest and most intricate 'Kolams' in front of their houses, and then decorate these Kolams at various points with pumpkin flowers. On more festive occasions, in the houses, temples and Tambalams (i.e. brass plates used in our houses) for Niranjana, these Kolams are done with various coloured powders. These Citras are naturally short-lived.

It is interesting to compare these short-lived or momentary patterns with those of the kaleidoscope, which are also passing structures 'such as those of snow crystals or certain types of radiolariara and diatomaceae' (Lévi-Strauss, *The Savage Mind*, p. 36).

5. Kolama — a pattern drawn in powder, in front of the main door, especially in Tamil Nadu, but in the South generally. The patterns are generally based on the hexagon, that is the overlapped triangles known in the West as the Star of David, but in India as the star of Laksmi. In fact the kolama pattern is especially connected with the worship of Laksmi, though a favourite motif to be found in the patterns is the three-leaved bilva branch, related by Tucci in his article on 'Earth in India and Tibet' (*Eranos Yearbook*, 1954) to the worship of Durga, but also important in Saivite ritual, being thought to relate to the three eyes of Siva. Probably a prototype of the kolama pattern would be an arrangement of flowers and leaves, like a sort of sacred garden, before the shrine or in front of the door of the home. Another favourite motif of kolama patterns are intertwined serpents, which are especially used to decorate the entrance of the home during the 'Nagapancmi' festivities (snake festival), but for other occasions also. One pattern is meant to depict the tortoise, and another the heads of crows — both are creatures around which there is a good deal of folk legend. In general the patterns are thought to protect the entrance of home or shrine against the spirits of the dead, and are drawn on festival days, but not on days when somebody has died in the house, or when the dead are commemorated.

< 204 >

6. Cf. D. N. Shukla, *Hindu Canons of Iconography and Painting*, p. 40.
7. When I say all sculptures were probably originally painted, I am of course not meaning metal sculptures, but sculptures which are part of architecture. These sculptures were probably mostly covered at first with a very thin fine plaster, and then decorated. But the Indian sun and rain has in general washed off most of the exterior decoration of sculptures (and most sculpture, except in caves, is exterior, for the inside of the Hindu temple is generally bare, except for a few cult images which quite often, at least in the middle ages, were executed in cast metal).
8. Susanna Millar, *The Psychology of Play*, p. 50. Piaget studied the development of logical thought in children, and his ideas about child-play are related to his theories concerning the processes of knowing.
9. According to some theorists in this field, the primal sense is not touch but taste. By 'touch' I mean something even more basic than a 'sense' as a differentiated faculty – a pure 'contact', as the young baby feels the 'contact' of his mother.
10. 'Varna' means strictly colour, but the varna system applies to the whole social system comprising the three principle castes.
11. Cf. Lévi-Strauss, *The Raw and the Cooked*.
12. Cf. Hargreaves, *Asian Christian Thinking*, on 'tree metaphors', p. 6.

Chapter 13: The tree at the centre of the garden of innocence

1. Joseph Campbell, 'The Symbol without Meaning', *Eranos Yearbook*, XXVI (pp. 415-75).
2. Krsna and the gopis are meant to dance together in a beautiful forest glade called Vrndavan which is in fact the garden of innocence. This is the myth behind that type of classical Indian dance called the raslila, which is thought to go back to ancient tribal forms of dance, being a round-dance with Krsna at the centre. A myth relates the origin of the Manipuri form of classical Indian dancing to the raslila of Siva. It is told that Siva and Parvati wanted to dance the raslila like Krsna and Radha, and so Siva searched out a beautiful valley with many trees and flowing streams, to be the stage for his love-dance with Parvati. This is in fact Manipur, the 'land of jewels'. 'Ras' means juice, and is not only related to the emotive quality of the dance, but probably to the whole dance of organic nature, in which the sap rises as a creative force.
3. Cf. R. Lannoy, *The Speaking Tree*, pp. 36-9.
4. Cf. Tucci, 'Earth in India and Tibet', *Eranos Yearbook*, XXII, pp. 323-64.
5. A fifteenth-century Bengali poem called Mansa-Kavya says, 'The goddess is to be worshipped in the form of a golden pot containing water with a twig of "sig" over the mouth of it.' The bilva is the bel tree (*Aegle Marmelos*). Cf. Thankappan Nair, *Tree Symbol Worship in India*.
6. According to W. D. O'Flaherty (*Asceticism and Eroticism in the Mythology of Siva*), Madan was probably an old tree-god, and the burning of Madan by the third eye of Siva probably relates to an ancient agricultural practice

< 205 >

when trees were burnt to ashes in order that the earth might be revitalized. It seems that this was given ritual form in the ceremonial burning of a sacred tree as a preparation for a new awakening of nature in spring.

7. The symbol of the swing hanging from the branches of a tree is used a great deal in Indian poetry.

8. Cf. A. Coomaraswamy, *Yaksas*, p. 17.

9. Cf. H. Prestler, *Primitive Religions in India*, p. 97. See also Thankappan Nair, op. cit. Tree marriages fulfil two functions. Firstly, by marrying a girl to a tree it is made known in the community that she is now marriageable, having entered puberty; secondly, by marrying a widow to a tree, she is able to marry subsequently another person, as the wrath of her former husband is directed towards the tree.

10. A variant of this story is found at the beginning of the Ramayana.

11. Notices of the Jains, received from Carukirti Acarya, their chief pontiff in Belligola, Mysore.

12. Zimmer, *Philosophies of India*, p. 282. The story concerning Sagara he gives is from the Mahabharata 3, 10.

13. Hypaethral — open to the sky, 'roofless'. According to Coomaraswamy, even the Buddhist 'caitya' developed in its form from ancient tree shrines to Yaksas. The word 'caitya' is meant to derive from the root 'ci' meaning to build up, or heap up — presumably stones at the foot of the tree as is still customary in village areas. There is a section on hypaethral temples in *Temples of South India*, by K. R. Srinivasan.

14. Cf. Anders Nygren, *Agape and Eros*, in which he describes how the word 'agape', meaning 'love', came in pre-Christian pagan custom to be used for the funerary meal held on the anniversary of the dead, and was absorbed into early Christian usage as the 'love-feast'. This was also closely derived from the Jewish Sabbath meal. After a preliminary blessing of the meal, the food was eaten in a joyous atmosphere. Tit-bits from the meal would be taken away by participants to be shared with others, very much like Prasada.

Chapter 14: Symbol of the serpent

1. Freud used this term solely to connote sexual energy and drive, which he believed to be basic to the unconscious. Jung used the word in a broader sense, to mean psychic energy as a whole, which he believed to contain many other elements besides the purely sexual. Thus though Freud invented the term, Jung's use of it is perhaps nearer to the Indian concept of the kundalini.

2. The collective unconscious is a concept defined and used by C. G. Jung. Freud held that the unconscious consisted wholly of the subliminal or repressed acquisitions of an individual's personal psychic life. From clinical observation, Jung felt there was more to the unconscious than the purely personal. He posited a collective unconscious (in addition to the personal unconscious) containing 'mythological associations, motifs and images that

< 206 >

can spring up anew any time anywhere' (Definition in C. G. Jung's *Psychological Types*, Routledge & Kegan Paul, 1971). See also *Man and his Symbols*, ed. C. G. Jung, p. 55.

3. In the great myth of Indra and his conquest of Vrtra, the cosmic serpent, we are told that the serpent enclosed the waters of life in his coils, and these had to be released by Indra who 'became like hair of the horse's tail'. The myth is clearly a creation myth, for when Vrtra is finally split open he becomes the sky and the earth. The name Vrtra may be related to Vrata (vow) and is also connected with the word Rtu, which is the ritual of life, the rhythm of the seasons. It seems to me the two opposites, Indra and Vrtra, horse and serpent (as we find it again in the St George and dragon myth) are in fact two aspects of time and energy. The horse, connected with the sun and the solar horse-sacrifice, is an out-going, piercing energy. The serpent is connected with the cosmic flood, with the cyclical rhythms of the seasons.

4. Lists of the various avataras of Visnu are given in various ancient Indian texts, such as the Mahabharata and Bhagavata Purana, but the well-accepted version of ten avataras is probably based on the Taittiriya Samhita, where the following divine incarnations are listed: 1. Matsya (Fish incarnation), 2. Kurma (Tortoise incarnation), 3. Varaha (Boar incarnation), 4. Narasimha (Man-Lion incarnation), 5. Vamana (Dwarf incarnation), 6. Parasurama (Brahmin incarnation), 7. Raghava Rama (Ksatriya incarnation), 8. Krsna, 9. Buddha, 10. Kalkin (incarnation to come). Of these, the first four incarnations seem clearly to arise from very ancient cosmological speculations concerning the creation of the universe from primal chaos, which is pictured as an ocean. (For further information see D. N. Shukla, *Hindu Canons of Iconography and Painting*).

5. Much is made in Indian symbolic thought of the relationship between hot and cold, which seems to fit in with Lévi-Strauss's idea of the 'raw' and the 'cooked'. The serpent, along with other cold-blooded creatures such as the tortoise and the lizard, is essentially a 'raw' creature, representing nature in its wild and instinctive form. It is both firm and fixed (tortoise) or changeable (lizard) but it is in essence the cosmic dharma, or wheel of existence in nature. And yet it is aspiring to an existence beyond the merely natural — perhaps we could call it the 'supernatural', which is characterized by fire (tapasya), the transforming of the merely emotive into the 'civilized'.

6. Ganesa is thought to originate in a pre-Aryan elephant god who was worshipped beneath trees along with the serpent, bull and monkey (cf. A. Getty, *Ganesa — A Monograph on the Elephant-faced God*, in particular the introduction by Foucher). Even now Ganesa idols are often found near snake stones. Getty points out that certain esoteric images of Ganesa show him with a naga spreading its hood over him. The relationship of Ganesa to serpents is also interpreted by Heras in his book *The Problem of Ganapati* with special reference to the relation of Ganesa to Subrahmanya.

7. Psychic wholeness is understood by Jung as the integration of opposites. See C. G. Jung, *Symbols of Transformation*, p. 303. Again, Jung speaks of 'the tension of opposites from which the divine child' (i.e. the symbol of the

< 207 >

individuated self) 'is born as the symbol of unity'. Cf. C. G. Jung, *Aion*, p. 31.

8. Cf. J. Fergusson, *Tree and Serpent Worship* (sacrifice in relation to serpent worship).

Chapter 15: Symbol of cosmic vitality

1. There is an interesting popular myth concerning the princess Sukanya and a sage in the forest who went into meditation. So deep was the meditation of this sage that ants built their castle around him, and he became completely hidden in the ant hill. The princess Sukanya, coming to the forest to bathe, was interested in the ant hill, and noticed two sparkling, gem-like points in its depth which were actually the eyes of the sage — the only part of him which the ants had not covered over. She tried to pull these gem-like things out, using a stick, and was horrified when blood began to flow from the wounded eyes of the sage. As a result of her injuring the sage, a plague spread in the kingdom, and eventually she confessed to what she had done in the forest. An embassy from the king went to the sage, who was now blinded, to ask what could be done in reparation for the sin committed by the princess. The sage asked that she should become his wife, which brought great grief to the king, who had hoped for a better future for his beautiful daughter. However, Sukanya agreed, and the plague left the kingdom. One day in the forest she met the Asvins, who are the twin healers of the gods, who tried to seduce her, but she resisted them. They then offered to heal her husband the sage, and not only give him sight, but youth as well, but only on one condition. They said they would make him look just like them-selves (and they were identical twins) and she would have to choose between the three of them. They then entered together with the blind sage, into the pool in the centre of the forest where originally Sukanya had come to bathe, and all the three were for a while lost to sight. When they emerged, they came forward as three beautiful youths, all identical. But the sage had told Sukanya that if she looked carefully, the eyes of the gods would not blink, whereas his own mortal eyes would, and in this way she was able to identify her true husband.

   Here we see the sexual significance of the eye in relation also to the lingam-like ant hill. Many reversals are noticed in the myth. The girl Sukanya ('kanya' means 'virgin') pokes at the eyes of the sage with a stick, causing bleeding. The bleeding eye here is a feminine symbol for the men-struating vagina. The stick is masculine. However, the male sage asks for the virgin to marry him as reparation for having blinded him. She remains a virgin resisting even the beautiful gods of life, who test her. They, together with the sage, enter the same pool where she had come to bathe. She recognizes her husband by the blinking of his eyes. What is old becomes young again.

2. I noticed the Kanappa myth depicted on one of the gopurams of Mylapore temple in Madras, a temple dedicated to the lingam, which was worshipped

< 208 >

by Parvati in the form of the peacock. The peacock also has eyes in its tail (see p. 194).

3. Essential to the transformation process is the notion of sacrifice. According to Lévi-Strauss (*The Savage Mind*, pp. 225-8), the sacrifice acts as a link between two absolutely different realities, in fact the fundamental polarities of the universe. One might note that the sacrifice of Christ on the Cross is between the opposites of the vertical and horizontal, heaven and earth. In the Narasimha myth we find the demon king sacrificed between the inner and outer, day and night. The sacrifice is also often accompanied by a ritual meal which is cooked in a vessel (we might note the connection with alchemy). The meal, according to Lévi-Strauss, is the link between production and consumption, so that every act of cooking is 'sacrificial' in this sense. The ritual meal integrates all opposites in society, and is, as it were, the mythic cauldron in which everything is put once more into the melting pot. And yet, by a curious inversion, though it unites, it is divided — it is distributed among those who have come to share the meal. The pot is thus a symbol of gathering in, and its breaking is a symbol of re-distribution and expenditure.

4. The mandorla probably goes back to Orphic symbolism. According to Cirlot (*Dictionary of Symbols*), it is meant to represent the interpenetration of heaven and earth, spirit and matter, and is a symbol 'of the perpetual sacrifice which regenerates creative force . . . morphologically it is cognate with the spindle of the Magna Mater, and with the magical spinners of thread.'

The mandorla was often used in Byzantine and early Medieval art, and in Russian icons, to enclose the figure of Christ in a sort of 'glory'. Placed vertically, like an opening door, it appears like a narrow gap in the fabric of this world, through which the Saviour is emerging, and behind Him is the light of eternity. Most frequently it is the Christ of the Transfiguration (Matt. 17; Mark 9; Luke 9) who is so framed, but sometimes it is the Pantocrator, or the Risen Christ.

5.   To gaze on Krsna was my greatest wish,
   Yet seeing him was filled with danger.
   Gazing has bewitched me, no will remains,
   I cannot speak or hear,
   Like monsoon clouds my eyes pour water.
(*Love Songs of Vidyapati*, trans. by Deban Bhattacharya, Orient Paperbacks)
   My eyes learn what their vision is for,
   Looking into his face, bright moon.
   A long time they were fasting, my eyes,
   Those thirsty Chakora birds whose sole food is moonbeams:
   Now they have found the round moon itself:
   Vasudeva Ghosh sings to his Gaura, his Golden one,
   Like a man blind from birth who has found his sight.
(In Praise of Krsná: *Songs from the Bengali*, Cape, London, 1967)

6. There are a group of sati stones in the Madras museum. On either side of the uplifted hand we see the sun and moon. The hand is meant to depict a vow taken before these deities.

< 209 >

Chapter 16: Complementary symbols and the idea of wholeness

1. Cassirer says that a myth is a statement about action, that the vital principle of myth is dynamic, not static. Further, Cassirer seems to believe that the primitive mentality does not invent myths, it experiences them. Myths are original revelations of the pre-conscious psyche, involuntary statements about unconscious psychic happenings.

2. Cf. Freud, *The Interpretation of Dreams*, London, Allen & Unwin, pp. 292–5. See also Fromm, *The Forgotten Language*. It seems that clothes symbolize in the human mind certain magical powers, hence to be without them is to be 'utterly powerless', as Freud puts it. Fromm sees clothes as symbols of authority. Certainly the examples of a priest or army man who feel 'naked' without their uniform, shows that clothes serve a magical-religious function, and are not merely to 'cover' the body, but are in some way intended to consecrate the body, and give it power.

3. Cf. C. S. Lewis, *The Allegory of Love*, Oxford University Press, London, 1936. Of course, the problem of the use of allegory cannot be disposed of easily. Allegory arises out of the extended simile, and therefore has intrinsic to it a basic dualism. On the other hand, a work of art, like myth itself, struggles to find identity rather than likeness. But in a masterly analysis of the rise of allegory in late classical and early medieval literature, C. S. Lewis shows how much allegory was related to an increased sense of internalization in a Western self-analytical mind. Thus, while realizing various forces within man such as courage and cowardice, love and hate, writers began to turn myth to serve ethics, and use the epic form to describe happenings inside the emotions of man. Man's passions were described as fighting each other in the same way as heroes fought each other of old. The first step, then, of 'allegory', is personification, as in the case of a 'temptation' which a St Augustine might describe as pulling him by the sleeve. Man is seen not as one, but as legion – an idea which is not merely a poetical device, but a reality all too poignantly felt by such mystics as St Anthony of the Desert, who, we are told by his biographer, fought with his passions which physically attacked him in the form of devils. It is on this basis of externalization of internal processes that we can see how the allegorical literature of the Middle Ages developed, which describes the fight between virtues and vices. C. S. Lewis points out that this tendency is to be found also in modern psychologists who speak of the 'censor', or 'ego' or 'super-ego' or 'id', as though these were characters in themselves and not aspects of the character of man. The modern equivalent of allegorical literature is thus often psychological. At this point we may ask whether the archetypes of Jung are myths or allegories? They could appear in both functions. In fact, as C. S. Lewis has shown, allegory was to begin with the death of all true myth – a way, in fact, in which the early Christian apologists were able to demythologize, for whereas they could speak of Venus as physical love, they could no longer accept her as a goddess. But on the other hand allegory was a rediscovery of myth, and a revitalizing of it.

4. Cf. Cassirer, in *Language and Myth* – 'The Power of the Metaphor'.

< 210 >

BIBLIOGRAPHY

Allchin, Bridget and Raymond, *The Birth of Indian Civilization*, Penguin, 1968.
Arneheim, Rudolph, *Art and Visual Perception: A Psychology of the Creative Eye*, University of California Press, 1954.
Auboyer, Jeannine (trans. S. W. Taylor), *Daily Life in Ancient India*, Weidenfeld & Nicolson, London, 1965.
Bharati, Agehananda, *The Tantric Tradition*, Rider, London, 1965.
Binyon, Lawrence, *The Spirit of Man in Asian Art*, Dover, 1966.
Brown, Clever Mackenzie, *God as Mother — Feminine Theology in India*, Hartfort, 1974.
Brown, Percy, *Indian Painting*, YMCA Publishing House, Delhi, 1965.
Campbell, Joseph, 'The Symbol without Meaning', *Eranos Yearbook*, vol. XXVI, Princeton University Press, 1957.
Campbell, Joseph, *The Hero with a Thousand Faces*, Princeton University Press, 1968.
Campbell, Joseph, *The Masks of God: Oriental Mythology*, Souvenir Press, 1974.
Cassirer, Ernst (trans. K. Langer), *Language and Myth*, Harper, 1946.
Chardin, Teilhard de, *The Phenomenon of Man*, Fontana, 1965.
Cirlot, J. E., *Dictionary of Symbols*, Routledge & Kegan Paul, 1962.
Coomaraswamy, Ananda K., *Yaksas*, Washington, 1928; reprinted Munshiram Manoharlal, Delhi, 1971.
Coomaraswamy, Ananda K., *Christian and Oriental Philosophy of Art*, Dover, 1956.
Coomaraswamy, Ananda K., *The Dance of Shiva*, Liban, 1968.
Danielou, Alain, *Hindu Polytheism*, Princeton University Press, 1964.
Diehl, C. G., *Church and Shrine*, Acta Univ. Ups. Hist. Rel. 2, Uppsala, 1965.
Diehl, C. G. *Instrument and Purpose*, G. W. K. Gleerup Lund, 1956.
Dowson, John, *A Classical Dictionary of Hindu Mythology and Religion*, Routledge & Kegan Paul, 1968.
Dubois, J. A., *Hindu Manners, Customs and Ceremonies*, Oxford University Press, 1906.
Eliade, Mircea (trans. Willard R. Trask), *Myth of the Eternal Return*, Routledge & Kegan Paul, 1954.
Eliade, Mircea, *Patterns of Comparative Religion*, Routledge & Kegan Paul, 1958.
Eliade, Mircea (trans. Willard R. Trask), *Yoga: Immortality and Freedom*, Routledge & Kegan Paul, 1958.
Eliade, Mircea, *Myths, Dreams and Mysteries*, Fontana, London, 1968.
Eliade, Mircea, *Two and the One*, Harville, New York, 1965.
Elwin, Verrier, *The Murias and their Ghotul*, Oxford University Press, India, 1947.

< 211 >

Fergusson, James, *History of Indian and Eastern Architecture*, Munshiram Manoharlal, Delhi, 1971.

Fergusson, James, *Tree and Serpent Worship*, Indological Book House, Delhi, 1971.

Fromm, Erich, *Man for Himself*, Routledge & Kegan Paul, 1949.

Fromm, Erich, *The Forgotten Language*, Grove Press, New York, 1951.

Getty, Alice, *Ganesa − A Monograph on the Elephant-faced God*, Munshiram Manoharlal, Delhi, 1972.

Gough, Archibald E., *The Philosophy of the Upanishads and Ancient Metaphysics*, Kegan Paul, London, 1903.

Harding, M. Esther, *Woman's Mysteries*, Rider, London, 1971.

Hargreaves, Cecil, *Asian Christian Thinking*, Christian Literature Society, Madras, 1972.

Havell, E. B., *The Himalayas in Indian Art*, John Murray, London, 1924.

Havell, E. B., *The Indian Sculpture and Painting*, John Murray, London, 1928.

Havell, E. B., *The Art Heritage of India Series*, comprising Indian sculpture, painting and ideals of Indian art, Taraporewala, Bombay, 1964.

Heras, H., *The Problem of Ganapati*, Indological Book House, Varanasi, 1972.

Ions, Veronica, *Indian Mythology*, Paul Hamlyn, London, 1967.

Jung, C. G., *Symbols of Transformation*, Routledge & Kegan Paul, 1956.

Jung, C. G., *Aion*, Routledge & Kegan Paul, 1959.

Jung, C. G. (ed.), *Man and His Symbols*, Aldus, London, 1964.

Jung, C. G., *Synchronicity*, Routledge & Kegan Paul, 1972.

Keith, A. Berriedale, *The Samkhya System*, YMCA Publishing House, Calcutta, 1949.

Kerenyi and Jung, *Introduction to a Science of Mythology*, Routledge & Kegan Paul, 1970.

Kirk, G. S., *Myth: Its Meaning and Functions in Ancient and Other Cultures*, Cambridge University Press, 1970.

Kosambi, D. D., *An Introduction to the Study of Indian History*, Vikas, New Delhi, 1970.

Kramrisch, Stella, *Indian Sculpture* (Heritage of India Series), YMCA Publishing House, Calcutta, 1933.

Kramrisch, Stella, 'Super Structure of the Hindu Temple', *Journal of the Indian Society of Oriental Art*, vol. XII, 1944.

Kramrisch, Stella, *The Art of India*, Phaidon, London, 1965.

Lannoy, Richard, *The Speaking Tree*, Oxford University Press, 1974.

Lévi-Strauss, Claude, *The Savage Mind*, Weidenfeld & Nicolson, London, 1966.

Lévi-Strauss, Claude, *The Raw and the Cooked*, Vol. I of *Introduction to a Science of Mythology*, Jonathan Cape, 1970.

Lorenz, Konrad, *Civilized Man's Eight Deadly Sins*, Methuen, London, 1974.

Madanjeet Singh, *Himalayan Art*, Macmillan, London, 1971.

Maritain, Jacques, *Art and Scholasticism*, Sheed & Ward, 1949.

Millar, Susanna, *The Psychology of Play*, Penguin, 1971.

Mukerjee, Ajit, *Tantric Art, Its Philosophy and Physics*, Ravi Rumar, New Delhi, 1966.

Mukerjee, Radhakamal, *The Cosmic Art of India* Allied Publishers, Bombay, 1965.

Narvane, V. S., *The Elephant and the Lotus: Essays in Philosophy and Culture*,

< 212 >

Bibliography

Asia Publishing House, Bombay, 1965.

Navaratnam, Ratna, *Kartikeya — The Divine Child,* Bhavan's Book University, Bharatiya Vidya Bhavan, Bombay, 1973.

Nygren, Anders, *Agape and Eros,* ISPCK, 1957.

O'Flaherty, W. D., *Asceticism and Eroticism in the Mythology of Siva,* Oxford University Press, Delhi, 1975.

O'Flaherty, W. D., *Hindu Myths — A Source Book,* Penguin, 1975.

Pandey, R. B., *Hindu Samskaras,* Motilal Banarsidas, Delhi, 1969.

Pathar, S. Viraswami, *Temple and its Significance,* Vanivilas Press, Trichy, 1974.

Prestler, Henry H., *Primitive Religions in India,* Christian Literature Society, India, 1971.

Pyyappan, P., *Lord Ayyappan — The Dharma Sastha,* Bhavan's Book University, Bharatiya Vidya Bhavan, Bombay, 1973.

Radin, Paul, *Primitive Man as Philosopher,* Dover, New York, 1957.

Reps, Paul (Compiled by), *Zen Flesh, Zen Bones,* Penguin, 1971.

Rowlands, Benjamin, *The Art and Architecture of India,* Harmondsworth, 1954.

Sen-Gupta, Sankar (ed.), *Tree Symbol Worship in India,* Calcutta, 1965.

Shukla, D. N., *Vastu Shastra* vol. II *Hindu Canons of Iconography and Painting,* Punjab University, 1958.

Singer, Milton (ed.), *Seminar on Indian Traditions,* Phild. 1959.

Singer, Milton (ed.), *Krisna: Myths, Rites and Attitudes,* Chicago Press, 1968.

Sitapati, P., *Sri Venkateswara, The Lord of the Seven Hills Tirupati,* Bhavan's Book University, Bharatiya Vidya Bhavan, Bombay, 1972.

Sperber, Dan (trans. by I. Morton), *Rethinking Symbolism,* Cambridge University Press, 1975.

Spratt, P., *Hindu Culture and Personality,* Manaktala, Bombay, 1966.

Srinivasan, K. R., *Temples of South India,* National Book Trust, India, 1971.

Suzuki, D. T., *An Introduction to Zen Buddhism* (with Foreword by C. G. Jung), Rider, London, 1969.

Tagore, Rabindranath, *Collected Poems,* Macmillan, 1936.

Thomas, P. T., *Savarimalai and its Sastha,* Christian Literature Society, Madras, 1973.

Tucci, Giuseppe, 'Earth in India and Tibet', *Spirit and Nature, Eranos Yearbook,* vol. XXII, Princeton University Press, 1953.

Tucci, Giuseppe, *The Theory and Practice of the Mandala,* Rider, London, 1961.

Vogel, J., *Indian Serpent Lore: The Nagas in Hindu Legend and Art,* Arthur Probsthain, London, 1926.

Volwahsen, Andreas, *Living Architecture: Indian,* Oxford and I.B.H. Publishing Co., Calcutta, 1969.

Wheeler, Sir Mortimer, *Civilizations of the Indus Valley and Beyond,* Thames & Hudson, 1966.

Whitehead, H., *Village Gods of South India,* Oxford University Press, Calcutta, 1921.

Zaehner, R. C., *Hinduism,* Oxford University Press, 1966.

Zimmer, Heinrich, *Philosophies of India,* Routledge & Kegan Paul, 1951.

Zimmer, Heinrich, *The King and the Corpse,* Princeton, 1971.

Zimmer, Heinrich, *Myths and Symbols in Indian Art and Civilization,* Princeton, 1963.

< 213 >

INDEX

<214>

<215>

<216>

Index

<217>

<218>

ARKANA – NEW-AGE BOOKS FOR MIND, BODY AND SPIRIT

With over 150 titles currently in print, Arkana is the leading name in quality new-age books for mind, body and spirit. Arkana encompasses the spirituality of both East and West, ancient and new, in fiction and non-fiction. A vast range of interests is covered, including Psychology and Transformation, Health, Science and Mysticism, Women's Spirituality and Astrology.

If you would like a catalogue of Arkana books, please write to:

Arkana Marketing Department
Penguin Books Ltd
27 Wright's Lane
London W8 5TZ

ARKANA – NEW-AGE BOOKS FOR MIND, BODY AND SPIRIT

A selection of titles already published or in preparation

The Networking Book: People Connecting with People
Jessica Lipnack and Jeffrey Stamps

Networking – forming human connections to link ideas and resources – is the natural form of organization for an era based on information technology. Principally concerned with those networks whose goal is a peaceful yet dynamic future for the world, *The Networking Book* – written by two world-famous experts – profiles hundreds of such organizations worldwide, operating at every level from global tele-communications to word of mouth.

Chinese Massage Therapy: A Handbook of Therapeutic Massage Compiled at the Anhui Medical School Hospital, China
Translated by Hor Ming Lee and Gregory Whincup

There is a growing movement among medical practitioners in China today to mine the treasures of traditional Chinese medicine – acupuncture, herbal medicine and massage therapy. Directly translated from a manual in use in Chinese hospitals, *Chinese Massage Therapy* offers a fresh understanding of this time-tested medical alternative.

Dialogues with Scientists and Sages: The Search for Unity
Renée Weber

In their own words, contemporary scientists and mystics – from the Dalai Lama to Stephen Hawking – share with us their richly diverse views on space, time, matter, energy, life, consciousness, creation and our place in the scheme of things. Through the immediacy of verbatim dialogue, we encounter scientists who endorse mysticism, and those who oppose it; mystics who dismiss science, and those who embrace it.

Zen and the Art of Calligraphy
Omōri Sōgen and Terayama Katsujo

Exploring every element of the relationship between Zen thought and the artistic expression of calligraphy, two long-time practitioners of Zen, calligraphy and swordsmanship show how Zen training provides a proper balance of body and mind, enabling the calligrapher to write more profoundly, freed from distraction or hesitation.

ARKANA – NEW-AGE BOOKS FOR MIND, BODY AND SPIRIT

A selection of titles already published or in preparation

Neal's Yard Natural Remedies Susan Curtis, Romy Fraser and Irene Kohler

Natural remedies for common ailments from the pioneering Neal's Yard Apothecary Shop. An invaluable resource for everyone wishing to take responsibility for their own health, enabling you to make your own choice from homeopathy, aromatherapy and herbalism.

The Arkana Dictionary of New Perspectives Stuart Holroyd

Clear, comprehensive and compact, this iconoclastic reference guide brings together the orthodox and the highly unorthodox, doing full justice to *every* facet of contemporary thought – psychology and parapsychology, culture and counter-culture, science and so-called pseudo-science.

The Absent Father: Crisis and Creativity Alix Pirani

Freud used Oedipus to explain human nature; but Alix Pirani believes that the myth of Danae and Perseus has most to teach an age which offers 'new responsibilities for women and challenging questions for men' – a myth which can help us face the darker side of our personalities and break the patterns inherited from our parents.

Woman Awake: A Celebration of Women's Wisdom Christina Feldman

In this inspiring book, Christina Feldman suggests that it *is* possible to break out of those negative patterns instilled into us by our social conditioning as women: confirmity, passivity and surrender of self. Through a growing awareness of the dignity of all life and its connection with us, we can regain our sense of power and worth.

Water and Sexuality Michel Odent

Taking as his starting point his world-famous work on underwater childbirth at Pithiviers, Michel Odent considers the meaning and importance of water as a symbol: in the past – expressed through myths and legends – and today, from an advertisers' tool to a metaphor for aspects of the psyche. Dr Odent also boldly suggests that the human species may have had an aquatic past.

ARKANA - NEW-AGE BOOKS FOR MIND, BODY AND SPIRIT

A selection of titles already published or in preparation

Women Mystics of the Twentieth Century   Anne Bancroft

Throughout history women have sought answers to eternal questions about existence and beyond – yet most gurus, philosophers and religious leaders have been men. Through exploring the teachings of fifteen women mystics – each with her own approach to what she calls 'the truth that goes beyond the ordinary' – Anne Bancroft gives a rare, cohesive and fascinating insight into the diversity of female approaches to mysticism.

Dynamics of the Unconscious: Seminars in Psychological Astrology Volume II   Liz Greene and Howard Sasportas

The authors of *The Development of the Personality* team up again to show how the dynamics of depth psychology interact with your birth chart. They shed new light on the psychology and astrology of aggression and depression – the darker elements of the adult personality that we must confront if we are to grow to find the wisdom within.

The Myth of Eternal Return: Cosmos and History   Mircea Eliade

'A luminous, profound, and extremely stimulating work . . . Eliade's thesis is that ancient man envisaged events not as constituting a linear, progressive history, but simply as so many creative repetitions of primordial archetypes . . . This is an essay which everyone interested in the history of religion and in the mentality of ancient man will have to read. It is difficult to speak too highly of it' – Theodore H. Gaster in *Review of Religion*.

Karma and Destiny in the I Ching   Guy Damian-Knight

This entirely original approach to the *I Ching*, achieved through mathematical rearrangement of the hexagrams, offers a new, more precise tool for self-understanding. Simple to use and yet profound, it gives the ancient Chinese classic a thoroughly contemporary relevance.

ARKANA – NEW-AGE BOOKS FOR MIND, BODY AND SPIRIT

A selection of titles already published or in preparation

Judo – The Gentle Way Alan Fromm and Nicolas Soames

Like many of the martial arts, Judo primarily originated not as a method of self-defence but as a system for self-development. This book reclaims the basic principles underlying the technique, re-emphasizing Judo as art rather than sport.

Women of Wisdom Tsultrim Allione

By gathering together the rich and vivid biographies of six Tibetan female mystics, and describing her own experiences of life as a Tibetan Buddhist nun and subsequently as a wife and mother, Tsultrim Allione tells the inspirational stories of women who have overcome every difficulty to attain enlightenment and liberation.

Natural Healers' Acupressure Handbook
Volume II: Advanced G-Jo Michael Blate

Volume I of this bestselling handbook taught the basic G-Jo – or acupressure – techniques, used to bring immediate relief to hundreds of symptoms. In Volume II Michael Blate teaches us to find and heal our own 'root organs' – the malfunctioning organs that are the true roots of disease and suffering – in order to restore balance and, with it, health and emotional contentment.

Shape Shifters: Shaman Women in Contemporary Society
Michele Jamal

Shape Shifters profiles 14 shaman women of today – women who, like the shamans of old, have passed through an initiatory crisis and emerged as spiritual leaders empowered to heal the pain of others.

'The shamanic women articulate what is intuitively felt by many "ordinary" women. I think this book has the potential to truly "change a life"' – Dr Jean Shinoda Bolen, author of *Goddesses in Everywoman*